A FRESH START AT THE CORNISH COUNTRY HOSPITAL

JO BARTLETT

Boldwood

First published in Great Britain in 2026 by Boldwood Books Ltd.

Copyright © Jo Bartlett, 2026

Cover Design by Lizzie Gardiner

Cover Images: Adobe Stock and Shutterstock

The moral right of Jo Bartlett to be identified as the author of this work has been asserted in accordance with the Copyright, Designs and Patents Act 1988.

Every effort has been made to obtain the necessary permissions with reference to copyright material, both illustrative and quoted. We apologise for any omissions in this respect and will be pleased to make the appropriate acknowledgements in any future edition.

A CIP catalogue record for this book is available from the British Library.

Paperback ISBN 978-1-80656-140-7

Large Print ISBN 978-1-80656-138-4

Hardback ISBN 978-1-80656-145-2

Trade Paperback ISBN 978-1-80656-141-4

Ebook ISBN 978-1-80656-142-1

Kindle ISBN 978-1-80656-134-6

Audio CD ISBN 978-1-80656-146-9

MP3 CD ISBN 978-1-80656-133-9

Digital audio download ISBN 978-1-80656-147-6

This book is printed on certified sustainable paper. Boldwood Books is dedicated to putting sustainability at the heart of our business. For more information please visit https://www.boldwoodbooks.com/about-us/sustainability/

Boldwood Books Ltd, 23 Bowerdean Street, London, SW6 3TN

www.boldwoodbooks.com

For Jean and her Michael, whose love is limitless and which no change or challenge could ever dim.

xx

PROLOGUE

Eve massaged her temples with small, circular movements, trying to stave off the headache that had been threatening for the last hour. Paracetamol wouldn't cut it; she needed sleep. It had been a long shift and this was the first chance she'd had to catch her breath and stop in the last three hours. All she wanted to do was to go home, get into her nice warm bed, sink into the memory foam mattress, and rest her head against Max's shoulder. Except that wasn't going to be an option.

'You look like I feel, Evie B, absolutely bloody knackered.' Vick Stanhope, the Lead Nurse in A&E, always said it like it was, in a broad Leeds accent and with a smile that very rarely slipped off her face no matter how tough a shift they were having. 'We've got half an hour left and then you can get yourself off home.'

'I wish I could, but I've got to pick Max up from his stag do.' Eve rolled her eyes, but even that was painful.

'Let him get a cab, the silly sod. What is this anyway, his fourteenth stag do?'

'Third. I realise it seems ridiculous, but you know Max. He's got so many friends and he makes more wherever he goes. He'd have needed to hire Elland Road to catch up with all of his mates in one go.'

It was an exaggeration, of course, to claim that Max could have filled Leeds United's football stadium with his friends, but there were a lot of them and they came from all walks of life, spanning two or three generations, the different hospitals he'd worked in and a wide range of interests. Tonight's third and final stag do – at least that's what Eve hoped it would be – was with a group of guys all more or less the same age as Max, and it was an old-school kind of night out. There'd have been plenty of drinking, a bit of dancing at one of the clubs once their inhibitions had been loosened, and right about now they'd probably be queuing for a kebab somewhere, refuelling before they went on to the next club. It was a stark contrast to his second stag do, which had involved watching Formula One racing in Monaco, with a group of friends and relatives who had more money than sense in Eve's opinion. Some of the friends stretched right back to Max's days at a prestigious private school in Berkshire, four counties away from his family home in Cornwall, but he got on with everybody and he didn't care what their background was. If Max liked you then you'd made a friend for life, and everybody loved him. There'd been times when Eve had felt a bit resentful. Everyone wanted a piece of Max and it ate into their time together.

They'd met on their first day at medical school and the magnetism that drew everyone to him had also worked its spell on Eve. She hadn't thought for a moment that her feelings for him would be reciprocated, but he'd made it clear almost straightaway that they were and they'd been together ever since. It was perfect; they shared so many of the same goals and values, and his family had welcomed her with open arms, something she valued more than she could have put into words. She'd lost her mother to cancer when she was just fourteen, and had moved in with her father and more-than-slightly resentful stepmother, whose plans to move to Spain had been scuppered by Eve's arrival. As soon as she'd started university, the plans were back on, and her father and stepmother now lived in southern Spain, running a bar and raising their beautiful twin sons, who probably thought of Eve as more of a distant cousin than a sister. Max's family, by contrast, had folded her into the centre of their lives and had made her feel welcome from the very first time he'd taken her home with him. She adored them and it was just one more reason she felt incredibly lucky to be marrying Max and taking another step towards the life they wanted.

Their careers were going just the way they'd wanted too. Eve had specialised in emergency medicine, having found her passion early on in the foundation stage of her training, and Max was two thirds of the way through his training to become a surgeon. They'd both worked at St James's Hospital, but for the second phase of his training, he'd moved to the nearby Leeds Children's Hospital to specialise in paediatrics. They were the type of couple who had five-, ten- and even twenty-year plans, because Eve needed the security of being able to picture their future. Her mother's diagnosis and subsequent death had made it feel as if the world had been ripped out from under her feet. Max brought the spontaneity and the fun, thinking nothing of booking them a holiday based on the toss of a coin, or something as simple as turning off the road when they travelled down to Cornwall, to check out a town or village he'd never been to before, just because he liked the sound of the name on the road sign. She knew without a shadow of a doubt that he was the person she was supposed to share her life with – and she wouldn't have minded if he wanted thirty-three stag dos, and she had to pick him up from every single one of them at the end of a long shift – as long as he felt the same way about her. And she knew he did.

'Oh yeah, I know what Max is like all right and to be honest, if he'd let me come, I'd have tagged along on one of his stag dos, instead of coming to your hen.' Vick gave a throaty laugh, throwing back her head and making the wooden beads at the end of her long braided hair knock together like wind chimes.

'Well, thanks a lot.' Despite her words, Eve was already laughing.

'You know I'm only joking, chick. I wouldn't have missed that for the world.' Vick gave her shoulders a squeeze. 'And I still think there's time for us to cram another one in, maybe even two. You can't let Max have all the fun and it's still nearly three weeks until the wedding.'

'One was enough for me and I've discovered that shift work and hangovers do not mix. It would probably take me the full three weeks to get over it, especially if you're in charge of the drinking games again.' It had been a brilliant weekend, hiring an Airbnb in the Peak District, which was a more-or-less halfway point between her life in Leeds and Max's family in Cornwall. His mother, sister and aunt had all joined Eve and her friends for the celebration and there was no way it could be topped. All the women who meant the most to her were there and she felt absolutely no need to repeat it.

'Spoilsport!' Vick laughed again. 'Still, I could always pretend I'm on a stag do, the amount of drunks we get here on a Friday night. Although, the usually endless stream does seem to have dried up in the last half an hour.'

'Vick, don't, that's almost as bad as saying that it's... well, you know, the word we never, *ever* say.' Eve widened her eyes in mock horror. They both knew better than to ever say it was *quiet*, because then the floodgates were guaranteed to open and they'd be back to being run off their feet for the rest of the shift.

'I'm not that daft, as soon as I opened my mouth they'd be—' She didn't even get a chance to finish the sentence before the red phone behind them started to ring. It meant a patient with a serious trauma was on the way in. Turning like a ballerina performing a flawless pirouette, Vick snatched up the phone, taking down the details of the call from the paramedics, before relaying them to the rest of the team.

'Male, early thirties with a serious head injury resulting from an assault and subsequent blow to the head from hitting the pavement. The paramedics suspect a skull fracture and possible serious frontal lobe bleed. He has a GCS score of four. Estimated time of arrival – five minutes.'

'Oh God, that doesn't sound good.' Eve hated these kinds of calls, someone so young whose life was now hanging in the balance, a life which would almost certainly be irrevocably changed even if he did survive. She couldn't allow herself to think too much about the tragedies she encountered every single day at work, they had a job to do. 'Right, let's get ready.'

Within minutes, Eve was standing by the doors to the emergency department with Vick by her side. She hadn't even realised it had been raining until now. Despite the fact that the sky was jet-black, it was still humid outside, summer in the city at its peak and steam rose off the ground as the rain hit the warm Tarmac. The wail of the siren heralded the approach of the ambulance, and the reflection of the flashing blue lights bounced off the wet road. This was their patient. She recognised Allie, the paramedic who was driving, who both she and Max had known since their early days at the hospital. Allie leapt out of the front of the ambulance, heading straight round to the back to open the doors. But then, as Eve and Vick moved towards the back of the ambulance too, Allie turned, her face draining of colour, and looking deathly white in the eerie light.

'Eve I don't know…' Allie shook her head and turned to look at Vick. 'She shouldn't be here, not for this.'

'What do you mean I shouldn't be here?' Even as she said the words, Eve knew what they meant, but she couldn't acknowledge them, because she couldn't allow it to be true. Then, any last semblance of hope she had that she might have misunderstood was taken from her. The world as she knew it, was being ripped away for the second time in her life, as Allie mumbled the words she so desperately didn't want her to say.

'It's Max.'

1

TWO YEARS LATER

Eve woke with a start, all four of her limbs flinching violently, almost as if she'd been electrocuted. She'd been back in that room again; standing by the side of Max's bed as one of her colleagues delivered the devastating news about his test results.

'The bleed in Max's brain has caused irrevocable damage. It's going to be life-changing. For both of you.' It was a moment she never wanted to relive, but every time she closed her eyes, she knew there was a good chance of that happening. Even when she didn't close her eyes, it could happen. Working in an emergency department, there were far too many triggers and reminders of that terrible night, meaning the possibility of being forced to relive it was always present. All it took was for another patient to be rushed in whose circumstances or injuries were an echo of Max's. Or a relative who was forced to hear the same fateful words and be told that their loved one would never be the same again.

The cases that Eve found especially hard were the ones that came out of nowhere, where the patient and their family had just been getting on with their lives, not expecting anything out of the ordinary to happen and then, bam, out of the blue they'd been hit by a sucker punch that changed everything. That's what had happened to Max, in every sense. A complete idiot, who Max and his friends had walked past, on their night out, had for some unknown reason taken offence to the group of thirty-somethings, laughing and having fun. Brandon Moorcroft was the name of the man who changed everything with a single punch directed to the back of Max's head, sending him sprawling forward, making him lose his footing and smack his head against the pavement.

Moorcroft had been half out of his mind on a combination of drugs and alcohol, having got wasted after splitting up with his partner. He hadn't been able to justify to the police why he'd attacked Max, except for the fact that he was wearing a T-shirt clearly marking him out as the stag. Moorcroft claimed that white-hot rage had washed over him because Max was getting married and he'd just been dumped. The attack was completely unprovoked, and Moorcroft had eventually sobbed in court, saying how desperately he wished he could take it back. But there was no rewind button. That decision, that single blow to the back of Max's head had ruined so many lives and Eve wasn't sure she'd ever be able to shut her eyes and know for certain that she wouldn't be back in that moment, one she'd have given anything not to have happened.

* * *

Less than half an hour after waking up, Eve was on her way to work. She ran to St Piran's whenever the timing of her shifts allowed. There were staff changing rooms, lockers and a couple of showers available. It meant she could try and run off some of the tension in her body before she started her day and change into her uniform once she was ready. The rucksack on her back contained everything else she needed and the meandering route she took to work allowed her to take in some of the scenery that made Cornwall so beautiful. She lived on the top floor of a converted former grain store, with far-reaching views of the countryside, but too far from the coast to get even a glimpse of the sea. If she'd run directly to the hospital, via the quickest route, it would have been less than a mile and a half. As it was, she always took a route of at least three miles, sometimes more than double that, depending on how much time she had to spare. She loved the rough terrain of the coastal path, not just for the beautiful views of aquamarine water and the dramatic cliffs jutting out of the waves, but because it required concentration, to avoid tripping or falling. It meant her mind was less busy with all the other things that usually dominated her thoughts; the worries and the fears, and sometimes even the regret. Not tripping and falling to her death, while running on the coastal path, was a form of mindfulness that Eve was pretty sure she'd invented. Maybe she should market it to others, because sometimes it felt like the only thing keeping her sane.

'Did you run here again?' Meg, one of the other A&E doctors widened her eyes when Eve nodded, as she emerged from the changing room, after showering and drying her hair. 'My God, you put us all to shame.'

'Not me.' Eden, a staff nurse in the Emergency Department, gave them a rueful grin. 'I have a four-year-old with autism to get ready and out of the door to nursery before I get to work, so I've already had my workout for the day.'

'Fair point and trust me, I fully intend to recoup the calories on my first break.' Eve tapped the side of her nose. 'Rumour has it that Gwen is bringing in one of her famous cakes to celebrate the fact that she's got another grandchild on the way.' Eve turned her palms towards the ceiling, indicating the futility of trying to resist the offer of cake. Gwen was the volunteer coordinator who ran the Friends of St Piran's Hospital shop and was like a stand-in mother come agony aunt to all the staff, and people rarely turned down any offer she might make.

'Has she? That's great news.' Aidan, the most senior nurse on duty beamed, before lowering his voice and exchanging a glance with Eve. 'Although I'm really glad Esther isn't in today. If she hears one more bit of a baby news, I think it might break her.'

'I think you might be right.' Eve sighed, thinking about Esther's reaction to one of their recent admissions; a young girl who'd taken two entire packets of birth control pills in a misguided and extremely dangerous attempt to end an unwanted pregnancy. Esther, who was the department's Lead Nurse, had gone about her duties as diligently as ever, caring for the young girl and staying by her side when her stomach was pumped, monitoring her condition in the hours that followed, while they waited for space on a ward, and even supporting her when she spoke to her parents. Afterwards though, when the girl had been taken up to the ward, Esther had broken down at the injustice of it all. She'd been trying for a baby with her husband, Joe, for over a year, she'd said; her own birth control pills having been consigned to the bin and replaced with multi-vitamins, folic acid and even a supplement that claimed to be a birth control detox. None of them had made any difference so far and she and Joe, a consultant psychiatrist at the hospital, had just been referred for fertility treatment.

'I'm sorry, my hormones are haywire.' Esther had taken a shuddering breath, as Eve had passed her a tissue, and Aidan had wrapped his arms around her shoulders, offering the hug she clearly so badly needed. Eve had been grateful he was there, because as much as she'd wanted to hug Esther, somehow she couldn't bring herself to do it. She'd been at the hospital for well over a year now and she was gradually getting to know them all better, but a stretch of personal leave in the middle of that had meant she still felt like the new girl in lots of ways, even though Meg and Eden had both joined after her. She was probably closest to the two of them, and had been out for drinks with the entire team a couple of times, but none of them knew the full story about why she'd left Leeds and ended up in Cornwall. In fact, they barely knew anything about her personal life at all. She kept herself so closed-up these days that she hadn't wanted to open the floodgates of her own emotions, by letting herself connect too closely with any grief her colleague was feeling.

All those unfulfilled plans, all the hopes and dreams that might never be realised had felt too close to home, even if their circumstances were completely different. Instead, Eve had offered to make tea. She could cope with that and had lost count of the number of times it had been offered to her in the wake of Max's accident. Before the night of his third stag do, she'd believed that Yorkshire Tea, the signature drink of her adopted county, really could work miracles. But she'd found out the hard way that sometimes the best it could do was to provide a brief distraction, or a reason for someone who had no idea how to offer mean-ingful comfort to take a break from trying to, just for a little while.

'I guess we better start this shift then.' Eve tightened the hair band that was tying back her long, dark brown ponytail. She'd grown her hair for the wedding, having chosen a half up, half down sort of beachy boho look that had felt perfectly in keeping with the venue, just ten miles from the hospital where she now stood. The hairdresser had never arrived to style her hair, her dress still hung in a wardrobe at Max's parents' house, unworn, and all the plans they'd made for their wedding had come to nothing in the end. Yet somehow, she couldn't bring herself to cut her hair, despite the fact that it would be so much more practical.

'Oh God, sorry to do this to you at handover.' Isla, one of the other nurses on the team, pushed open the door to the staffroom, cutting off any response that Eve's colleagues might have been about to make. 'But we've just had a call on the red phone. A tourist in a hire car lost control coming down the hill into the harbour in Port Agnes and ended up pinning two pedestrians against the wall and hitting another. ETA is ten minutes.'

'Here we go again.' Meg grimaced, as they all moved to follow Isla, and all Eve could do was nod mutely. Here they went again, indeed, facing another incident when someone's life might have been changed forever, even destroyed. It never got any easier facing up to these moments, but Eve had to do it if she was going to be able to carry on doing her job. And sometimes, just lately, it felt as if being a doctor in A&E was the only part of her old self that Eve had left.

* * *

Oakwood Park, as the name suggested, was a twelve-acre site dominated by the mature oak trees dotted around the grounds and the beautiful Victorian former manor house, which now housed a charitable foundation providing twenty-four-hour nursing, neuro-rehabilitation, educational services, respite, and supported living accommodation for people with a range of head injuries from those needing minor care to maintain their independence, to those with complex disabilities. It had been Max's home since his discharge from hospital fourteen months ago, and it was somewhere Eve felt she could have negotiated the journey to with her eyes shut. It had been too late to visit Max the day before, after a shift that had started with three badly injured pedestrians and a driver who it turned out hadn't simply lost control of his car, but had suffered a heart attack at the wheel.

That had set the tone for the day and the shift had been non-stop. Eve had ended up staying on later than planned, because of the backlog of patients still waiting when the nightshift team had arrived, already short-staffed due to a sickness bug that was going around. She hadn't admitted, even to herself, that the idea of staying on at work was preferable to heading home and then driving over to see Max. Just the thought made her feel horribly guilty, but his moods seemed to have darkened over the past couple of weeks and Eve increasingly felt like she'd become his whipping boy of choice.

Today, there was no option to stay on late, and she couldn't come up with a justifiable excuse to Max's mother, because she was off work and Annie knew it. Annabel, or Annie as she was known to her nearest and dearest, had begun asking Eve for copies of her work schedule as soon as she had started at St Piran's, and now it was a habit it seemed impossible to break, no matter how much she might want to.

'Oh, Eve, thank goodness.' Annie folded her into a highly perfumed hug, the moment she entered the lounge that Max shared with three other residents. They all had their own bedrooms, but this communal area was viewed as a stepping stone to Max being able to move to one of the supported living bungalows in the grounds of Oakwood Park. 'We were beginning to wonder if you'd decided not to come again.'

Annie's voice was falsely bright, so the tone didn't sound accusatory, even if the words were. Part of Eve wanted to tell her not-quite-mother-in-law that it wasn't an option she could choose, because no one could withstand the guilt trip that decision would result in. Instead, she painted on a smile and swallowed back the words that were trying to escape. Coming to see Max was hard, because he still looked a lot like *her* Max, the man she had loved with every fibre of her being, but it wasn't *her* Max.

He'd died on the night of his third stag do, and no amount of rehabilitation or outright denial on his mother's part was ever going to bring him back. She almost wished he'd changed as much physically as he had in personality, then maybe it would be easier to accept this new person, but she wasn't sure that would have made any real difference, because a lot of the time Max seemed to resent Eve's very existence. It was almost as if she was the reason he'd ended up at Oakwood Park, and in a way she supposed that was true. If they'd never met and fallen in love, he wouldn't have proposed and he wouldn't have been out on that stag night, on the very evening that Brandon Moorcroft was. If Max had made one different decision anywhere along the line he wouldn't have been in that precise place at that precise time, connecting with the blow that had floored him and ended all the plans they had for the future. Then there was the fact that she had been the one to help his mother choose Oakwood Park.

'He'll need to be near to us and close to a hospital, not just for his treatment but for when you relocate for work.' Annie had made it sound like a *fait accompli,* and the truth was it had been. The relocation had never been in question as far as Max's mother was concerned. Eve had wanted to follow Max, of course she had, but her medical training meant she couldn't wear the same blinkers as his mother, burying her head in the sand and pretending that 'one day soon' they'd get the old Max back. She knew he was gone for good and that the changes to his personality that had turned him into an entirely different person would not be reversed. She'd already lost the person she loved most in the world, and relocating to Cornwall meant leaving behind her closest friends.

Oakwood Park was less than ten minutes' drive from his parents' house in Carrick Water, a tiny hamlet between Port Agnes and Port Kara. It meant that Eve could also visit every day after work *if she wanted to*. Those last four words were loaded. If she'd admitted to anyone else, even herself, that she didn't always want to, she would have sounded like the worst person in the world. She knew that, because she already felt like the worst person in the world. If Max had still been *her* Max, and as happy to see her as he used to be, of course she'd have wanted to go every single day. But when someone made you feel about as welcome as a case of athlete's foot it was much harder to feel inclined to visit at the end of a long day.

'Have you heard anything from Lily?' Annie fired the question at Eve, after she'd kissed her on both cheeks in a way that some-times felt more like aggression than affection. It wasn't because Annie didn't love Eve, she knew Max's mother adored her. It was because ever since the assault, Annie had been in a state of high alert, that made it slightly unnerving – and very far from relaxing – to be around her.

'She's sent me a few photos and I've seen some updates on her Instagram stories, but if you're asking me whether she's mentioned anything about coming home, then no, she hasn't.' Eve gave Annie a sympathetic smile. She knew how desperately Max's mother wanted her daughter, Lily, to come home from California. She also knew why Lily didn't want to, but that wasn't something she was willing to share with Annie. She was already hanging by a thread and Eve wasn't going to be the one to cut it. Annie's behaviour, and the expectations she'd put on her daughter in the wake of Max's assault, had pushed Lily to a point where she'd admitted to Eve that she wasn't sure she wanted to go on. She'd been exhausted physically and mentally trying to live up to her mother's demands, and by the time Max was moved to Oakwood Park she was already at breaking point. When her American boyfriend, Scott, had been offered a job back home and had asked Lily to go with him, it had been the life raft she'd needed. Annie hadn't taken it well at all and it had led to her own mental health spiralling even further which, in turn, had necessitated Eve taking time off work. Now that Annie was finally back to just about holding it all together, Eve wasn't about to shatter her hopes by telling her she wasn't sure Lily would ever come home.

'She FaceTimes me on a Sunday, but the rest of the time it's just WhatsApps, because of the time difference.' Annie's mouth was downturned at the corners, but then it veered between that and false brightness far too much these days. It was just one more thing that broke Eve's heart, because Annie had been the definition of *joie de vivre* before all of this. She could create a party out of nowhere and her infectious laughter had rung around the Pascoe family home. Having more or less retired from Carew's, her maternal family's law firm, in the wake of Max's assault, Annie now had three obsessions; bringing about her son's complete recovery, getting Brandon Moorcroft's case reviewed to ensure he was assigned with a sentence she considered 'just', and persuading her daughter to move back home. Only the last of those had a possibility of happening, and based on the messages Eve had received from Lily, even that was very remote.

Brandon Moorcroft had been sentenced to three years. Eve had to agree with Annie and Max's father, Nigel, that it wasn't nearly long enough. But Brandon had been high on methamphetamine after the breakdown of his relationship, and seemingly not just repentant but distraught at the damage he had caused. His barrister had offered up a defence centring around his difficult childhood as mitigation for his behaviour, and his former partner as the one solid presence in his life. When she'd left, he'd unravelled, and Max had just been in the wrong place at the wrong time. It couldn't excuse what Moorcroft had done, but it did impact on the sentencing, and they'd all been distraught when his prison term was handed out. In the early days it had felt as if the injustice of it all would eat Eve alive, and she could see it doing the same thing to Annie.

For Eve, the turning point had come in learning more about Brandon Moorcroft's background and the counselling she'd undertaken in the months following his sentencing. Her therapist had told her that holding onto the anger would harm her more than it would ever hurt Moorcroft, and she'd known from how twisted up she felt inside that he was right. She'd needed to find a way to let go of the sense of making things right by punishing Brandon Moorcroft, because no sentence would ever be enough. Her therapist had suggested that she look into restorative justice, which would give her the opportunity to sit across the table from Brandon – if he agreed to be part of it – and talk to him about the impact his actions had had on her life, and try to understand how he could have got to the point he'd reached on that fateful night. Eve had felt more and more lately that it was something she wanted to do, and she wanted to suggest it to Annie, to stop the bitterness from continuing to eat Max's mother from the inside out. But that was something Annie was nowhere near ready to hear, and Eve had a feeling she never would be.

'I'm sure Lily will come home for a visit soon.' Eve squeezed Annie's hand, hoping her words would offer some reassurance, despite the fact she knew they were a lie.

'Thank goodness I've got my bonus daughter.' Max's mother gave her a wobbly smile and Eve forced herself to return it. She loved Annie and Nigel as if they really were her parents, but they didn't know what was in her heart and she was terrified that if they ever found out, they wouldn't just stop loving her, they'd never want to see her again.

'Where's Max?'

'He's with the occupational therapist, they're working on the targets they've set him to achieve before he'll be allowed to move into one of the bungalows. But he should be back any minute.' Annie smiled again and Eve nodded. There were five shared bungalows for semi-independent living on the Oakwood Park estate, where the residents could move to as a step towards possibly moving into supported lodgings in the community, and sometimes even to full independence at some point in the future. The thought of that outcome made Eve shiver. What would everyone expect of her if Max was allowed to leave Oakwood Park? Whatever it was, she had a feeling she was destined to fall short.

'How's he getting on with—'

'Oh, here he is, talk of the devil!' Annie cut Eve off, clapping her hands in delight as Max came back into the room.

'I'm not the devil, you silly old woman.' It was a term Max had teased his mother with in the past, but back then it had come with so much love and affection, off the back of her struggling to download a new app on her phone, or losing her glasses when they were perched on the top of her head. Now it sounded like he meant it.

'I was just teasing, sweetheart.' Annie hugged him tightly. If his words cut her, she wasn't showing it. 'Look who's here, darling. It's Eve.'

'Hi.' Max sounded like a truculent teen and, as Eve took a step closer, he wrinkled his nose. 'You stink.'

'Don't be silly, of course she doesn't.' The laugh that accompanied Annie's words sounded forced and Max clearly wasn't going to be put off his stride.

'Yes, she does, she stinks.'

'I've come straight from work, it's probably the smell of the hospital.' Eve forced another smile, trying to remind herself just how triggering those kinds of smells must be for Max. She'd changed her clothes, but maybe the smell of antiseptic was clinging to her skin and her hair. He'd spent far too long in hospital in the weeks after the assault and then there was the fact that the person he'd been, the trainee surgeon who'd lived for his career, would never go back to a hospital in that capacity again. No wonder he resented any reminder.

'Well, I don't want to smell it.' Max folded his arms across his chest, suddenly going from sounding like a stroppy teenager to looking like a toddler.

'Let's go outside, shall we? Spring is definitely on the way and it's lovely out there.' Annie was doing her best to smooth over the situation, as she always did. Desperately trying to pretend everything would all be okay if they could just get through all of this. She seemed determined not to accept that 'all of this' was the new normal and there was no getting through it. At least not to the place where they'd come from.

'Okay, but the wind better not blow the smell in my direction.' Max stalked out of the door before either of them could answer, and as Eve exchanged a look with his mother, Annie just shrugged.

'Just give it a bit more time,' she said, the way she had so often before and Eve wanted to ask how much time would be enough for her to give, because she knew forever wouldn't be long enough and just lately even one more day felt like more than she could bear.

2

Felix closed the door behind him and let out a long breath. He'd known how lucky he was to find this place, one of six purpose-built apartments, or 'flats' as his sister insisted on calling them; teasing him as she always did for becoming so Americanised during his time in San Francisco. Whatever Eden wanted to call it, his new home was just what he'd hoped for when moving back to the UK. The big windows meant that it was full of light, even on the dullest of days, and Felix had a good-sized balcony with a view of the sea. There was even a shared garden, which had a gate on one side leading to a footpath that went all the way to the beach. He'd wanted a dog for as long as he could remember, but his apartment in San Francisco hadn't been pet friendly in the slightest and then there'd been Meredith. He'd wondered for a while if getting a dog might help, give her something to focus on other than the demons that had so often felt as if they were on the verge of overwhelming her. The way things had become, in the end, he couldn't have trusted her to look after herself – let alone a dog – she might even have sold it when he was at work one day. Anything was possible when she needed to score her next hit.

Now he could get a dog if he wanted one and come home from work knowing that it had been looked after by whatever doggy-daycare service he booked it into. There were no more calls from Meredith at all hours of the day and night, telling him she was in trouble and needed his help. The only person he had to look after was himself and it was a huge relief not to be responsible for anyone or anything else. It was weird, though, the way the human psyche worked, because he also felt strangely bereft, as though something was missing. He didn't want to go back to that life, but the void that trying to help Meredith had left behind was what had led him to volunteer for Domusamare, a local charity. It had been set up initially to try to combat homelessness, but now the charity also supported addicts, recovering addicts and victims of domestic abuse. His first day volunteering there had taken him back to some of his darkest days in San Francisco, trying to help fentanyl addicts, most of whom had long ago lost the desire to try and help themselves. A colleague at the hospital where he'd worked in San Francisco had asked if he would help out and, as an occupational therapist, he'd truly believed he had some skills that could be useful to people whose long-term use of the drug had resulted in a huge physical toll on their bodies, as well as their minds.

The clinic Felix volunteered at, By the Bay Recovery, was where he had met Meredith. A former addict herself, but five years clean, she'd retrained as a therapist to help others as a way of giving back to those who had saved her. It had been incredibly easy to fall in love with her and he had barely given her past a thought when their relationship had moved from friendship to something he'd hope would last forever. Felix had always known that alcoholics and drug addicts were in recovery for life, but at first he'd felt sure that Meredith had banished her demons. He could never have guessed the day he met her, or in the months that followed as their relationship deepened, that she was constantly teetering frighteningly close to a relapse. Meredith seemed to have it all together and she ran five miles every day, saying it kept her mind and body in the kind of condition she owed them, after all the abuse she'd put them through. It wasn't just a routine, it was essential to her wellbeing and, looking back, maybe that had also been an addiction of sorts. Felix just didn't realise because all he could see was the woman he loved. He'd felt guilty ever since for not seeing the signs in her when he should have been able to. Growing up with an alcoholic mother who hadn't managed to break the cycle until he was an adult, Felix knew that sobriety often balanced on a knife edge. His mother had tried numerous times in the past and had 'fallen off the wagon', and even when she did manage to quit drinking there was always a fear in the back of his mind that at any moment she could start again. All of that made it even harder to forgive himself for not truly considering that possibility when it came to the woman he'd shared his life and home with.

Meredith was almost the quintessential Californian girl when it came to her appearance, long blonde hair, bluey grey eyes that looked like they'd been colour matched to the water in San Francisco Bay and a broad, bright smile that made it look for all the world as though she'd never encountered a major problem in her life. And the truth was, by some standards, she hadn't. Instead Meredith had a pre-disposition to poor mental health, where even minor knocks and blows could feel catastrophic and leave her desperate to numb her resulting anxiety. It had started off with alcohol when she was still at school and progressed through an addiction to prescriptions painkillers after a minor accident, and eventually on to Class A drugs, until she was no longer functioning at all. That seemed to be far behind her by the time they met, but then she'd lost a client she'd grown close to, and all the years of therapy and studying, and helping others overcome their own demons, just melted away. Meredith had spiralled back into addiction in a way that had been terrifyingly quick and nothing that Felix had tried had been able to pull her out again. She'd left the home they shared, telling him he didn't understand her and that he never would because he hadn't had to fight his own addiction.

He'd been desperate to get Meredith the support she needed to get well again. At first, she'd rung him at all hours of the day and night asking for help, mainly in the form of money she claimed she needed for food, but they both knew she didn't care whether she ate or not. All she cared about was the next hit. Then she disappeared altogether. Someone had told Felix they'd heard she'd gone back into rehab, but she'd stopped calling him, or even picking up when he tried to get hold of her and he'd discovered that she'd racked up thousands of dollars' worth of debt on credit cards she'd taken out in his name. Felix had done everything he could to track her down, working with her family to try and save the woman they all loved, and in the end, it had pushed him to the edge of his own limits and he'd been forced to make the decision to leave San Francisco, to give himself some peace of mind.

His friend, Karl, still worked at the clinic, and Felix had asked him to keep trying to find Meredith and to let him know if she turned up, because if there was anything he could do to help her, he wouldn't hesitate. The love he'd felt for Meredith was still there, but it had morphed from romantic love to a kind of compassionate sorrow. He really hoped she was getting the help she needed and that this time it might actually work, but coming home to Cornwall had saved him from living half a life, constantly on edge. He'd taken a job as an occupational therapist at St Piran's Hospital. It was a world away from his life in California and, even though addiction problems existed everywhere, the rugged beauty of the coastline in the area where he'd grown up, had soothed his soul from the moment he got back.

Most of his patients were rehabilitating from injuries, or strokes, and he felt as though he could really help them make meaningful steps towards recovery, or at least find new ways to function that would improve their quality of life. Yet as the weeks ticked by, the void had opened up inside him and the desire to do more to help people like Meredith had grown with it. She haunted his dreams and when Drew, his sister's boyfriend, had told him about his own volunteering at Domusamare, it had felt like the outlet he needed. That had proved to be true, but he'd almost forgotten there'd be days like this. Days when it hit home that sometimes there was nothing that could be done to change the outcome everyone was working so desperately hard to try and avoid. Days when he'd be reminded so sharply of Meredith that it would feel almost impossible to breathe.

* * *

Knock... Knock-knock-knock... Knock. It was almost like Morse code, the way his sister knocked on the door, announcing who it was without her having to say a word. It was a code they'd come up with as kids, when their rooms had been their sanctuaries and they didn't want to let anyone in, except one another. Their mother had been in the grip of alcoholism back them, but their father had made his own mistakes, enabling his wife and trying to cover up what was going on. Even when Felix had told his dad that he and Eden felt unsafe when their mother was on one of her drunken rampages, he hadn't forced her to get help. Instead of making his wife face the consequences of her actions, he'd fitted locks to both of his children's bedroom doors, so that they could 'feel safe' by locking their mother out. That wasn't the way to make children feel safe, but it had at least provided a physical barrier to keep both of their parents away from them. They started using their keys to lock the doors when they went out, too, after their mother had got horribly drunk one day and ripped all the posters off Eden's walls and torn them to shreds in a fit of rage.

The locks allowed them to ignore the knocking and the ranting of their mother when her demands to be let in went unanswered. Instead they'd stay silent and hope she might believe they'd gone out. It was why Eden had come up with their 'secret' knock, the code that meant they'd know who was at the door. It was silly all these years down the line, with their mother and father both completely transformed from the people they'd been, but the 'secret' knock endured all the same.

Felix opened the door a few inches. 'I don't interact with cold callers.' His attempt at keeping his tone serious and his expression neutral failed almost instantly, and he laughed as she rolled her eyes.

'You've got three freezing callers out here, never mind cold ones, so just let us in, will you?'

'You should have said Teddie was here.' His heart instantly lifted at the sight of his four-year-old nephew in the arms of Eden's partner, Drew. When Teddie reached out towards Felix, everything in the world was good again. Eden's little boy had been diagnosed with autism and, until very recently, had been completely non-verbal. Now he was beginning to say things, but the development of his speech was quite different to that of most children, who would learn individual words and eventually begin to string them together. Teddie had what was called Gestalt language processing and as soon as he started to speak it was in phrases, rather than individual words. The phrases had a unique meaning to Teddie and weren't always easily decipherable to those who didn't know him. One of the earliest examples, had been when he'd memorised the phrase 'we all fall down' from the 'Ring-A-Ring-A-Roses' nursery rhyme. Now, every time Teddie hurt himself, whether it involved falling over or not, he'd say 'we all fall down.' The speech and language therapist had told Eden that the phrases were stepping stones to the development of more fluid speech, where the set phrases would eventually progress to single words, but she'd been so delighted for him to say anything at all that she wouldn't have minded what his first words had been.

'Twinkle, twinkle.' Teddie repeated the phrase with the same rhythm it had in the nursery rhyme, but Felix knew exactly what his nephew wanted and it wasn't a singalong.

'Okay, sweetheart. Let's get inside and I'll get your toy box out for you.' Lifting Teddie into his arms, Felix carried him through to the large open plan living area, one corner of which had been given over to sensory equipment for his nephew. There was a big wooden toy box containing all the toys that Felix had bought for him, the most recent additions were a set of shatterproof tubes that were filled with liquid and glitter, that twirled and danced when they were turned over or shaken. There were also some squidgy toys in different shapes, filled with sequins and sparkly beads providing sensory stimulation when they were held up to the light box. Teddie loved the feel of them, and the new additions had quickly become firm favourites, Felix had sung the nursery rhyme 'Twinkle, Twinkle, Little Star' to Teddie, when he'd first bought the toys and noticed that some of the sequins were star-shaped. Now 'twinkle, twinkle' had become his nephew's way of verbalising the intention to play with them.

Felix had had an affinity with Teddie from the first time they'd met and, despite the fact that he'd come and gone from his nephew's life because he'd only returned to Cornwall for all-too-brief visits when he'd been living in the States, they'd always had a close bond. Felix was able to understand what the little boy wanted in a way that was only matched by Eden and Drew, and he found the development of Teddie's language fascinating. If the human mind could create those kinds of building blocks for speech, when the usual path to language development was closed off, then surely it was capable of all kinds of things that the medical field didn't even know about yet. Felix lived in hope that there'd eventually be huge leaps of progress in terms of under-standing the relationship between addiction and brain chemistry, leading to the development of far more effective treatments. It would be too late for far too many people, but there were so many others who needed help. He'd spent all day dealing with the consequences of what happened when they were out of treat-ment options, and it never got any less devastating.

'You've got a knack of choosing toys he loves. Mum bought him a gorgeous wooden fort, but the only thing he likes about it is the feel of running his hands along the battlements. It doesn't matter how many times she retrieves the little wooden soldiers and puts them all back in the fort, the first thing Teddie does is to grab them all out again and hurl them to the furthest corner of the room. She still doesn't quite seem to grasp the fact that Teddie doesn't play the way she expects him to. But she's trying.'

'She is and you know, Mum, she just wants everything to be *okay* and she struggles when that doesn't look the way she expects it to. But we know Teddie isn't just okay, he's perfect.' Felix gave his sister's waist a squeeze. 'Now what can I get you guys to drink?'

'You don't have to get us anything, we just came to check that you were okay.' Drew looked puzzled when his statement was met with another eye roll from Eden. He'd clearly let the cat out of the bag in his usual direct style, but it was one of the things that Felix liked best about him and there was a lot to like. Drew had come into his sister's life in the last year and it was as if he'd been made to fit there. He was a pathologist at St Piran's Hospital and he had high-functioning autism, which allowed him to understand Teddie in a way that perhaps not even Eden could. Drew clearly adored both her and Teddie, and it was wonderful to see her happier than Felix could ever remember her being, especially after the hell that Teddie's father had put her through.

Eden had had so much on her plate that Felix had never told her about Meredith. It had been easy to keep his private life private, when he was living thousands of miles away. Eden would have warned him off getting involved with someone with addiction problems and repeating the cycle in the same way she had with Teddie's father. It was ironic when he'd been the one to caution her against that, but he'd done it himself anyway and it had ended in exactly the way she'd probably have predicted. Maybe it had been mapped out in their DNA after all they'd gone through as kids, but his sister's newfound happiness with Drew made him happy too and it gave him hope for a future that wouldn't have any echoes of their past. The last thing he wanted Eden to do was to worry about him now that he was home, but there were some things he knew he couldn't keep from her forever.

'I'm fine.' Felix tried to sound as if he meant it, but he'd been unable to fully shake off his sadness at the loss of another life to addiction. 'It was an overdose and when we sign up to volunteer at Domusamare we know that sometimes these things are going to happen, don't we?'

'Yes, but it's still a kick in the gut when they do.' Drew gave him a level look and all he could manage in response was a small nod. 'It's especially hard when you think you're making progress and that someone is on the road to recovery and then it all falls apart.'

When Felix still didn't answer, Drew continued. 'You did everything you could. Everyone at the charity did. You've got to shake off the feeling of being responsible for the people we work with. We can't force them to take the help that's offered or to stay away from the drugs.'

Drew ran a hand through his hair, breaking eye contact. He wasn't being flippant or trite and Felix knew what he was saying was true. If you took these things home with you then you'd be no good to the next person who needed your help, but it wasn't easy, especially not when you'd loved an addict, or been parented by one. Felix had done both of those things. It was why he was so determined to continue trying to help others, but it was also what made the blows when they came all the harder to bear. Drew was right, though, he had to be able to separate those things out from his own life.

'I'm all for shaking it off, what do you suggest?' He looked at Drew, a suspicion of what the other man might say making him raise his eyebrows. 'Although if you suggest another cold water swim it might be the end of our friendship and it'll almost certainly be the end of any hope I've got of becoming a father one day. It's still only March and I thought my testicles were never going to recover from the last one.'

'Too much information, big bro, too much information.' Eden shook her head, but she was laughing. 'Now you can see why I keep refusing to go and I haven't even got testicles.'

'You don't know what you're missing out on. All those endorphins that come rushing to the surface, not to mention the improvements to your circulation and your mental resilience.'

Drew could spout all the science he wanted about his newfound passion for sea swimming all year round, but Felix's toes weren't the only things curling in on themselves at the thought of it. Even if he had wanted to make it a daily habit, he definitely wouldn't have chosen March to start.

'Eden might not have tried it, but I know exactly what I'm missing out on and I intend to keep it that way.' Felix grinned again, already feeling much better just for spending time with people he loved and who he knew loved him in return. It was certainly far more appealing than plunging back into the Atlantic and trying not to release a string of expletives about just how cold it was. Otherwise, he'd have turned the air as blue as his testicles.

'I don't need to try it when there are plenty of other ways to get an endorphin rush.' Eden said as she shook her head and Felix raised his eyebrows for a second time.

'I think it might be my turn to caution you about too much information.'

'Not that.' She stuck out her tongue. 'Boys are so basic. What I was going to suggest was that we all head for dinner at Penrose Plaice. When we went in there with Teddie last month, I told Brae, the guy who runs the place, that he'll only eat chicken nuggets from McDonald's or Birdseye, so there'd be no point ordering anything for him. You know what Teddie's like, nuggets might be one of his safe foods, but if they deviate even slightly from what he's expecting, we might as well be asking him to eat a whole trout with its head still on.'

'He's got a discerning palate.' A wave of love for his gorgeous nephew, and all the little quirks that made Teddie who he was, washed over Felix as Eden nodded.

'He has indeed and it turns out that Brae was more than willing to cater to it. The next time we went in, he said he had a stash of Birdseye nuggets ready and waiting for Teddie's visit. So my vote for the endorphin rush we all need is a family dinner at Penrose Plaice and a wander around the harbour in Port Agnes to look at the winter lights before they take them down. Teddie loves them.'

Port Agnes was the neighbouring village to Port Kara and for the first time this year they were keeping some of the lights that had been put up at Christmas on display until the first official day of spring on the twentieth of March. It had been billed as 'light in the dark' and a way of encouraging visitors in the quietest months of the year. Teddie would have been happy to see the lights up all year round and anything that made his nephew happy was a good idea as far as Felix was concerned.

'That sounds perfect. Thank you.' Bending slightly, he dropped a kiss on his little sister's head. This was why he'd come home. Family was everything and no medicine or therapy would ever be able to take its place.

3

Eve's decision to go to Oakwood Park before work meant that there was a firm cut-off point for when she'd be able to leave. If she went after work, and Annie was there, no reason or excuse would feel good enough for why she couldn't stay for longer. It didn't matter that most of the time Max didn't even seem to want her there, preferring instead to hang out with his new friends, gaming or watching TV. Annie would look at her in that way she did, her eyes slightly narrowed, saying something that sounded innocuous enough on the surface, but that was loaded with hidden meaning.

'You're always in such a rush. I do feel for you, having to spread your time so thinly, I don't know how you and Max ever managed to spend any time together before the assault. Although, I suppose if something is enough of a priority then you can always find the time.'

Annie's tone would always be light, there was no emphasis on the words that would make it obvious she was having a dig, but Eve felt the sharp stab of reproach all the same. Maybe it was because she was searching for excuses not to spend as much time with Max as she could have done and Annie could see right through the reasons she came up with.

When she arrived at Oakwood Park, there was no sign of Annie, but her heart lifted a little at the sight of Felix, the occupational therapist working with Max on both his physical and cognitive rehabilitation. Max had been having regular sessions with the occupational therapy team at the hospital, but just recently Felix had been assigned to work with him in preparation for the next phase of his rehabilitation and the proposed moved to semi-independent living in one of the shared bungalows. As a result, Felix was now coming out to see Max in his own environment for some of their scheduled sessions. Eve had been introduced to Felix before he'd even started working at the hospital, because his sister, Eden, was one of her colleagues and perhaps the closest thing to a new friend she'd made since moving to Cornwall.

Eve had liked him straightaway and she'd been delighted when she'd discovered that he was Max's assigned occupational therapist. Sometimes conversations with the medical professionals supporting Max could be difficult and she'd broken down when she'd been asked by one of the doctors about how his behavioural changes were affecting her, wondering if the other woman was judging her as harshly as she was judging herself. Eve felt as if she could be honest with Felix and that he wouldn't judge her. She knew about some of the difficulties he and Eden had experienced in their own family, and that he would be unlikely to see things in black and white the way she feared other people might. They probably didn't, after all, the medical team supporting Max would have seen all of this before and the way injuries like his could change everything. But Eve felt judged, because she knew nothing about these people and they knew far more about her than she wanted them to. With Felix it felt like there was more of a balance.

'Hi, Eve, how are you? We were just talking about you.' Felix greeted her with the smile he always seemed to be wearing whenever she saw him and she found herself wondering if he was really as carefree as he seemed. She doubted it, in a job like his, but she found her mood lifting just from being around him. He had the same dark hair and bright blue eyes as his sister, but aside from their colouring, they didn't really look alike, despite the fact that they were both very attractive. Felix was hanging onto the last vestiges of the tan he'd been sporting when they first met and he was like a much-needed dose of sunshine on a grey March day.

'I'm good, thanks, but should I be worried when you say you've been talking about me.'

'All good things.' Felix was still smiling, but she saw a flicker of something in his eyes that gave away the lie even before Max interjected.

'I told him that you couldn't wait to get your knickers off when we met.' Max gave a brittle laugh. It was completely different from the sound of his laughter that she remembered so vividly. Things like that were what made it all the harder to believe *her* Max was still in there. The feeling deepened as he turned towards Felix, with a smirk on his face. 'Gagging for it she was, like a bitch on heat!'

Eve caught her breath, unable to speak. Max would *never* have said anything like that before the assault, not even to his friends in the sort of inanely laddish way some men did. It was so far removed from the sort of person he'd been that she couldn't even bring herself to respond, but Felix could.

'You need to stop talking like that, Max. This is exactly the kind of inappropriate comment we were speaking about just now.' Felix's voice was calm and measured, which would have made his words hard to argue with, even if Max had felt like it, but he just shrugged.

'I don't see why. It's not an insult.'

'There are parts of a relationship that are supposed to remain private and you need to make sure that Eve feels comfortable with the sort of things you're sharing.'

'You don't care, do you?' Max looked at Eve as if any protest she might make would have surprised the hell out of him; as if no one could possibly be offended by being described as a 'bitch on heat'. 'We used to have loads of sex; it's nothing to be ashamed of.'

'It's like Felix said, I don't think other people need to know about that and I very much doubt they want to hear about it either.' Eve tried to keep the same note of calm in her voice as Felix had adopted, but she didn't manage it. Instead her tone was tight and strained. Coupled with holding back the urge to cry, it left her throat feeling raw with suppressed emotion.

'They bloody well do want to hear about it. Jamie said he could imagine what you liked doing and that he'd have given anything to see your—'

'Darling!' Annie swept into the room, thankfully cutting off whatever it was that Max had been about to say.

'Christ, not you again. Why don't you just go into work if you're that bored that you need to come here all the time.' Max sounded like a huffy teenager, but if Annie was offended she wasn't showing it and she just laughed. It was something she was far better at than Eve could ever imagine herself being, but deep down the changes in Max must be every bit as agonising for Annie as they were for Eve.

'I only work one or two days a week now, darling, for the express reason that it allows me to be with you as much as possible.' Annie made it sound like her greatest pleasure and Eve experienced such a powerful stab of guilt she was surprised it hadn't skewered her to the wall.

'Well, you needn't bother. I don't need you here. Either of you.' Max cast a pointed look in Eve's direction. 'I've got things to talk about with Felix that I don't need you listening in on.'

'There's nothing you can't say in front of us, is there, Eve?' Annie didn't wait for her to respond. 'In fact there's not a thing you could do or say that would make us want to be anywhere but here with you.'

There was the guilt again, stabbing so hard this time that it made Eve catch her breath and all she could do was nod mutely. As if that somehow made it less of a lie than saying yes out loud.

'So Max is making good progress, Felix?' Annie's tone made it sound more like an expectation than a question, but Felix's smile was undimmed.

'I'm making you work hard, aren't I, Max?'

'Too fucking hard sometimes.' Max gave another unrecognisable laugh and Annie wagged a finger at him.

'We don't use language like that, Maximus. We never have.' Annie's use of Max's full name had always made Eve want to laugh before the assault, but now nothing about Max made her want to laugh.

'For Christ's sake. Everyone says fuck. Everyone except you.' The petulant teen was back, but Felix did his best to defuse the situation.

'I'd say we can see all the hard work starting to pay off, especially with the physical rehabilitation and adaptive techniques. I think if you keep working at this pace, Max, you should be on track for that move to the bungalow.' Felix never spoke about

Max, always to him. It was something Eve had noticed from the outset and she appreciated it, she hoped Annie did too. As for Max, she had no idea if he noticed or even cared these days, but the old Max, *her* Max, would definitely have done.

'That's excellent.' Annie gave a little clap of her hands, genuine delight spreading across her face. 'It's another step along the road and, who knows, we could be back to making wedding plans by this time next year.'

'Who knows.' Even to her own ears, Eve's words sounded dull and unconvincing. As she caught Felix's eye for a moment, he gave just the briefest, almost imperceptible shake of his head, as if he knew as well as she did that they wouldn't be planning a wedding this time next year. They wouldn't ever be planning a wedding again, because the one person who wanted that even less than Eve did was Max.

* * *

'Why are you still crying for God's sake?' Max's irritation would have been obvious even if it hadn't been spelt out in his words and Eve's heart felt like a lead weight in her chest. She was sure if she'd been floating in water that she'd have sunk to the bottom and would never have been able to make it back to the surface.

'Georgia lost her mum and she's devastated.' Eve could barely get the words out, her throat burning from the effort of not bursting into the kind of noisy sobs that would probably have pushed Max over the edge, but she was powerless to stop the silent tears rolling down her cheeks and he was clearly infuriated.

'She just works here, she's not your friend and you didn't even know her mum, so why are you so upset?' Max looked at her with such disdain that she wanted to cry again. What made it worse is that he'd have been the one person she could have gone to in the past, who would have given her unconditional love and support, and he'd have understood why this had hit her so hard without her having to say a word. Georgia, one of the carers at Oakwood Park, was back at work for the first time after her mother's death. It had been sudden, a heart attack, not cancer like Eve's own mum – and Georgia was in her early twenties, not fourteen as Eve had been – but she'd still felt a powerful bond of understanding when the young woman had burst into tears upon seeing Eve, and they'd exchanged a hug.

'I just miss her so much already and no one is ever going to take her place. How am I supposed to get through the rest of my life without her?' Georgia had looked at Eve helplessly, clearly desperate for her to impart some wisdom that would help ease the pain, but sometimes there were no words. Eve still had to try.

'You'll always miss her and wish she was here, but she will be in lots of ways. I still remember things Mum used to say to me when I'm struggling with something, and it's like she's still around giving me advice.' Eve had squeezed Georgia's hand.

'Thank you. You're so kind.'

'Can we go now? I want to eat the food before it gets cold.' Max had cut in. 'I hate it when that happens. There's nothing worse than soggy chips.'

For a moment, Eve almost laughed with incredulity at the bitter irony of his words. She'd been comforting Georgia after a terrible loss, but Max genuinely couldn't think of anything worse than soggy chips from the takeaway that Eve had just driven him to collect. There was nothing funny about it, though, and her heart broke at the way Max had acted. There was no point telling him, now they were back in his room, that some of her tears had been for Georgia, but some had been for herself. The young woman's sadness had brought back feelings that Eve tried so hard to push down, about the pain of losing her own mum. She wanted a hug and for Max to tell her it was okay to cry, the way he would have done before the assault. He'd have held her and reassured her that as much as she missed her mum, and as hard as the years after her death have been for Eve, she had him now, and his family, and she'd never have to feel alone again. Except that was never going to happen, instead Max gave another heavy sigh as he looked at her again.

'Are you going to answer me? I said why are you so upset when you don't even know the woman who died and you barely know Georgia. It's ridiculous.'

'Do you remember when we talked about empathy, Max?' The voice behind Eve made her jump and she turned in surprise to see Felix standing in the open doorway.

'Yeah, yeah.' Max rolled his eyes. 'I'm supposed to practise it as much as I practise the physical stuff, but I just can't see how being upset for someone you don't even know makes any sense. People have too many emotions in my opinion. Especially Eve.'

'I'm just going to get some air.' Eve all but pushed past Felix on the way out, leaving him to continue the conversation with Max. She was embarrassed that he'd seen her like that, with such raw emotion spilling out of her, and that he'd overheard at least part of her conversation with Max. She knew there wasn't much privacy at Oakwood Park, and the door to Max's room had been open, meaning that anyone walking down the corridor could have heard, but she still wished it hadn't been Felix. She wasn't sure quite why the idea bothered her so much, but it did. She felt ashamed that he might have overheard her vulnerability and Max's rejection of her feelings. Felix knew Max was her fiancé and he probably felt sorry for her, or worse still judged her for her relationship with Max. She'd had to get outside and take some big gulps of air to try and regain control of her emotions. But even five minutes later, having walked backwards and forwards across the lawn in front of Oakwood Park House, her throat was still burning and she knew more tears could come all too easily.

'Are you okay?' Felix's voice caught her by surprise for a second time and, even though she'd fully intended to nod, she shook her head.

'I'm sorry. I know it's silly getting so upset like that over Georgia's news and then getting even more upset about Max's reaction, but whenever I hear about someone losing their mum it just brings back the feeling of losing mine.'

'There's nothing silly about the way you reacted and there's definitely no need to apologise. You're an amazing person, Eve, and Max is really lucky to be surrounded by so much love and support, but I know he doesn't always see it that way.' There was such warmth in Felix's voice, it was almost like being wrapped in a hug, and to Eve's horror she found herself imagining what that might be like. She hadn't felt anything close to amazing in a very long time, that was the only reason Felix's words were affecting her so much. Desperately trying to shake the unwanted thought off, she nodded mutely, and Felix continued. 'It must be incredibly tough at times, dealing with the impact of the TBI on all of you.'

Eve wished she wasn't so familiar with the language that surrounded Max's injury. A TBI was shorthand for Traumatic Brain Injury, which was what he'd suffered. Sometimes, in the wake of the assault, she'd even wished she wasn't a doctor, then she might not have known quite how extensive his injury was and that the changes in Max's personality were lifelong. She might still have had hope, if she was in some other occupation, but just lately she seemed to have next to no hope left.

'I know it's not his fault, but he used to have so much empathy. He'd have been the first person to hug Georgia and he'd probably have cried too. Maybe not in front of her, because he's right, this is her grief and not mine, but he would have done later. Her sadness would definitely have touched him, but now... He says it's because he barely knows Georgia, so why would he get upset, but he knows me and I find it so hard that he can't even be there when I need him any more.'

'When someone's empathy is affected in that way, it can be one of the toughest things for loved ones to cope with. That's why we work on it in all the forms of therapy we offer patients who've had a TBI. Some people with frontal lobe damage can never regain cognitive and emotional empathy, but we can work on developing compassionate empathy. It's the form of empathy that focuses more on actions and behaviours, rather than feelings, so it tends to be something people with TBIs can get their heads around a bit more easily. All of the professionals working with Max are trying to incorporate that into his therapy, so I don't want you to think there's no hope of things changing.'

It was almost as if Felix had read her mind and, as she turned to look at him, his striking blue eyes meeting hers, the temperature suddenly seemed to rise by twenty degrees. Her pulse was racing too. *Oh God, no. This absolutely wasn't happening.* She wasn't going to get a schoolgirl crush on Felix, just because he was so incredibly lovely, or because he looked every bit as beautiful on the outside as he was on the inside. *No. Absolutely not. No way.* That would have been ridiculous and she wasn't allowing it to happen. It would make her even more pathetic than still trying to turn to Max for support, like she had in the old days, when he was the one who needed it most. She wasn't going to let herself go down that road. She had to nip this in the bud and say it out loud, to spell it out to herself and Felix.

'We just all really want Max to continue making progress, so that we can get things back to where they always should have been.' The smile Eve painted onto her face was so forced it hurt. She knew getting Max back to who'd he'd been before was never going to happen, but she had to keep pretending. Only now the charade wasn't solely for Annie's sake, it was also to protect herself, from looking like a total idiot by falling for Felix, when all he was trying to do was help.

4

Lots of people looked forward to the weekend and woke on Friday mornings with a spring in their steps and the *thank God, it's Friday* mantra on their lips. Working in A&E was a different story. It was often more like Freaky Friday than TGIF. It was the day of the week that seemed to bring out all the people hell-bent on self-destruction. Throw in a stag do of twenty lads, determined to help their mate enjoy his last weekend of freedom at 'all costs' and you had a recipe for disaster. Not to mention a very over-crowded waiting room.

'How many of the stag party are receiving treatment or waiting to be seen?' Danni Carter was Clinical Lead in the emergency department and it was her job, along with Lead Nurse, Esther, to try and ensure that all the patients who needed care would receive it within the guidelines set by the trust, despite the constraints of staffing and other resources. It wasn't a job for the faint-hearted.

'Six, but they all came in from Port Tremellien by cab. There's a seventh one on his way in by ambulance, the best man apparently.' Esther shook her head and let out a long sigh, looking from

Danni to Eve. 'Although I use the term loosely, as apparently, he was demonstrating how to do a scissor kick while he was walking along a half-height wall. As you can imagine, it didn't end well and he's got an open fracture. Another group of lads in the area were watching when he fell and they laughed. That's when the fight broke out that landed the rest of them in here.'

'I don't envy the bride marrying into that kind of friendship group.' Danni wrinkled her nose. 'I've got no idea why they want to spend the money hiring an Airbnb for the weekend just to get horribly drunk and only remember the weekend at all because of the injuries they end up with.'

'I hate stag dos.' Eve hadn't intended to say the words out loud, because the last thing she wanted was to have to explain why just hearing the term 'stag do' was enough to make her shudder, but they'd slipped out of her mouth before she could stop them. Luckily, when it came to her colleagues, she didn't need to give any rationale for her hatred of stag dos. Esther was already nodding vigorously.

'God, me too. And hen dos and anything else that involves binge drinking, as well as losing all your inhibitions and parking your ability to think rationally at the door. I try really hard to be sympathetic to all my patients, but some of them don't make it easy, sitting there covered in their own vomit, with injuries inflicted by stupidity, while other people who are here through no fault of their own are having to wait longer as a result.' Esther suddenly stopped. 'Oh no, hark at me. It's official, isn't it? I'm getting old. I sound like the kind of grumpy old killjoy I swore I'd never turn into.'

'No, you sound like the mum you're going to be before you know it.' Danni squeezed Esther's shoulder. Not only were they best friends, they were also sisters-in-law, as Esther was married to Danni's brother, Joe. Most of the team knew Esther and Joe were trying for a baby, but Eve would never have dreamt of bringing the subject up, she wasn't close enough to any of the team to initiate that kind of conversation.

'I really hope you're right.' Esther smiled.

'It's going to happen, I know it.' Danni returned her smile. 'And as a mum who's just about to face toddler tantrums, I'm going to get in some practice at laying down the rules and assign some chores to you both. Would you be able to lead on dealing with the patient who's on his way in, with the compound fracture, please, Eve? You'll need to liaise with the surgeons from orthopaedics by the sound of things.'

'Absolutely.' Eve nodded, stilling her breath at the thought of what she might be about to face as she moved off to await the ambulance. She had to remind herself that it was okay. They already knew what injuries the best man had sustained. He'd been assessed by the paramedics and there were no concerns about life-threatening injuries. The break had been stabilised as much as possible and she just needed to take immediate action to reduce the risk of infection, compartment syndrome, or a thromboembolism. Whilst the latter could be life threatening, if a blood clot formed near the injury site and travelled to the lungs or brain, treatment in a hospital environment would be relatively straightforward. Eve would ensure that antibiotics were administered and decide whether any further action was immediately necessary. The surgical team would then carry out an assessment and it was quite likely they'd decide to operate, after which the patient would continue to receive medication to prevent blood clots until his mobility was sufficiently restored. This wasn't an injury that could be compared to the one Max had sustained on his stag night, but that didn't stop Eve's stomach churning like a washing machine on a spin cycle as she awaited the arrival of the ambulance.

'Are you okay, Eve?' Meg's voice was louder than it needed to be, given that she was only a few feet away from where Eve had been standing.

'Yes, why?' She blinked her eyes a couple of times in order to focus. For a moment she'd been miles away, back in Leeds, on the night that had changed everything. But she had a job to do, and she had to shake the memory off.

'It's just that I spoke to you three times and you didn't answer.'

'Sorry, I was just thinking about what an absolute nightmare stag dos are.'

'Definitely. It would put me off marriage, if I hadn't already decided that I'm going to stay single and have about ten dogs instead of a husband.' Meg laughed. 'I came out to try and track down one of the men from the stag do, who Isla triaged. He needs treatment for a superficial head wound, but one of his mates just told me that he's got a cab back to Port Tremellien to get to the pub before it closes.'

'I can't imagine why you'd ever want to stay single, when there are men like that around. He sounds great.' Eve laughed as well, immediately feeling better. The atmosphere was completely different to how it had felt on the night of Max's assault. She had to stop comparing every incident that had any similarity to that night, otherwise she'd spend far too many shifts in a state of unbearable tension.

'Hmm. Give me a Labrador any day.' Meg was already walking away. 'Right. I'd better get back into the thick of it. Eden was trying to persuade one of them to put his trousers back on when I came out. Apparently, he couldn't get it into his head that there was no need to take them off when his only injury is a suspected broken knuckle.'

'We should get danger money and patients like that should be fined to pay it.'

'I'd vote for that.'

Just as Meg disappeared back through the doors, Eve's patient arrived and she breathed a sigh of relief to see him laughing and joking with two of the paramedics, Julia and Dean, who quickly outlined the handover information.

'Anything else I should know?' Eve looked towards Julia after the briefing and the other woman pulled a face.

'Tom here is a bit handsy, aren't you, Tom?' She gave him a stern look and, to his credit, he managed to look contrite. 'But I've told him if he does it again, he might wake up from this op to discover it's not just his injured leg that's been shaved.'

'It's the groom who's supposed to wake up with no eyebrows.' Tom's voice had taken on a whiney tone.

'Who said anything about your eyebrows?' Julia gave a wicked grin and Eve couldn't help laughing.

'I promise to be good.' Tom gave a mock salute, but he was laughing too. 'And thanks for looking after me.'

'I would say no problem, but my mum always told me not to lie.' Julia winked. 'Come on then, Deano, let's go and see what other reprobates we can pick up on our travels.'

'Am I really going to need surgery?' Tom's eyes were round with concern as he looked at Eve after the paramedics left. All the cockiness and swagger that had made him think it was a good idea to demonstrate a scissor kick on a wall had clearly deserted him.

'I think so, I'm just going to do an initial examination and we'll set up an IV for antibiotics. I'd usually have a colleague with me, but we're stretched very thin tonight and all the nurses are already busy. So you're stuck with just me for now, at least until the surgeons from orthopaedics come to see you.'

'Hazza's Mrs is going to kill me if I miss the wedding.'

'I take it that's the groom?' Before Tom could answer, another man burst into the room.

'Oi, oi, Tommy boy, are they going to amputate?' The man had a huge grin on his face and an ever bigger black eye.

'I might ask them to, if it's a choice between that and facing Beth. She told me to make sure Hazza didn't do anything stupid, but I can just imagine what she's going to say about having me in the photos with a cast on, or crutches.'

'Yeah, I think I'd rather face a chainsaw than Beth when she's on the warpath. Where is Hazza anyway? Last time I saw him he was having a bet with James about who could last longest in the water and they said they were going in.'

'I thought he was here.' Tom's face seemed to drain of all colour as he spoke, and Eve felt as if her blood had turned to ice, exactly like the water would feel this late at night in March.

'Have you tried phoning him?' Eve's tone was urgent and both men looked at her in surprise.

'I don't really know what happened to my phone.' Tom patted the pocket of his shirt as if it might suddenly appear and the other man shrugged.

'Yeah, I tried but it went straight to voicemail.' His lack of concern made Eve want to shake him.

'Well, try again.' She was raising her voice now, but she couldn't seem to keep control of her emotions. 'Where exactly was he when you last saw him? Why didn't you do anything to stop him going for a swim?'

'Christ, I think Beth's got competition.' The man with the black eye laughed, and Eve completely lost control.

'You bloody idiot. You're standing there laughing and your friends could be out there suffering from hyperthermia or worse still, drowning. What kind of moron are you?' She was really shouting now, barely aware of what Tom and his friend were saying in response, as Meg suddenly appeared in the cubicle.

'Are you okay, Eve?' It was a repeat of the question she'd asked earlier, but it was clear from the look on her face that she already knew Eve was far from okay.

'These idiots have let the groom and another of their friends go into the sea. It's pitch-black and freezing out there and even if they don't drown, they could still die.' A sob caught in Eve's throat and suddenly tears were streaming down her face. She'd never met the groom, or his friend, so she couldn't explain why she was crying for them. Except deep down, she knew her tears weren't for these strangers.

'I don't know why she's going so mental.' The man with the black eye gestured towards Eve. 'Hazza's all talk, he wouldn't really get in the sea in this weather. He thought it was cold when we went to Croatia for my stag, so he's not going to go swimming in Cornwall in March.'

'Who says I won't?' Another man came strolling into the cubicle.

'Hazza!' The man with the black eye slapped him on the shoulder. 'You've got this doctor shouting at me like I'm a five-year-old for apparently letting you drown or freeze to death.'

'Nah, James bottled it.' Hazza shrugged and all the adrenaline that had been racing around Eve's body seemed to drain out of her, but she still couldn't stop crying.

'Christ, can't you give her a Valium or something.' Black-eye man was on a roll now.

'I'm going to have to ask you both to go out to the waiting room if you aren't receiving treatment. Your friend needs to be seen by the orthopaedic surgeons and I'll let you know when you can come and see him.' Meg's tone was calm but forceful, brooking no argument and to Eve's surprise, both Hazza and the man with the black eye complied without protest.

'You don't have to ask me twice. If I wanted to be moaned at, I could have stayed at home. Come on, Hazza.' Black-eye man put an arm around the groom-to-be's shoulders. 'Let's get out of here. We'll come back and see Tom when we know whether they're going to chop off his leg.'

Cackling with laughter, the two of them left and Meg turned back towards the patient. 'I'm going to call the orthopaedic surgeons and ask them to come down and see you now, but in the meantime, I'll get one of the nurses to set up an IV with some antibiotics.'

'Yeah, she said that's what you were going to do.' Tom threw a look towards Eve, who didn't trust herself to speak, tears still streaming down her face.

'Eve, do you want to take a bit of a break? I can handle things here.'

'It's too busy and I—'

Meg cut her off, putting a hand on her arm. 'You need a break. It's fine. I can take it from here.'

Eve had been about to argue again, but she knew Meg was right and in the end, she just nodded, wiping her eyes with the back of her hand and trying desperately to halt the tears that wouldn't seem to stop coming.

* * *

'I feel like such an idiot.' Eve took the cup that Eden passed her in the staffroom at the end of the shift. The tea looked as if a spoon could have stood up straight in it, it was so strong. When she took a mouthful, it was sickly sweet as well and it was all she could do to swallow it.

'I know you don't usually take sugar, but they say strong, sweet tea cures everything, don't they?' Eden briefly rested a hand on her shoulder. 'And you're not an idiot, sometimes it just all gets too much.'

'It wasn't even like I was in the middle of a life-and-death moment, though. I don't know why the thought of those two guys going into the sea on a night like this freaked me out so much.' It was a blatant lie, but Eve couldn't face admitting the truth.

'I do,' Meg interjected. 'I've seen patients brought in who've been pulled from the sea and far too often it doesn't end well. I've also seen other stupid decisions that have cost people their lives and it's such an awful waste. Those men on the stag do were about our age, far too young to end up on a slab in the mortuary, and sometimes the stupidity and pointlessness of people's actions gets to you in a way you can't just shake off. I know, I've been there.'

It would have been obvious that Meg was speaking from personal experience, even if her eyes hadn't darkened at that moment, a shadow seeming to fall across her whole face at the recollection of events she clearly wished she hadn't witnessed. For a moment Eve thought about asking her more, but if Meg had wanted to share the details she would have done, and Eve knew better than anyone that there were some things that needed to be kept shut down inside if there was going to be any hope of getting through the day.

'I guess so.' Eve tried to inject some lightness she didn't feel into her tone, and when she caught Isla's eye it was harder still. 'I've just been more reactive to situations lately than I should have been.'

Isla gave an almost imperceptible nod, but Eve saw it all the same, and when Isla and Eden exchanged a look, she knew for certain what they were thinking. They'd witnessed her losing it before, when an eighteen-year-old called Callum Sinclair had been rushed in after collapsing on the rugby pitch, his hysterical mother begging the medics to save her son. Eve had known that they wouldn't be able to save him and that his mother's pain wouldn't be fleeting, it would last forever. There'd be no looking back to the moment her son had *almost* died, because he was dead and there was nothing anyone could do to change that.

There'd been so many emotions racing through Eve's head. There'd been echoes of the night Max was brought in, the tension in the air, the team throwing everything at the situation to try and save a young life, but the outcome had been different and what had thrown Eve the most was the unwanted thought that had come into her head. Perhaps it would have been better if Max *hadn't* survived. She didn't want to think that way, and she didn't really believe it, but the truth was *her* Max *had* died that night. She'd lost him, but she hadn't been able to grieve for him in the way she would have done if the team hadn't managed to save him. Annie hadn't had to say goodbye to her son, the way Callum's mother had, but she'd lost a big part of who Max was. She just wasn't ready to accept it and that made it even harder for Eve to be able to express her grief. All the pushing down of her feelings wasn't good for her, she knew that, and she could almost feel them poisoning her. But she was going to have to get a handle on how it was making her react to things, otherwise there was a chance she might not be able to do the job she loved any more. She couldn't lose that, because she was scared if she lost one more thing she might not survive it.

'We all have things that trigger us.' Isla's voice was gentle. 'It's like that for me if someone comes in and it looks like it might be cancer. Or if there's a middle-aged man who reminds me of Dad, and the symptoms of Huntington's. We're all human and if we didn't have those emotions, if we didn't care about people going through hard times, I think it would be far worse for our patients.'

'It would.' Eve managed a weak smile, thankful that Isla hadn't asked what it was that had triggered her. She was just grateful to have her colleagues' support, maybe if she allowed them in a little bit more, she could even call them friends. She had to take steps to bring joy to this new life she'd found herself in, and that seemed like as good a place to start as any.

5

Eve had only intended to make a flying visit to see Max to drop off some shopping he'd requested. She needed to get home to make a long overdue video call to his sister, Lily, and she didn't want to say what she planned to say in front of him. She'd been hoping to drop the shopping off and have a quick chat with Max, who probably wouldn't even take off his gaming headset, just so she could reassure herself and Annie that he was okay. She might have felt guilty about the intended haste of her visit, if it hadn't been her fifth one of the past seven days and if Max had made her feel like he'd actually wanted her there on any of the previous four occasions. She knew Annie had already been in that morning, so he'd almost certainly be glad just to be given his shopping and allowed to get on with his game. Except when she got to Oakwood Park there was no sign of him.

'I don't suppose you know where Max is, do you?' she asked Jeanine, one of the staff, who was walking down the corridor when Eve came back out of his room.

'He's in the kitchen. Having an OT session with Felix, but it's not a problem if you want to go in and join them.' Jeanine smiled and stopped walking, clearly expecting Eve to say thank you and walk past her towards the kitchen, when what she really wanted to do was make a bolt for the door. She knew how grouchy Max could be when he got frustrated during his OT sessions, and she really wasn't in the mood to witness that. She didn't want to see Felix again just yet, either. She was still trying to get a handle on the unwanted wave of attraction she'd felt towards him the last time they'd been together, and it had been a long week already, with far too many heightened emotions to deal with. But Jeanine was still watching her, so she squared her shoulders and nodded.

'Thanks, I'll pop in, but this is only a flying visit. I can't stay long, I've got a meeting tonight.' Eve was doing that overexplaining thing she always did when she was trying to justify a decision she thought someone else might judge her for. She shouldn't have to justify herself and the truth was she didn't, because Jeanine probably wouldn't think anything of it either way, or judge her even if she did walk straight out of the front door. She was the one who was judging herself for it, and all the overexplaining in the world would never overcome the guilt she felt at wanting to turn in the other direction and go home. That's why she couldn't do it.

'I'm sure Max will be pleased to see you.' Jeanine smiled again, but it didn't reach her eyes and they both knew she was lying.

'Why can't I do it my own way, for Christ's sake?' Eve heard Max before she saw him, but when she did, he was snatching a pan back from Felix, who cried out as hot liquid splashed over his hand.

'Ow, Max, please be careful. You're going to get a nasty injury if you don't slow down.'

'Er, duh.' Max set the pain down on the stove with a crash and jabbed a finger towards his head. 'In case you didn't know that's already happened. Dickhead.' He almost spat the last word and Eve couldn't prevent herself from reacting.

'Stop it, Max! Felix is just trying to help you and the least you can do is to show a bit of appreciation.'

'For what? Being made to feel like a baby, who doesn't even know how to cook baked beans? I just wanted to put them in the sodding microwave for Christ's sake!'

'I know and I get that, I really do.' Felix's voice was calm and measured, and there wasn't a hint of anything even approaching anger on his face. 'But I explained to you that we need to sign off a certain number of sessions using the hob for cooking, in readiness for your move to one of the bungalows. It wouldn't matter if it was baked beans, a tin of soup, or stroganoff, we need to make sure it's safe.'

'Bollocks to this, I'm going back to my room.' Max wrenched off the apron he was wearing and threw it in the sink. 'I've got already got a GCSE in Food Tech. I don't need this shit.'

It was as he stalked out in the wake of that grand declaration that Eve caught Felix's eye and the laughter started to bubble up inside her. She put a hand over her mouth to try and hold it in, but her whole body started to shake and she realised that Felix was laughing too.

'GCSE Food Tech. That told me.'

'Don't!' She had tears streaming down her face now and it wasn't just the reference to GCSEs that made her feel as if she was back at school. It was that same kind of uncontrollable laughter she'd sometimes got sitting next to one of her friends in class, when they knew they weren't allowed to laugh, but nothing could prevent it from happening.

'I need to up my game, that's for sure,' Felix said, his smile not wavering, and she finally managed to answer in a voice still choked with half-hysterical laughter.

'At least look up what's on the A Level syllabus.' Maybe she should have felt mean for laughing, but wasn't laughing *at* Max, she was laughing at how absurd their lives had become. The truth was, in moments like this, if she didn't laugh, she'd cry, and she did that far more than she should already.

'That'll be my homework for tonight.' Felix passed her a piece of kitchen towel, suddenly looking a bit more serious. 'Sorry you had to see that; Max can just get very frustrated during our sessions when he finds things tougher than he thinks they should be. Thanks for saying what you did, though.'

'I just thought it might help to hear how much we all appreciate what you're doing for him.'

'It does and I know deep down he appreciates the help I'm trying to give him. Sometimes he even shows it, in his own way.' Felix's smile stopped halfway this time. 'I just hope you can feel that, or someone else is telling you that, because all the things you do for Max are incredible. I can only imagine how hard it must be sometimes, when it feels like he's throwing that back in your face.'

'It feels like that a lot.' Eve wasn't sure she'd ever been so honest with anyone before and she couldn't afford for Max to become her confidante in a way that no one else was. Not if she was going to stand any chance of keeping her feelings for him in check.

'I see how much difference you make to Max's life and I know it helps him in ways he doesn't even realise, let alone express.'

'Thank you.' She nodded, needing to get out of there before the tears of laughter, which had been streaming down her face moments before, turned into tears of another kind. 'I'd better go and help Max unpack the shopping I brought in for him, but I'll see you soon, I'm sure.'

'I hope so, Eve.' She turned and walked out of the door then, unable able to look at Felix, because she was terrified that the connection she felt between them might not just be in her imagination. Whatever difference she might make to Max's life, the draw she felt towards Felix meant she was betraying him and that had to stop. Right now.

* * *

As Eve waited for the FaceTime call to connect, she slowed her breathing, not wanting all the things she had to say to Max's sister to come out in a rush, or for her to say anything she might later wish she hadn't said. She and Lily had fast become friends, from the moment he'd introduced them. Lily was two years younger than her brother, which made her a year younger than Eve. She was a lawyer, who was now specialising in social justice, after a change of direction. Nine months after Max had been attacked, Lily had made the decision to move to the US. Every time they spoke she urged Eve to be honest and to tell Annie that she couldn't carry on visiting every day and holding down a demanding job, as well as being the person to prop Annie up when she needed it, but there was no way Eve could do that now that Lily had left. Max's sister had escaped the weight of Annie's expectations, but they had fallen all the heavier onto Eve's shoulders as a result. It would have been selfish of her to hold that against Lily, especially when she knew just how much stress she'd been under before she'd made the decision to go to the US. It had been Eve who'd encouraged Lily to go, before it became too much to cope with, but she still couldn't help hoping her friend might feel ready to come home now.

'Hey, Eve.' Lily gave her a beaming smile, so reminiscent of the ones her brother used to wear that for a moment Eve could barely catch her breath to reply, but somehow she managed to respond.

'Hi, Lily, you look great.' It was true. Max's little sister looked like the weight of the world had been lifted these days, and the girl with the shadows under her eyes in the months after his assault, seemed to have disappeared altogether. Getting away had clearly been the right decision.

'Thanks, I want to say the same about you, and you do look as beautiful as ever...' Lily hesitated for a moment, before continuing. 'But you also look absolutely knackered. You can't go on like this, Eve, using all your time off to visit Max and support Mum and Dad. You never get any time to yourself, or have the chance to rest. You've got to step back before this ends up making you really ill.'

'It's not that easy.' Eve's words were barely more than a whisper, but they carried a heaviness that seemed to push her deeper into the floor, pinning her down to this life she hadn't chosen. She might as well have been wearing boots made of concrete for all the chance she had of walking away, especially if Lily wasn't ready to come home. Someone had to be there for Annie, and the truth was Eve's motivation wasn't entirely selfless. Lily's parents would always love her, no matter what choices she made, even if they thought she'd walked away when they needed her most, because she was their daughter. The love was unconditional. Eve was another matter. She had to earn her place in the family and it mattered far more that she was able to live up to Annie and Nigel's expectations. She couldn't just walk away, not if she ever wanted to be welcomed back. When she'd thought Lily might crack from all the pressure she was under, it had been a easy decision to encourage her to go, yet Eve couldn't heed her own advice. It wasn't that straightforward for her, no matter what Lily thought.

'It could be that easy, if you made the decision to put yourself first.' Lily sighed. 'I know you find that difficult, but I also know that this wouldn't be what Max would have wanted, if he was still the old Max.'

'Your mum wouldn't see it that way. I don't think she'd cope if I stopped visiting Max as often.' It was Eve's turn to sigh. 'If I'm honest the visits are more for her benefit than his. A lot of the time I think he'd rather I didn't visit at all. I don't know if it's because I remind him of how much has changed, or if I just get on his nerves these days.'

She gave a hollow little laugh that didn't have a trace of real humour in it; not surprising really, when it was all she could do to stop herself from crying yet again.

'Oh, Evie.' The use of the pet name Max's family had given her just made her feel more emotional. They were the only family she had and walking away from them wasn't an option. Her father's lack of interest in her life sometimes made her wonder if she'd imagined that he existed at all. She might as well have done for all the involvement they had with one another. His disinterest and the coldness of her stepmother had hurt like hell in the wake of her mother's death. Once she had become a part of Max's family, it hadn't felt nearly so much like she was missing out and she didn't want to give that up, because it would break her heart if she did. But Lily couldn't see that; she'd been born into this family and she didn't have to worry that her place in it might one day disappear. 'Mum must see what this is doing to you and, even if she doesn't, I'm more than willing to set her straight.'

'Please, don't.' Eve knew that Lily would happily deliver on her promise, but Annie had been hurt enough by what had happened to Max, and she didn't want to be the cause of any more suffering. The only thing she could do was to try and find a compromise that eased the pressure on her, but didn't create a rift with Max's mother. She had a feeling that was going to be a very difficult balance to strike. 'When are you coming home for a visit?'

Eve had done her best to keep her tone light, but she could hear the pleading note in her voice. If Lily had picked up on it, she wasn't letting it influence her response. 'We're trying to buy the apartment we've been renting, but it'll take every cent we've got and a bit more besides, so there's no money for a trip over right now. We've got a guest room so I keep telling Mum and Dad to come out here instead, and I've love you to come over for a visit too.'

'I couldn't leave Max for that long.'

'Yes, you could, the staff at Oakwood Park look after him really well.'

'Your mum then, I can't just leave her.'

'She's not your responsibility.' Lily's tone was insistent and Eve wanted to agree and say *no, she's not, she's your responsibility*, but that wouldn't have been fair or true. None of them were responsible for Annie, she was a grown woman in her mid-sixties, but that didn't stop Eve feeling responsible for her, despite Lily's continued attempts to persuade her otherwise.

'You *can* leave Mum, but the longer you stay, the harder it's going to get. I had to get out before I drowned, Eve, you were the one who helped me see that, but knowing you're still there makes me feel as though I sailed away on a life raft and left you to drown instead. I grew up with my mother's high expectations of me and that was okay. I'm the great-granddaughter of Anna Carew and I was supposed to grow up and spend my entire career in the family law firm like Mum and Aunt Jules. I did all of that and I just about managed the weight of those expectations, then Max got hurt and suddenly it was all on me. I still had to fulfil the legacy of the family I was born into, but somehow I had to fill the gap Max had left behind too.' She paused for a moment, letting out a long sigh before continuing.

'All of the hopes and dreams she had for him fell on my shoulders. She wanted me to take the lead in the business with Jules, but she also wanted me around in every minute of my spare time. She was so paranoid about me getting hurt too, and then she started talking about when me and Scott were going to get married and start a family. I had to give her every dream she'd ever wanted for her children, so that it wouldn't hurt as much that Max was never going to do any of the things she'd hoped he would. I just couldn't be everything she wanted, Evie, it was suffocating me, and you certainly can't.

'Mum needs to accept that Max has changed forever, and any dreams she has for him now are going to need to be completely different. She needs counselling or some kind of professional help. It's not our job to help her get to that point and I don't think either of us could, even if we spent our whole lives trying. What I'm most worried about is that you will.'

Lily looked close to tears now too and Eve wished they were face to face, so that she could hug the woman she'd thought of as a sister for so long. She'd seen the pressure that Lily had always been under and had handled so well. Max's great-grandmother, Anna Carew, had by all accounts been a force of nature and groundbreaking in so many ways. The legal profession hadn't even been open to women until the 1920s, but Anna was amongst the first to qualify and be called to the bar, eventually starting her own practice. She married, automatically losing her surname as women did in those days, and had two daughters, Joanna and Hannah, incorporating her first name into both of theirs and a tradition was born. Joanna also became a lawyer, and had two daughters of her own – Annabel, or Annie as she was known, and her sister Julianna, who everyone in the family called Jules, both of whom joined the family law firm. Lily's full name was Lilyanna and so the profession she would go into had never really been in question. She'd looked set to spend her entire career at Carews, a renowned and very well-respected firm specialising in high profile divorces and family law, but Max's assault had changed everything, and her new focus was a world away from the path she'd been born to follow.

'I won't allow things to stay like they are right now forever, I promise.' Eve wasn't entirely sure whether she was making the vow to Lily or herself, but either way she was determined to keep it. Max's sister was right about one thing, she couldn't go on like this indefinitely.

'So, what is your plan?' Lily's tone was gentler this time, but her brow was furrowed, as if she was trying to work out the solution to an impossibly difficult equation, which wasn't far from the truth.

'I wanted to try and persuade your mum to consider restorative justice.' Almost before the words were even out of Eve's mouth, Lily gave a snort of laughter.

'I think you might have more chance of being able to fly out here for a holiday just by flapping your arms.' She must have seen Eve's face fall and her expression softened. 'I'm sorry, Evie, because I really think it could help, but Mum doesn't want to understand what motivated the crime, and even less so, to consider any form of forgiveness. She wants revenge.'

Eve nodded, knowing it was true. Restorative justice would give Max's parents the opportunity to sit down and talk to the man who'd changed all their lives as a result of one punch. It was an approach that had allowed other victims of crime and their families to witness the perpetrator taking responsibility for their actions. It might never provide closure, or the ability to move on, but it could help people to move forward. That was something Annie desperately needed, because right now she was stuck clinging to the forlorn hope that Max might somehow make a full recovery. The only other thing that seemed to make Annie come alive was the campaign she'd launched to get Brandon Moorcroft's sentence reviewed and extended, and the civil case she was intending to bring in an attempt to ensure he was financially ruined for the rest of his life. Lily was right, she wanted revenge, but even if she got it, it would never be enough because it would never give her back Max the way he used to be.

'I've got to try because I know Max wouldn't have wanted your mum to be like this. He wanted to be a surgeon so he could help fix people who were broken, and it was obvious that Brandon Moorcroft was a broken man when he decided to lash out. Max would have wanted Moorcroft to get help, ruining two lives isn't the solution.'

'You don't have to sell it to me, I agree that's exactly what Max would have wanted.' Lily managed a half smile, before it melted off her face again. 'I just don't think you'll ever convince Mum of that.'

'All I can do is try.' Eve let go of a long breath, making herself another vow. She was going to get the ball rolling with this, whether Annie chose to be involved or not. She didn't want anyone else to go through the things that Max's loved ones had been through. If meeting Brandon Moorcroft could help prevent him hurting anyone else in the future, that alone had to mean some good had come out of all this pain. And maybe, just maybe, it would be another step along the road to finding a more hopeful future for them all.

6

As fundraisers went, this one was heavy on the fun, but then as Eve had quickly found out, any event organised by Gwen Jones, who was the volunteer coordinator for the Friends of St Piran's, was always going to meet that definition. It was taking place in the Old Town Hall in Port Tremellien, but it had been decked out to look more like a bar in the Wild West. There was axe throwing, a bucking bronco ride, a tin can alley and a lasso game. The event had been opened with a line dancing display by Gwen and some of her friends, which the crowd were then invited to join in with. Funds were being raised through the sale of tickets, as well as food and a silent auction. The money collected would be split between the hospital and Domusamare. Eve had been persuaded to come along by Eden, Meg and Isla, the three of whom she'd definitely grown closer to since the night of her meltdown. They still didn't know the full story about Max yet, although Eve wondered if Eden might have been told by Felix. Even if she had been, she wouldn't be able to say anything, because it might put her brother's job at risk if she did.

Moving to Cornwall had been a wrench in so many ways.

She'd loved her job at Jimmy's, the nickname given to St James's Hospital in Leeds, and in lots of ways it had felt like starting again, in terms of her career. Leaving behind her closest friends had been even harder and she'd kept her guard up since starting at St Piran's, not wanting to get close to anyone. She wanted to keep the situation with Max private, for his sake but also because the last thing she wanted was for anyone to feel sorry for her. Then there was the fact that getting close to anyone raised the potential of getting hurt. It felt as if she'd lost so many people she cared about over the years, and it had begun to feel safer not to allow herself to get close to anyone else. Yet her colleagues at the hospital had found a way of getting under her skin. She liked them all, even the ones she hadn't expected to find anything in common with. Like Gary, a nurse in his fifties – happily married to Wendy, the head of housekeeping – who had an endless supply of cracker-style dad jokes, which had kept her smiling through many a late shift, despite the fact that they were more likely to make her groan than laugh out loud.

Aidan, another of the male nurses, had a quick wit and relaxed charm that made him easy to be around. Zahir, like Danni, was one of the more senior doctors, and he had a reputation for being ferociously competitive, as he was demonstrating now, pacing out the ideal distance from which to throw his axe. But he was supportive rather than competitive when it came to work, and when he'd been acting Clinical Lead, during Danni's maternity leave, he'd bent over backwards to accommodate Eve when she'd needed to take extended leave for what she'd told him was a family crisis. He hadn't pushed for too many more details and she'd been grateful for that. Annie had collapsed, after barely eating or sleeping following Lily's move to the US, and Eve had stepped in. Nigel was a lovely guy, but he was holding the family together financially with all the money Annie had poured into trying to pursue some kind of justice for Max. Nigel was at the top of his field in cosmetic dentistry and he worked very long hours and travelled internationally to see some of his clients, which put even more pressure on Eve to be there for Annie.

When Meg had been brought in to cover for her, Eve had been worried about her own job, fearful that she might be permanently replaced. What she hadn't admitted to anyone, even herself, was that a tiny part of her would have been relieved, because it would have given her a reason to go back to Leeds and escape the pressure of being there for Max and Annie. But the team at St Piran's had welcomed her back, despite Meg being given a permanent contract too. Even then she hadn't been able to let down her guard and admit why she'd been forced to take so much time off work. Now, as she stood next to Eden, waiting for her turn to throw the axe again and see if this time she could actually get it to hit the target, it really did feel like she was out with friends. They were all laughing as Zahir took a professional-looking swing and promptly sent the axe straight into the wooden floor about three feet shy of the target.

When Vick, her best friend from Leeds, had asked her if there was anyone at St Piran's she might be 'interested' in, Eve had scoffed. Even if it had been an option, she wouldn't have been 'interested' in any of the men from the team in A&E, no matter how nice they were, or how much she liked them as people. That side of her seemed to have frozen when she'd realised that the Max she'd known and loved with all her heart was never coming back to her. So she couldn't have explained why, as Eden's brother, Felix approached, she was suddenly smoothing her hair and worrying if the chilli con carne she'd eaten had been too garlicky.

'You should be good at this.' He grinned as he drew level with his sister. 'If the way you used to throw your shoes at my head when I annoyed you is anything to go by.'

'If you want to encourage me, you could go over and stand by the target, that will give me something to aim for.' Eden nudged Felix, laughing. 'Anyway you should be a sure thing for winning a prize at the tin can alley game. You used to line up all my dolls and try to knock them off the wall with your catapult.'

'Sounds like the work of a trainee serial killer to me.' Eve raised her eyebrows, but Felix couldn't have looked less like a serial killer if he'd tried. Especially when he shot her a smile, his blue eyes twinkling with amusement.

'My sister is prone to exaggeration, I can assure you. I'm much nicer than she'd have you believe.'

'Actually, he is nice.' Eden briefly laid her head on his shoulder, before turning back towards Eve. 'Teddie adores him and my son is the best judge of character I know, even if he is only four. I think his autism gives him superpowers in that respect.'

'I can also vouch for the fact that Felix is a good guy.' Gwen, who was doing the rounds trying to drum up more bids for the silent auction, stopped to join in the conversation and locked eyes with Eve. 'You're still fairly new to the area and I know Felix hasn't been back long, but he grew up here, so if you need someone to show you around, he's your man.'

Gwen was renowned for her attempts to act as a matchmaker, whether or not the people involved had expressed any interest in finding someone to date. So Eve shouldn't have been surprised, but heat coloured her cheeks all the same. Felix would probably have been mortified at the thought. Especially as he knew she had a fiancé, and she couldn't even look at him as she spoke.

'Work doesn't give me a lot of time for anything else, and I'd like to use any spare time I do have to get involved in something community based. When I looked up Domusamare it sounded like the sort of thing I'm looking for.' It wasn't a lie, or even an excuse to get Gwen off her back, she really did want to find out whether she could get involved with the charity's work. Their website said one of their aims was to help people who were struggling with reintegrating into society after serving prison sentences, and help them deal with the issues at the root of their offending. If she could talk to Annie about the difference that was making to some of Domusamare's clients, it might be the evidence she needed to persuade her to consider restorative justice, or at least to let go of her obsession with increasing Moorcroft's sentence. It might also mean she could play a tiny part in helping to prevent the kind of repeat offending that could result in more crimes like the one Max had been the victim of. The thought of that had become her new fixation, and maybe in her own way she was every bit as obsessed as Annie. They both needed to do something that might make a difference of some kind, because they were completely powerless to alter the one thing they really wanted to change, and that was the prognosis for Max's recovery.

'I volunteer for Domusamare.' Felix smiled again. Of course he did. Why wouldn't he do something like that; something that made him seem even lovelier than he already did. 'I can introduce you to Henry, who runs the charity if you like, so you can discuss what kinds of things you might like to get involved with? I'm sure he'd love to have you onboard.'

'And I bet he's not the only one!' Before Eve had even been able to respond, Gwen had given Felix a playful nudge and dropped a perfect wink.

'You're incorrigible, Gwen!' Felix laughed and Eve wished she could just laugh it off as easily, but heat had swept over her again and she'd have been more than happy if a giant crater had opened up beneath her and she'd disappeared forever. Instead, she cut in before Gwen could take things any further.

'Thanks. I'd really appreciate the introduction, because I can't think of anything I'd rather do with my free time than support the charity.' Eve's tone sounded haughty, even to her own ears, as if spending time with Felix was something she'd have to endure in order to achieve her aim of working with the charity. She didn't want him to think she was some kind of snob, but it was the lesser of two evils, because the idea of him thinking she was interested in him 'like that' was far more mortifying. The worst part of it all was that she had a sneaking suspicion she *was* interested in Felix, and that was something she couldn't even admit to herself let alone anyone else.

7

'Oh God, I shouldn't have had those tequila shots. I feel like I'm still paying for it two days later and surely all of the alcohol has to be out of my system by now.' Esther dropped her head into her hands, as the team sat in the staffroom waiting for Danni to give a briefing about handover from the night shift, during which there'd been a major incident following a fire at a holiday park ten miles down the coast. Esther's bloodshot eyes made it look as if she'd come straight to work from a bar, but Eve knew there was no way she'd risk being hungover at work, let alone coming in drunk.

'I told you now that we're banging on the door of forty, it takes three days to get over a drinking session, not three hours.' Aidan gave her a wicked grin and Esther shook her head, before grabbing hold of it, as if her head might fall off if she didn't.

'I am not *nearly* forty, I'm only mid-thirties and you're hurting my bloody head.' Esther didn't look amused, and Eve would have known there was more to her bad mood than a headache even if she hadn't sworn. Okay, bloody was pretty mild in the scheme of things, but she didn't think she'd ever heard Esther swear before. 'It's all

Gwen's fault for plying me with the shots at the end of the fundraiser, just because I said I might as well get drunk if I'm not pregnant.'

There it was, the real reason she was so unhappy and it had nothing to do with tequila, or being teased about her age. Although the latter might have hit home harder than it would have done otherwise, given that Esther would be all too aware of the tick-tock of the clock that any woman trying for a baby desperately wanted to ignore.

'Okay, but even so, you know tequila slammers are the territory of the under twenty-fives. Once your frontal lobe is fully developed, they're far too dangerous.' Aidan grinned and looked towards where Eve and Eden were standing together. 'That's why these two look so fresh-faced and ready for action. They didn't get into a shot-drinking contest with Gwen, who even in her seventies was always going to drink the rest of us under the table. But she's the exception that proves the rule.'

'God, I so want to be Gwen when I grow up,' Eden said.

'Me too.' Eve's response surprised her, because she realised it was true, but it had nothing to do with the ability Gwen evidently had to drink whatever she wanted and not suffer for it afterwards. It was Gwen's zest for life she wanted to harness, she was involved in so many different things and found joy in all of them from what Eve could see. Joy had been missing from Eve's own life for a long time, and it felt as if life was passing her by. She didn't want to spend another two years like that, let alone another ten, or even worse, the rest of her life. Something had to change.

'Everyone wants to be Gwen when they grow up, but right now I just want my head to stop feeling like it's stuffed with cotton wool, at the same time as being crushed in a vice.'

'You don't think there's any chance it's the supplements you're taking that are causing the headache, do you?' Meg gave Esther a questioning look. 'It's not normal to still be suffering two days later, even if Gwen is the one pouring the drinks, and a lot of prenatal supplements have high doses of vitamin A, which can cause headaches.'

'And you know this how?' Aidan raised his eyebrows. 'Is there something you're not telling us, Meg?'

'I'm a doctor, Aidan and some of us medics know our stuff. Just because you spend all your time scrolling through pictures of Timothée Chalamet!' She stuck out her tongue and then laughed, her reaction making it clear that he hadn't hit a nerve with her, and he pulled a face of mock outrage.

'I only look at his pictures because I'm trying to work out if his haircut would suit me.'

'You'd need to buy a toupee first.' Gary's response was so deadpan that for a moment no one reacted, but then they all started to laugh, even Esther.

'They call them hair systems these days actually, old man, but you'd know that if you hadn't been around when man first made fire.' Aidan nudged his friend and a warm glow settled in Eve's stomach. She loved this, the easy banter between her colleagues that she was finally starting to feel a part of. She might not be right in the thick of it yet, but she was getting there and she no longer saw herself as a complete outsider. St Piran's was beginning to feel like home.

'Sorry about the delay.' Danni offered up the apology as she came into the staffroom. 'I was with Zahir and we were waiting to hear whether any more of the patients we've been keeping stable in the department are being transferred to the specialist burns unit in Bristol, or whether they still need to wait for a bed in ICU. Isla just took a call to say that the burns unit has accepted the last of the patients with more serious burns, so it looks like the crisis is over and we should be in for just another normal day at the office.'

'You know you're not allowed to say that!' Esther pulled a face. 'That's the first rule of A&E, and you can't even blame baby brain any more. I mean when I eventually get pregnant, I fully intend to blame my children for all eternity for ruining my washboard abs, even though I've never actually been able to find them, but you looked like a supermodel a week after giving birth. If you weren't my best friend and I didn't love you so much, I might actually hate you!'

'Don't worry, there's not a chance of there being any washboard abs under here either.' Danni smiled, but there was a troubled look in her eyes and Eve sensed Eden stiffening beside her.

'Right, come on then, let's get to work.' Danni headed out of the door first and Eve slowed her pace, falling in line with Eden at the back of the group.

'Was it just me or did Danni look at bit worried about something?' Eve kept her voice low. 'You don't think there's anything wrong, do you?'

'No.' Eden's response was assured, but when Eve turned to look at her, she had the same troubled expression on her face as Danni had worn. 'I think she's pregnant again.'

* * *

Eve held her breath as the paramedics rushed towards her. Paediatric emergencies were always enough to make her heart sink to the floor, but she knew just from the sight of the tiny little boy lying on the stretcher, who couldn't have been more than three, how serious it was. His skin had a blueish grey undertone and his abdomen appeared distended, as he coughed and tried to pull the oxygen mask off his face. Eve had answered the red phone when the paramedic team had called to say the little boy was on the way, so she knew the cause of his symptoms even before Jeff, one of the paramedics, outlined what had happened.

'This is Carter, he's three years old. He was found face down in a garden pond by his mother and he wasn't breathing at the time of discovery. She managed to resuscitate him with support from the 999 call handler, but no one saw Carter go into the water and we don't know how long he was in there for.'

Eve's stomach roiled as she looked at the tiny child in front of her, unable to stop herself from thinking about just how different the outcome could have been for him if his mother had found him a few minutes later, or if she hadn't known what to do to resuscitate him. She'd seen children brought in who hadn't made it. Her training at St James's had made her more adaptable than many A&E doctors, because she'd specialised in emergency medicine with a sub specialism in paediatric emergency medicine. It meant she'd witnessed more tragedies than she wanted to think about and seeing Carter looking so vulnerable hurt her heart. The only positive was that if she'd been forced to bet on it, she'd put her stake on him being okay, because he was alert and had enough strength to fight against the oxygen mask.

He wasn't completely out of the woods yet, though, due to a phenomenon called secondary or delayed drowning, which had the potential to cause respiratory failure and death, even days after a near-drowning incident. Carter was safe for the time being and he'd be monitored for any signs once his condition was stabilised and his symptoms treated. It was the what-ifs that Eve found so much harder to shake off, especially since Max's attack. Things could have ended so differently for him that night, if he'd only left the club five minutes earlier or five minutes later, or taken another route through the city. It seemed impossible to her that their lives could have changed so catastrophically because of such tiny, almost meaningless decisions. Sometimes the thought crippled her, when she was forced to choose between two seemingly innocuous decisions. It was such a waste of energy thinking that way, because no amount of considering the what-ifs could change the outcome, but she seemed powerless to stop. Shaking off thoughts of Max, she looked at Jeff.

'Given that he's likely to have ingested pond water, we'll need to get him on IV antibiotics and warmed IV fluids to bring his temperature up. I also want a scan to rule out any injuries he might had sustained from falling or jumping into the pond. Even if all that's clear he'll need to be monitored for at least eight hours. Where's his mum?'

Meg and Esther hurried towards Eve, as she looked past the paramedics, expecting to see Carter's mother there. She might well need treatment herself, after the shock and trauma of what she'd witnessed, but there was no sign of her.

'She's coming along separately, with the police.' Jeff had a grim expression on his face.

'Do they think it wasn't accidental?' Meg looked horrified and the question had taken the words right out of Eve's mouth.

'I'm not sure, but it was clear she was known to them and the social worker is also on the way. Poor kid.'

'I hope they lock the mother up and throw away the key.' Meg's eyes had darkened and Eve had never heard her sound so hard. It was understandable given what had nearly happened to Carter, but they were supposed to keep some degree of impartiality, especially as his mother might need treatment, and they didn't even know if the woman had been charged with anything yet. But Esther was nodding vigorously.

'It makes me sick to my stomach that there are people out there who don't prioritise their kids at all and yet seem to be able to have them without any difficulty whatsoever, when me and Joe would do anything to have a child and we'd build our whole world around them.'

'All we can do is make sure Carter gets the care and attention he deserves now. We'll deal with the problem of his mother if and when she turns up.' Eve didn't give the others any opportunity to respond, instead detailing what she needed Meg and Esther to do, before arranging his scan and calling the children's ward to ascertain availability of a bed, if they decided it was safe to move Carter there for observation. Technically Eve wasn't Meg's superior, but she had far more experience when it came to paediatric emergency medicine and there was no room for ego in A&E. At least there shouldn't be.

* * *

'I just wanna know he's okay, I'm his mum for God's sake and you've got no right to stop me from seeing him.' As soon as Eve heard the woman shouting, forty-five minutes after Carter had been admitted, she knew who it was and, when the woman clearly didn't get what she wanted, she started screaming a string of expletives. Her little boy was stable and he was going to be okay, maybe hearing that would be enough to calm her down. For the other patients' sakes, Eve had to try.

Hurrying down the corridor she went through to the waiting area and found a painfully thin woman with greasy, dark blonde hair and hollows beneath her eyes that made her look like a skeleton come to life. She was a poster girl for addiction and Eve's heart hurt even more for the beautiful little boy who'd almost lost his life. There was no sign of the police. But a harassed looking woman wearing a lanyard with the Cornish County Council logo, who Eve assumed was the social worker, was trying to calm Carter's mother down, as she paced around the waiting area ranting; the other patients watching her, like she was an animal in a zoo.

'I've called security.' Cheryl, one of the receptionists, hissed as Eve approached and she nodded, hoping that by the time they came this would all be over. Taking a deep breath she approached the woman, and began to speak, keeping her tone deliberately soft.

'Hi, I'm Eve Bellingham, one of the doctors and I've been looking after Carter.' For a split second it crossed her mind that she may have got it wrong and that this might not be his mum after all, but the expression on the other woman's face told her she was right before she even responded.

'Is he okay?' There was such desperation in the woman's tone, that, in that instant, Eve's heart ached for her. Most people who came to the kind of addiction she would have sworn this woman was in the grip of, had been through trauma of their own and the haunted expression in the woman's eyes told their own story.

'He's stable and breathing without assistance, but we won't know for a while yet whether the submersion in the water has caused any further complications. He has two cracked ribs, likely to be from when the CPR was performed.'

'Oh thank God, and thank you so much.' Carter's mother seemed to lose all her fight as she clasped Eve's hand. And as her face relaxed there was a softness there that wouldn't have seemed possible a moment or two before.

'Can you be certain that's what caused the injury?' The social worked narrowed her eyes and Carter's mother immediately tensed again, her arms flying upwards and nearly knocking Eve back.

'I'd never hurt Carter, not on purpose and you fucking know that, Pippa. I'm in a bad place and I wasn't watching him like I should have been. You know it wasn't deliberate and so do the police, otherwise they'd be here.'

'If you don't calm down, Sophie, I'll be calling them back and they almost certainly are going to be charging you with neglect. Getting angry and getting arrested at the hospital isn't going to help.'

'You love this, don't you? You've been wanting to take him off me since before he was even born, every time I see your face I want to—'

Eve saw Sophie draw back her hand and instinctively she grabbed her wrist. Sophie might be tiny and painfully thin, but she was fuelled by desperation and it took all of Eve's strength to hold onto her.

'Don't do it. If you want to see Carter, you need to step back and just breathe.' Eve's voice sounded melodic, even to her own ears, almost like the words were a lullaby.

'Can I really see him?' Sophie's eyes widened and as Eve nodded, she yanked her hand free and threw her arms around Eve, almost knocking her backwards for a second time with the force of her embrace and the smell of unwashed skin. Sophie clearly loved her son and yet her actions had nearly killed him. It was one more reminder that sometimes love just wasn't enough.

8

Sophie had sobbed throughout the time she'd spent at Carter's bedside, her hands clenching and unclenching as she'd begged for his forgiveness, revealing nails that had been bitten down so far that some of them were bleeding. There were obvious scars on her arms, from what Eve could almost guarantee were self-harm injuries. Her wrists were so thin the shape of her bones was visible through the skin and she had the look of a baby bird that had fallen out of its nest weeks before it was ready. The reality wasn't far off and she barely looked more than a child herself.

'They're going to take him for good this time. I've blown my last chance.' Sophie had turned towards Eve when she'd told her she needed to leave, her bloodshot eyes pleading for a just a little longer, even before the words came out of her mouth. 'Please don't make me go, I don't know when they'll let me see him again. Just five more minutes. *Please.*'

There'd been none of the aggression in her tone that she'd directed towards her social worker earlier, perhaps because Pippa had decided to use the opportunity to go off and make some phone calls to determine what would happen once Carter was ready to be released from hospital. Sophie herself was assessed as not needing treatment, at least not by the team in A&E, but it was obvious to anyone that she needed help. It was why Eve couldn't bear the thought of her just walking out of the department and heading who knew where and, worse still, with God knows who.

'You can have ten more minutes with Carter, but only if you agree to stay on with me afterwards, and make a plan for what you're going to do next.' Eve had held her gaze and Sophie had nodded slowly. If it meant getting to spend more time with her son, Eve had been pretty sure the other woman would have agreed to pretty much anything. What soon became clear was that making a plan for Sophie wasn't going to be nearly as easy as getting her to agree to stay and discuss it.

Eve had known that Sophie's explanation of what had been going on in her life would be hard to listen to, but it was even worse than she'd been expecting.

'My landlord kicked us out, that was why we were sofa surfing and staying at my friend's place. I'd forgotten she even had a pond in the garden. I couldn't pay the rent and my bastard of a landlord decided that paying it in another way wasn't working for him any more.' Sophie curled her lip. 'It didn't seem to bother him last month, but I suppose that was a novelty. Or maybe this month he's got someone else willing to lay down and think of England, while the fat old bastard climbs on top of them and gives a few half-hearted thrusts before it's all over. That was the small mercy of it all, I suppose. Between his bulk and the smell of chip fat, I could barely breathe.'

'That's no way to live.' Eve tried not to judge, and in her job she'd seen pretty much everything, but sometimes it was incredibly hard. In this instance, she was judging Sophie's landlord far more harshly than she judged the woman herself.

'I know it's not.' There was an edge of defensive to Sophie's tone and a defiant tilt of the chin. 'Don't you think I want more for Carter? Of course I do. You've got no idea how bloody hard it is though, someone like you. None of you lot do.'

'You're right, I don't, but maybe it would help if you told me.' Eve locked eyes with her for a second time and, after what seemed like an interminable silence, Sophie's chin dropped and she nodded slowly.

'My dad was never around and Mum always had boyfriends. Some of them were nice and some of them weren't. Eventually she moved one of them in and he was always far more interested in me than he should have been. Coming into my room uninvited and pulling me onto his lap for cuddles and kissing me on the mouth. I was still just a kid for Christ's sake.' Sophie let go of a shuddering sigh and Eve had to clamp her arms to the side of her body to stop herself from reaching out. 'I stayed out all hours just so I didn't have to be around him, but I made some bad choices and when I ended up pregnant with Carter, my mum didn't want to know. So we were on our own.'

Sophie shook her head, unable to continue and Eve couldn't hold back from putting an arm around the other woman's shoulders. What surprised her most was that Sophie didn't shrug her off.

'I can't imagine how hard that was.' Eve really couldn't. She might have lost her mother at a relatively young age and her father might have been emotionally distant, but she'd always had a roof over her head. Yet she'd still felt a huge gap in her life, so the void Sophie had experienced must have seemed unbridgeable. She wanted to promise this incredibly vulnerable young woman that everything would be okay from this point onwards, but she knew it wasn't something she could say and the last thing Sophie needed was even more broken promises.

'No, you can't, and maybe if I'd known just how hard it was

going to get, I might just have ended things there and then. The harder things got, the worse I felt about myself and the more I needed something to numb that. It started off with drinking and a bit of weed, but it kept spiralling until I was on far worse than that. I want to get clean, I really do, and I've tried for Carter, but social services are right. I must be a shit mum, because I can't do it, not even for him.'

Sophie started to sob then, her whole body heaving with emotion and Eve wrapped her arms around her this time, holding her as tightly as she could, able to feel just how painfully thin the other woman was. 'It's an incredibly hard thing to do, but it's obvious you love Carter and that you want to make things right. If there was a chance to try again, would you want to take it?'

'Of course I would.' Sophie's head shot back. 'But who's going to give me a chance? I've already messed up all the stuff Pippa has tried to sort for me, and she told me last time that it was the end of the road.'

'I might know someone who can help.' Eve crossed her fingers, hoping that she wasn't raising Sophie's hopes with no chance of delivering.

'I'll do anything.' She looked at Eve with such desperation that all Eve could do was nod. Now, she had to deliver. She knew that both Drew and Felix volunteered for Domusamare. So, as soon as she left Sophie's side, she put in a call to Drew, only to discover he was in the middle of an autopsy and couldn't be disturbed. The person who had answered the phone hadn't even been able to tell her how long he might be. That just left Felix and, as much as Eve had vowed to try and avoid him, at least until she could get a handle on the attraction she felt towards him and preferably make it disappear, she knew she had to put her own feelings to one side for Sophie's sake. That was why she was on her way to the Occupational Therapy Department to find him, silently praying that he might be able to offer Sophie the lifeline she so desperately needed.

Felix stared at the number displayed on his phone. It was a call from the US, but not a contact he had stored. It could be anything from a scam call to a catch-up with an old friend who just happened to have changed their number, or even one who was taking the opportunity to call him from work. But, as he looked at it again, and a feeling of dread washed over him he just knew it was Meredith and he had a horrible feeling he knew what she wanted. He could just have rejected the call, or let it ring out and ignore the voicemail message she would inevitably leave. It would be far easier that way and he'd be able to go on trying to pretend that Meredith didn't exist outside the bubble of the life he'd lived in America. He'd kept so much of that hidden even from his own family. If he'd told Eden that he'd fallen in love with a former drug addict, she'd rightly have called him a hypocrite and asked what the hell he thought he was doing after all the warnings he'd given her. Yet, he'd been arrogant enough to think he was different. Growing up with an alcoholic mother, both he and Eden had developed a kind of saviour complex, wanting to step in and help people who were struggling with addictions of their own.

Felix had been certain that he could handle it; had felt as though he had all this compassion for people in the grip of addiction that had nowhere to go and, when he'd moved to the States, volunteering at an addiction crisis centre had felt like a natural step. But Meredith had taken Felix to the edge and coming home had been the only way to break the cycle. Now she was calling, he was sure of it, the ringtone on his phone loud and insistent. He could so easily cut off the call and block the number, but instead he found himself reaching for the green icon to answer it.

'Hello.' There was still a part of him that hoped it wouldn't be Meredith, but he recognised the sigh she omitted, even before she began to talk.

'Felix, thank God. I've missed you so much.' He wished he couldn't detect the lack of sincerity in Meredith's voice, but it was obvious. She was speaking so quickly, like she was rushing to get to the point and, before he could even respond, she laid the ground work for what he was certain was going to come next.

'I really need your help.'

'Okay, I'm back in the UK, but Karl can arrange whatever help you need to get you back into rehab.' He held his breath, hoping against hope that she'd say that was what she wanted, but he knew deep down that getting back into rehab wasn't why she'd called him. Meredith knew where to go for that kind of help, but she'd cut off every single person who'd tried to persuade her to get it, changing her number and telling them to get out of her life. Despite the fact she'd done the same thing with her own family, Felix knew they'd still be desperately waiting for her call, ready to do anything and drop everything to get her the help she needed. But she wasn't contacting him because she wanted to quit the drugs, and he'd promised her family he wouldn't do anything to jeopardise her finally reaching the point where she accepted that getting clean was the only option left.

'Felix, I owe some nasty people a lot of money. I thought I'd got together everything I needed to pay them back, but then I got mugged and now they're telling me that if I don't deliver they'll make me pay some other way.' It sounded like a line from a bad made-for-TV movie and when she started to sob down the phone, his mind raced. He knew she was lying about having got the money together and it being stolen. She might even have been lying about the 'nasty people', although he knew they existed and that if Meredith owed them money for drugs, they were more than capable of making her pay 'one way or another'. Whatever the situation, any money he sent her would be going straight to the suppliers and even if she cleared her debts that wouldn't be the end of it. She'd just run up another set of debts getting her hands on more drugs. It was a cycle she'd repeated with everyone who loved her, until she'd cut off contact with them altogether. Her family had been advised by professionals to make the hardest decision possible and to refuse Meredith any further financial support so that she could hit rock bottom and finally admit the kind of help she really needed. It made sense, but it was a terrifying leap of faith all the same. Felix couldn't go against their best chance of saving Meredith from herself, but that didn't make it any less agonising. If there was any way of reaching a compromise to keep her safe in the meantime, he was going to take it and he was certain her family would feel the same.

'If you arrange to meet Karl to get back into rehab, I can get the money to him, or your parents can. How much money are we talking about, Merri?'

He hadn't meant to use the derivative of her name, it sounded too intimate, as if they were still a part of one another's lives. He didn't want her to think she could manipulate him because of what they'd once been to each other, but the desire to step in and solve her problems was a hard habit to break.

'Five grand should solve the immediate problem.' The way she said it made it sound as though she was asking for five dollars.

'And what then? You'll cut us all off again, until the next time you need bailing out.'

'Don't be a such a baby, Felix. Christ, you think life's such a fucking fairytale, don't you? That because your mom kicked her habit, the rest of us should too. Well, maybe I don't want to. Have you ever considered that? Maybe I like life better when I'm high. It's my life and I get to choose how to mess it up if I want to.'

'Yeah, you do, but you can't expect the rest of us to bail you out.' Felix sighed, already knowing how this was going to go and feeling a horrible mixture of desperate sadness and frustration. 'I haven't got that kind of money just lying around, but if you let me speak to Ashleigh or your parents—'

'No!' Her response was sharp, but then she changed tack, a pleading tone to her voice. 'Come on, Felix, please, there must be a way you can get your hands on the money. I promise you I'll pay you back as soon as I can. If you don't help me... God knows what these people are capable of.'

'Let me talk to your family.' He repeated the request and she all but screamed her response.

'I said no!'

'You've already asked them for money, haven't you?'

'They're as bad as you, trying to make me go back to rehab. I haven't got time for any of that shit. If these people get their hands on me, they'll kill me long before I have the chance to get clean.'

'Go to the police, tell them what's happening. They'll protect you and get you some help, if you're willing to take it.'

'Jesus, Felix, you really do you live in a fairytale, don't you? If I don't get the money I could be dead by this time next week.'

'And if you don't get some help with your addiction you could be dead by this time tomorrow. Every time you take that stuff you're playing Russian roulette. I can't be responsible for funding that and I can't send you money unless I know you're at least going to try to use this as a wake-up call.'

'Did you and my parents write this speech together, because it sounds like you're reading from the same fucking script?'

'We all just care about you, Merri and—'

'Do you know what you sound like, you pious piece of shit?' Any pretence she might have maintained that she cared about Felix as anything other than a human cashpoint had been dispensed with.

'I hate what the drugs are doing to you. All those people you tried to help. Why did you do that, if you don't even think you're worth saving?'

'I can't do anything until I've paid off my debt.'

'So, if I find a way to send you the money, you'll check yourself back into rehab?'

'Yeah.' She couldn't even manage to make that one word sound convincing. 'I just need a bit more time to be ready.'

'I wish I could believe you.' He sounded as exhausted as he felt, but Meredith clearly hadn't given up the fight.

'Are you going to give me the money or not?'

'No, but if you let me call Karl, or your—' He didn't even get to finish the sentence before the sound of the call disconnecting cut off the final string of expletives she had unleashed. No doubt she was still ranting about him somewhere thousands of miles away. There was nothing he could do about that and as tempting as it was to call her back now that he had a contact number, and offer her the money she wanted, just to know she'd stay safe for a little while longer, he knew he couldn't do it. The only thing he could do was put in a call to her parents and Karl at the clinic, and hope to God that someone else could get through to Meredith, in every sense.

By the time he'd finished the second of the two phone calls, it felt as if a little bit of the burden had lifted off Felix's shoulders and the guilt didn't have quite such a tight stranglehold on his throat, after Meredith's parents and Karl had all told him he'd done the right thing. Karl had worked with Meredith for more than two years and he understood her situation well, having been there to witness her relapse and all of Felix's desperate attempts to help her. Karl had promised to do what he could to track Meredith down and put in a package of support, just in case this was the time when she was finally willing to give rehab another shot. Her parents had told her that if she agreed to check into rehab today, the money she needed was ready and waiting. If she was in genuine danger, then surely she'd have to accept. But no matter how much support she was offered, the ball remained in her court. She had to want the help, not just money, and sadly Felix wasn't holding out much hope of that. He'd barely ended the second call when there was a knock on the door of the OT consultation room that he'd used to give himself some privacy. Breathing out slowly, he put his mobile back in his pocket and tried to push his fears for Meredith back down where he'd been keeping them before she'd got in touch. He had a job to do and judging by the frantic nature of the knocking on the door, someone needed him urgently.

'Come in.' Whatever the person on the other side of the door wanted, he was certain it would be far easier to help them than it was to help Meredith.

'Hi, Felix, I'm really sorry to bother you.' Eve had been almost the last person he'd expected to see push open the door. She had a pinched look on her face, her eyes round with concern, as they so often looked. Never more so than when he'd bumped into her at Oakwood Park, visiting Max. He'd wanted to ask her about their relationship, after Annie had described her as Max's fiancée. Max didn't seem to view her that way any more and Felix couldn't help thinking how difficult it must be for Eve to come to terms with the consequences of Max's head injury, but he sensed she didn't want to be pushed into talking about it. He could tell from conversations with Eden that Eve hadn't told his sister about Max, and he doubted she'd told anyone else at the hospital that she had a fiancé living at Oakwood Park. Whatever Eve's reasons for keeping Max a secret, it wasn't Felix's place to tell anyone else what he knew, not even his sister. He could admit that there was a part of him that hoped her relationship with Max might be as platonic as it appeared to be, but he had no right to hope for that and no idea what he'd have done about it even it were true. He didn't need any complications in his life right now, and Eve definitely didn't. So it was much better if he kept his mouth shut.

'No problem at all. Come in, what can I do for you?'

'I've got a patient. Well strictly speaking she's the mother of a little boy who's my patient, but she's homeless and clearly in the grip of some kind of addiction and I'm scared that if she leaves the hospital with nowhere to go, it won't end well.'

'Right.' Felix couldn't stop his shoulders from slumping. After Meredith's call, he wished to God that Eve wanted something else from him. Anything but his support in trying to help another addict, but she was looking at him with so much sadness in her eyes and maybe this time would be different. Maybe they would be able to help this woman. After all, wasn't this why he volunteered with the charity? If it wasn't, he'd have to admit that his motivation came from somewhere else – guilt at feeling like he'd failed Meredith – and he didn't want that to be true.

'If you can tell me as much as you know, I can put a call into the team at Domusamare. I'm sure there's something they can do to help.' He smiled and, as Eve began to outline the situation, he willed his words to be true. He couldn't bear the thought of letting one more person down and he wanted to lift some of the sadness that Eve seemed to carry around off her shoulders. Whatever it took.

* * *

The team at Domusamare had swung into action and found Sophie a bed, as well as a key worker, assigning a staff member to oversee her stay and support her in accessing the services she would need, in order to take the steps she'd claimed she wanted to take towards getting clean. Felix knew only too well how easy it was for addicts to 'talk the talk', and Sophie was far more convincing than Meredith had been when she'd called him. Once upon a time, Meredith had made the same kind of promises that Sophie was currently making, but she couldn't even do that any more. He'd heard them far too many times to be fooled, and she seemed to know that. Instead she'd used the threat of something happening to her as leverage, but something was going to happen to her either way if she didn't get help. It was a vicious cycle and the only way to break it was for Meredith to decide *she* wanted to change, even more than she wanted the drugs. She clearly wasn't there yet and the real tragedy was that he didn't think she ever would be again. There was still hope for Sophie. She seemed to have the motivation to help herself, in the shape of her little boy, and as Felix and Eve crossed the car park, outside the Domusamare hostel where they'd left Sophie in the care of the staff, Eve voiced the same thought that was going through his head.

'Do you think she'll take the help they're offering?'

'I hope so.' He wished he could give Eve more than that, but he wasn't going to paint this as an easy fix, or promise her that there were any guarantees for Sophie, even though Domusamare had agreed to support her.

'Me too. Her little boy...' Eve shook her head. 'He could so easily have died and I think it shocked her to the core, but she's tried to beat this before and it hasn't worked.'

'It often doesn't.' There he was again, being far more down-beat than he wanted to be and he didn't miss the look of disappointment that had clouded Eve's face.

'Sorry, I'm being a proper misery.' He forced a smile. 'The team at Domusamare are brilliant and she's getting the best possible help. They'll liaise with the mental health team at St Piran's and all the other services she'll need. In the meantime, they're giving her somewhere safe to stay and three decent meals a day. She couldn't ask for better than that and she's really lucky you were at the hospital when her son was admitted and that you cared enough to want to help her. Not everyone would do that for her in those circumstances. A lot of people couldn't see past the danger she'd put her little boy in.'

'I'm not sure I could have done if she hadn't told me about her past. I lost my mum when I was fourteen and I never really felt secure about anything after that.' She paused for a moment, before meeting his eyes. 'At least not until I met Max, and I came to really feel like part of a family again. I don't think Sophie has had that for a long time and no one has ever put her first from what I can tell.'

'I'm sorry you lost your mum.' It was his turn to hesitate and he wanted to take the opportunity to ask her more about Max, but that had to come from Eve, if and when she was willing to share it. 'I think it takes a degree of personal experience to really understand what could drive someone down a path of addiction and retain sympathy for their plight. Most people see it as self-inflicted, but it's rarely as simple as that.'

'It must have been hard for you and Eden.' She stopped again and gave him a half smile. 'Sorry, you probably don't want to talk about all of that with someone you hardly know, but she's told me a little bit about your mum's problems with alcohol and how that affected her, and I guess it was the same for you.'

'Yes, it moulds who you are and it wasn't just Mum.' Felix was so close to telling her about Meredith that he could feel the shape of her name in his mouth, but then he shook his head, pushing all the feelings that came with talking about her, back down again. 'We worried about Dad a lot as well and he spent so much time covering up for Mum that it felt as if neither of them were ever going to find the strength to make a change. Thank God they did, but I know the impact that addiction can have on families, and I really hope that Sophie can do this for her sake, as well as for her son.'

'Me too.' Eve stopped as they reached her car and she smiled, her amber-brown eyes almost sparkling, in a way he wasn't sure he'd seen before, and he found himself wondering if she'd looked like that all the time, before Max had sustained his head injury. He felt an inexplicable and ridiculous stab of envy that Max might have been on the receiving end of that smile every single day, but Eve really was beautiful, her dark hair shining in the glow of the streetlight above their heads. 'And, thank you, Felix. I owe you a big favour for sorting this out. I bet the last thing you wanted after a long shift was me knocking on your door and asking for help. If there's anything I can do in return, just name it.'

He came so close to suggesting that going for a drink together would more than settle the score, he had to inhale sharply to draw the words back in before they could escape. It would be such an inappropriate suggestion, given what he knew about her relationship with Max, not to mention the fact that he was Max's OT. He also knew from his sister that Eve could be a closed book, and it had taken her a long time to even begin to open up. But he really liked her, and if all they could ever become was friends, he knew he wanted that. He didn't want to risk doing anything that might put a stop to that.

'You don't owe me anything, I'm always happy to help, but if Gwen ever brings one of her cakes into the hospital shop and you get to it while there's still some left, then you'll have my undying gratitude if you grab me a slice, and I promise I'll do the same for you. Trust me, it's not to be missed.'

'Oh, I know, I was this close to proposing to her when I tried her lemon drizzle cake.' Eve pinched her thumb and forefinger together, with just a tiny gap between them, the matching dimples on either side of her mouth making an appearance as she grinned.

'You'll have to get in the queue. I'm first if her husband Barry ever does a runner.' Felix laughed, although he had to admit it was no joke.

It wasn't that he genuinely wanted to be Gwen's second husband, of course, but he did want to find the kind of relationship she had with Barry. They'd been married for fifty years, but he'd seen newlyweds with less excitement at being around one another. The first time he'd met them, he'd asked Eden if they were as mad about each other as they seemed, and his sister had told him everyone talked about their relationship being something special.

They just seemed to get each other and to find adventure in the every day. So many people strove for a big house, or to jet off on as many trips as they could, but Felix knew those things didn't buy happiness.

They certainly hadn't for Meredith. He'd thought they could learn to be happy with the simple things, just because they were together, but Meredith had carried this emptiness inside her that nothing seemed to fill. He'd tried so hard and he hated that he'd failed, but he knew know that she had to want something to fill the emptiness; something that wasn't drugs. Maybe these things were pre-destined, wired into the DNA, and he just hoped that next time he entered into a relationship he'd be able to spot the signs if the other person was damaged so badly that they didn't want to be helped.

Maybe it was for the best that between work and volunteering he didn't have time to do anything about meeting someone else, at least for now. But as he looked at Eve, all he knew was that spending time with her felt good. 'So is that a deal?'

'Absolutely. I promise to always get you a piece of Gwen's cake when it's on offer.' She shook his hand and he tried to ignore how much he wanted to know what it would feel like to kiss her. The last thing Eve needed was him hitting on her and even if she hadn't already got a fiancé, his head was all over the place after Meredith's call. He might have needed to leave the US for the sake of his own sanity, but that didn't mean he could just stop caring. The day he did that, would be the day he knew he was in the wrong job. People like him and Eve had to care, even when it caused them pain. It was what made them who they were, and all they could do was hope they helped enough people to make all the hard days worth it. They were both counting on Sophie's ability to turn her life around, more than Sophie herself would ever know.

9

'What's the weirdest reason you've had someone come into A&E?' Aidan put his coffee down on the table as he asked the question. 'I think mine was the girl who came in with blue hands and we all thought she had something terribly wrong with her heart... turns out she'd bought the jeans she was wearing from a market stall and the dye had come off on her hands. When she took them off, her legs were bright blue too. She looked part human, part Smurf, bless her.'

'Oh God, I've had jeans like that in the past, thank goodness I've never mistaken the dye transfer for pulmonary heart disease.' Isla grinned. 'I think the weirdest one was the day Amy and I were on duty together and this woman came in with a huge purple finger. It genuinely looked like it belonged on Barney the Dinosaur.'

'Can we guess the cause?' Eden's question took the words out of Eve's mouth. She'd agreed to go for coffee at the end of the shift with Felix's sister, as well as Isla and Aidan. They'd been on an early shift and she was planning to go to Oakwood Park after work to see Max, as she did most days, but half an hour to stop for a coffee couldn't hurt and it might even be a relief to him. Sometimes Max seemed happy that she was there, but lately those occasions were more and more infrequent and his mood swings were completely unpredictable. He'd always been so relentlessly upbeat before the assault, able to lift Eve if she felt down.

Mostly it had been wonderful to have a walking, talking ray of sunshine like Max in her life, but just occasionally it had been frustrating that he'd wanted to brush off all her concerns with his 'it'll all be okay' mantra. Sometimes she'd just wanted him to acknowledge that things were crap. Like when her stepmother had planned a sixtieth birthday party for Eve's father, inviting friends right back to his school days, but not even telling his daughter, let alone inviting her. When she and Max had flown out to Spain on holiday once, they hadn't even bothered suggesting that they stay with her dad and stepmother, but they had asked if they could get together. After a lot of to-ing and fro-ing, her stepmother, Carol, had eventually suggested that Eve and Max come over to their villa for a 'nice family dinner'. It had been a surprise and even more so when Carol had gone to the trouble of asking if there were any foods they didn't like. Max would eat just about anything, so that had been easy, but Eve had been sure to tell her stepmother that she didn't like mushrooms or prawns, and Carol had assured her that would be no problem. When they arrived to discover that she'd made garlic mushrooms to start, followed by a prawn curry it had felt like a personal attack to Eve. Max had laughed it off and encouraged her to see the funny side, telling her that it was just because Carol was jealous of her, and the fact that Eve represented the life her father had lived before. What she'd wanted was for Max to tell her that her upset and anger was justified, and to join in with a rant about just what a nasty piece of work her stepmother was. She'd needed him to admit that life wasn't all sunshine and roses, and that the chances were Carol hadn't just made a silly mistake. She'd done it on purpose, but that wasn't who Max was.

She was sure his relentless optimism was encouraging to his patients, but she'd often wondered if there was a side to him she didn't see; a side where he was forced to admit that sometimes things were rubbish and that sometimes no matter how hard you tried, things couldn't be made right. He must have needed to acknowledge that in order to be able to do his job, but when he'd decided to move on from St James's Hospital, so that he could specialise in paediatric surgery at the Leeds Children's Hospital, it was a great fit for his personality. He even insisted the kids all called him Dr Max, instead of using his surname. He was a wonderful man and it hurt Eve's heart that he wouldn't even have recognised himself these days. She'd have given anything to have that relentless sunshine back, but by the time he'd been at Oakwood for six months, she'd been forced to accept it was never going to happen. It had been almost two years since the assault and Annie still hadn't got there, maybe that's where Max had got his eternal optimism from. Whatever the reason, Eve had needed this coffee with colleagues, on the bistro tables outside the Friends of St Piran's Hospital shop, and she knew the old Max wouldn't have begrudged her that for a second.

'I don't think it would take you long to guess the reason.' Isla turned towards Eden and waited for her to respond.

'Her ring was too tight?' Eden asked.

'Ding-ding-ding, we have a winner!' Isla held up a hand. 'But it's the reason she'd put the ring on in the first place that was interesting. Her best friend, who was also her flatmate, had got engaged, but the ring needed resizing to fit her properly, so she was keeping it in a drawer in her bedroom. What the newly engaged woman didn't know was that her so-called best friend was also sleeping with her fiancé. The girl with the massive purple finger, let's call her Emma, had decided that it should have been her he proposed to, so she'd swiped the ring and had worn it to get... well, down and dirty, I suppose, with the fiancé, as a kind of slap in the face to her friend, who was away at her parents' place for the weekend. Emma had fallen asleep in the fiancé's arms, only to wake up with what looked like one of those foam fingers they use at sporting events. When she told him what had happened, he tried to wrench it off her finger, but it only caused more damage. She completely freaked out when we told her we were going to have to cut it off.'

'Her finger?' Eve nearly choked on the coffee she was drinking.

'No, the ring, you eejit!' Aidan started laughing and, as everyone else joined in, it felt so normal, so much like the old days in Leeds, but for once it didn't hurt as much to make the comparison. There would always be an ache for everything and everyone she'd lost, but time was finally dulling the pain of leaving that part of her life behind and it felt as if she'd begun to reach the acceptance stage in grieving for what had happened to Max, at last. She just wished Annie could reach the same point.

'So, what happened to Emma? Did she have to confess to her friend?' Eden leant forward in her seat as she spoke, but Isla just shrugged.

'That's the worst part of working in A&E. Amy and I were desperate to know what the fallout of it all was, and Amy even did a bit of internet stalking after Emma left to see if she could find anything out, but there was nothing. No viral social media posts or articles in *Chat* magazine or *Take a Break*. Nothing!' Isla shook her head. 'Ames and I had to make up our own scenario instead. I just hope the girl who got cheated on had the last laugh one way or another.'

'I miss Amy so much,' Gwen said, as she came to join them at the table. She'd told them she was closing the shop after she'd served them and she was never one to pass up the chance of a coffee and a chat. 'How is she enjoying life as a popstar's girlfriend?'

'She's having a great time.' Isla smiled. 'You know her and Lijah, they act more like the couple next door than my actual neighbours, and they like keeping things low key rather than living any kind of celebrity lifestyle, but she's getting to see so many amazing places. Despite all of that she keeps claiming she misses hospital life and she's still insistent she'll be working some shifts as bank staff when they finally get back to Cornwall, but I'll believe it when I see it.'

'Oh, I can easily believe she misses all of this. There's never a dull moment, is there?' Gwen paused for a moment. 'Although after almost fifty years as a midwife, I reckon I've got more funny stories then you lot put together.'

'Treat us to one, Gwen. You know we love it when you're gloriously indiscreet.' Aidan gave her a gentle nudge and it was all the encouragement she needed.

'Let me think... okay, how about this one, from when I was working at a hospital. I won't say which one, but it was before the midwifery unit in Port Agnes opened. I told the father-to-be to put scrubs on and he didn't realise they were meant to go *over* his clothes, I turned away for a moment to check the foetal monitor and, when I looked back, he'd stripped everything off and was just pulling the top of the scrubs over his head.'

'So, you got an eyeful, Gwen. I bet it wasn't the first time or the last?' Aidan waggled his eyebrows at her. 'Although that's a bit tamer than I was expecting if I'm honest.'

'That's because I haven't finished yet.' Gwen wagged a finger at him. 'His pubic hair had been sprayed green and shaved into what was apparently supposed to be a four-leaf clover, although it looked more like wispy grass that could do with a good drink of water.'

This time Eve really did choke on her coffee and Isla had to pat her on the back as Gwen continued the story.

'The baby decided to arrive four weeks' early, and he'd had to fly back from his brother's stag do in Dublin to be at the birth. He told me he'd been forced by the rest of the stag party to do it as forfeit, after being the first one to be sick. His mates had assured him that the dye would wash out, but even scrubbing it in the shower hadn't made a difference and he'd had to grab the next available flight to get home in time for the birth. I'll never understand men sometimes, but it made me laugh so much I thought my own waters were going to break and I wasn't even pregnant!'

'I should have known we could trust you to come up with a corker, Gwen.' Aidan laughed again.

'Trust me that's just the tip of the iceberg, in fact there's a story I could tell you that would make having a four-leaf clover down there seem like—'

'Help, someone help us, please!' The woman's shout cut Gwen off and Eve shot straight to her feet, instinctively knowing that this wasn't just someone being overly dramatic; the utter desperation in her tone couldn't be faked. She rushed towards the wild-eyed woman, who had one arm around the waist of a much taller man, his face completely drained of colour. The man's hand was wrapped in what looked like a tea towel and there was already blood dripping down onto the floor where he stood, with a blank expression on his face, as if he couldn't see anything at all.

'It's okay we can get you some help, what's happened?' Eve did her best to keep her voice level, as the others followed her over to where the woman was standing, visibly shaking with what was almost certainly shock.

'I couldn't get the car anywhere near the emergency department and Dan was bleeding so much.' She was crying now. 'We've been renovating our house and I didn't realise he was using the table to steady himself when he bent down to pick up the pieces of wood I'd been cutting to make the framing for a new stud wall. And when I lowered the mitre saw again it took three of his fingers off.'

She took a huge gulping breath and lifted up the clear plastic bag of ice she was holding in her other hand, all three of the man's fingers were clearly visible, one of them still wearing a shiny gold wedding band.

* * *

'Please tell me you can sew his fingers back on.' Dan's wife, whose name turned out to be Sienna had begged Eve to make her the promise, as they hurried her husband away from the hospital shop to the emergency department, with the aid of a wheelchair Aidan had quickly found. Eve had wanted to be able to reassure Sienna and tell her that it was all going to be okay, but she wasn't a surgeon and she knew there were a lot of factors that could affect the viability of reattachment. Fingers were far easier to attach than a whole arm and the fact that it was a clean cut with a mitre saw, rather than a crush injury, or a blunt blade, like a lawnmower, all went in Dan's favour. It would still be up to the surgeons to decide if they wanted to attempt reattachment and, even if they did, there was no guarantee of how successful it would be. Dan might be better off without the fingers, if the reattachment served no purpose other than to get in the way of him adapting to his new normal.

Imogen Turner, one of the orthopaedic surgeons, who held a specialism in hand and microsurgery, had arrived in A&E within minutes of Eve putting in the call. Her assessment had brought good news. She was confident that the digits could be reattached with a good chance of achieving at least partial function, and Eve had expected Sienna to be overcome with relief. But as Dan was wheeled away to face surgery, his wife began to whimper.

'I did this to him. We've only been married a month and I've chopped off three of his fingers. How the hell are we supposed to get through this? Every time he looks down at his hand, he's going to remember what I did. Even if they manage to reattach his fingers, he's never going to be *normal* again, is he?'

'The surgeons are incredible, but the most important thing is that whatever happens Dan has lived to tell the tale. You can cope with anything else.'

'He did two tours of Afghanistan without getting seriously injured and now I do this to him. I don't deserve him. I've never deserved him and now he's going to realise he should have picked someone else. If he'd chosen anyone but me, he'd still be okay. I should've just cut my own bloody fingers off.'

'It was an accident and you had the presence of mind to pack his fingers in ice. He won't forget what you had to go through trying to help him and I'm sure the last thing on earth he'd have wanted was for you to get hurt.'

'I can't bear the thought of him looking down and seeing a hand that's dead, with all its function lost. He's left-handed, so it's even worse. We were going to start trying for our first child when the house renovation is done, but what if he can't even hold the baby properly. I'll have robbed them both of all those bonding moments, all because I wasn't concentrating when I should have been.' Sienna's voice had gone several octaves higher and nothing Eve was saying seemed to be making a difference. Sienna needed some kind of practical reassurance; to speak to someone who knew more about it than Eve did, and hear that there could be a good outcome, no matter how bad it looked right now.

'Would it help you to talk to someone who'll be involved in Dan's rehabilitation after the operation? He'll be able to tell you how likely it is that Dan will regain certain functions and what can be done to adapt to any permanent injuries.'

'I think it really would.' Sienna turned towards her with such hope in her eyes and Eve nodded.

'Okay, just give me couple of minutes and I'll see what I can do.'

'Thank you.' Sienna seemed to slump with relief as Eve headed off to make the call, she just hoped she'd be able to deliver on her promise.

'It's Eve, I need to ask another favour.' She blurted out the request as soon as Felix picked up the phone.

'I'm not sure Domusamare have got any beds left.' There was a slightly teasing tone to his voice and she could picture the slow smile spreading across his face. He had a beautiful smile and she knew that in a different time and place she'd have asked Eden more about her brother, but her life was far too complicated already and this was strictly work related.

'I've got a patient who's in surgery to have three severed fingers reattached. His wife was operating the mitre saw that cut them off and she's convinced herself his life is ruined and that he's going to hate her. She just needs to know there's some hope and I wondered if you'd be willing to talk to her, please?'

'Of course. I've just finished with my last patient of the day, so I can head down now.'

'Thanks, Felix, you're a star. See you in a bit.' As she ended the call, Eve hoped she didn't sound as patronising as she feared she might. She was probably overthinking things; it seemed to be her speciality these days. It was probably no surprise given how much of her time she spent attempting to hide her true feelings from Annie and trying to second guess if she was saying and doing the right things to keep up the pretence that her feelings for Max hadn't changed.

* * *

'So, as you can see, there are lots of things we can do to help someone adapt to losing fingers, even if the worst comes to the worst. But the chances are we'll be working on rehab to get the function back with Dan. Either way, I promise it isn't the end of the world.' Felix's tone was reassuring as Sienna handed his phone back, having watched the video he'd shown her of the kind of work he did with other patients like Dan.

'Thank you so much.' Sienna's face had flooded with relief almost as soon as Felix had begun talking, and her whole demeanour had changed from the woman who'd felt completely hopeless just half an hour earlier. 'Both of you have been so kind.'

'It's what we're here for.' Felix smiled, not offering any indication of the fact that neither of them were on the clock any more. It was just one more suggestion of what a good guy he was and there didn't seem to be any evidence to the contrary. Eve had heard Max giving Felix a really hard time during their OT sessions. She was sure he got his fair share of that from a lot of his patients, who must often had been frustrated and in physical and emotional pain, but it never seemed to faze him. She was half hoping that some deep, dark secret would come to light, something that would make Felix far less attractive, but the more time she spent with him, the harder it was to imagine.

'Sienna, oh baby, are you okay?' A man who looked to be in his mid-sixties swept into the relatives' room, followed by a woman of a similar age, both of them hugging Sienna in turn as she offered a muffled response.

'I've done something terrible, Dad... Oh, Mum, I thought I was going to lose him.'

'It's all right, darling, everything's going to be okay.' Sienna's mother still had her daughter wrapped in a tight embrace as she spoke, and her father turned towards Eve and Felix.

'Can you give me any update on my son-in-law, please? When Sienna rang us, she was so upset she wasn't making any sense.'

'Dan's in theatre and the surgical team were hopeful of being able to reattach his fingers, but there are never any guarantees with these things.' Eve tried to make her tone hopeful without over-promising, and Sienna's father seemed to take it in the spirit it was intended and nodded slowly.

'Thank you so much. That sounds like good news to me, sweetheart.' He said turning back towards his daughter. 'Dan's made of tough stuff, and if anyone can get through something like this unscathed, it's him.'

'What if he hates me for it, Dad? I can't lose him. I was terrified the whole time he was on active service that was going to happen. Now he's working locally and he should be safe, but then I go and do something as stupid as this.'

'It was an accident, darling.' Sienna's father repeated what Eve had told her more than once. 'And Dan must have put his fingers on the base of the saw to steady himself. Neither of you did those things because you wanted this to happen, and of course he's not going to hate you, he worships the ground you walk on.'

'I just love him so much.' Sienna gave into tears again and Eve bit her lip. She'd felt every bit as terrified as Sienna when Max had been admitted to hospital after his assault, except there'd been no miracle recovery for him. Rehab hadn't managed to undo the personality-altering impact of his injuries and now she knew it never would. Despite the fact that Max had been training to be a surgeon, she'd have given anything for his injury to have been the same as Dan's, even if meant he had to change career. At least he'd still be Max. It was crazy to envy a woman in Sienna's position, but she did.

'Now that your parents are here, we'll leave you to wait for one of the surgical team to come down with an update. If you decide to leave the relatives' room, just let one of the reception team know where to find you.' Eve forced a smile as she looked at Sienna. She had to get away soon or there was a chance she might blurt out how lucky she thought the other woman was that Dan's injuries would only change him physically. It wouldn't have been professional or even fair to make the comparison, but the words felt as though they were bubbling up inside her, all the same.

'Thank you both again, so much.' Sienna broke free from her parents and hugged both Eve and Felix, before they left in a flurry of further thank yous from both her and her parents.

'Are you okay?' Felix turned to her almost as soon as they were outside in the corridor and she had to blink furiously to stop the threatened tears.

'I just wish Max's injuries were that easy to deal with.'

'I can only imagine how hard it's been.' Felix put a hand over hers in a totally innocent gesture, but an unwanted bolt of desire shot through her body. It had been almost two years since Max had held her hand in a way that meant anything, and these days he was more likely to bat her away. She longed to have that feeling again, of wanting someone and being wanted in return. She couldn't deny it any longer. She wanted to walk hand in hand with someone she loved, and to be held by a man who loved her more than he loved anyone else. Max was never going to do that again, she knew that for certain now and it hurt like hell, but she couldn't walk away, because she couldn't bear the thought of completely closing the door on everything they'd been to one another and just disappearing out of his life. What made it even more impossible was everything else she stood to lose, if she was no longer Max's fiancée. She'd have nothing left at all.

'Can I ask you something?' Felix's voice was soft and she nodded slowly in response, bracing herself for what he might be about to ask. 'Why doesn't Eden know about Max? Does anyone here know what happened?'

'No.' Eve's response was barely audible and she wondered for a moment if she'd even said it out loud. She couldn't look Felix in the eye as she continued. 'Coming to work is my escape from it all, a place where I don't have to think about the fact that I've got a fiancé who is never going to be the same person he was before he was attacked, or that the woman who should have become my mother-in-law absolutely refuses to acknowledge the truth. I spend my life being forced to play along with Annie's fantasy that one day we'll get back to where we were. I just need somewhere that I can be Eve Bellingham, a doctor trying to do the best by her patients. I can't bring Max into this world, otherwise I won't get any respite from how much it hurts that I've lost him, even when he's still sitting there in front of me.'

She hadn't meant to say all of that and she definitely hadn't mean to allow the tears to finally start falling. But they came faster still when Felix pulled her towards him and held her in a way she'd ached to be held for two long years.

'I'm so sorry, Eve. I wish there was something I could do or say that would really help, but I want you to know that I'm here if you ever want to offload. I might not ever fully understand what it feels like to have a partner who has suffered a head injury like Max's, but I do know what it's like to have a partner who seems to have changed into another person altogether and how awful it feels to know you can't do anything about it.'

'I hate it so much. I just want things to go back to how they were and it kills me that they never will.' It was all she could manage to say in a voice thick with tears. There was so much she wanted to ask him about what he'd just said, but right now she couldn't find the words. All she could do was lean against him and hold on tight, hoping that this brief moment of being held, and feeling understood, would sustain her for whatever came next.

10

Max's birthday used to be a big occasion and he always made sure that Eve's birthday was even bigger. He knew how to do celebrations in style and that had probably stemmed from the way that Annie handled those kinds of events. Despite her success and her determination to honour her maternal family's legacy, Annie was far from being the stereotypical lawyer, and was obsessed with family rather than work. Max had followed his mother's example by making Eve's birthday special from the start of their relationship. It always began with her favourite breakfast and a carefully selected gift, and he'd always book a celebratory meal somewhere wonderful. But it hadn't ended there. When he'd discovered more about Eve's experiences of birthdays after her mum had died, and the event had stopped being marked in any significant way, he'd decided that she ought to have a birthday week to make up for it.

Her father's idea of making an effort had been a twenty-pound note stuffed into a generic birthday card – the kind that came in a multiple pack, rather than the sort that said '*Happy Birthday to a Special Daughter*.' On more than one occasion the card had arrived late and, once she'd reached the age of twenty-five, the cards had stopped arriving altogether. It hadn't mattered as much as it might have done, because by then she'd become one of the Pascoe clan, sucked into Max's family in a way that had made her feel loved *and* valued. She'd spent a long time before that wondering how different things might have been if her mother hadn't died when she was barely in her teens, but she'd finally been able to let go of all those what-ifs, because the void created by her mother's absence had no longer felt so overwhelmingly huge.

Even after Max's assault, when he had no longer cared when Eve's birthday was, Annie had never allowed it to pass without fanfare. She'd always insisted on a special family dinner, and there'd be beautifully wrapped gifts from her and Nigel, as well as from Max himself; no one acknowledging that Annie had bought and wrapped those as well. Max had been in an induced coma on the first of the family birthdays that came around after he was assaulted, but the ones after that had been marked by Annie as if nothing had changed, just as Eve knew Max's birthday would be this year. He was thirty-three and should have been just a year off qualifying as a surgeon, except now he often needed help with the most basic of tasks, becoming incredibly angry when he couldn't do something as simple as fastening a button by himself and wrenching it off in fury. Did Annie really believe it was just a matter of time before Max returned to his old self? She was an intelligent woman, but she was also a loving mother, so Eve understood why it might be preferable not to face reality. It was why they were all dressing up to go out for his birthday lunch, at Bocca Felice, a restaurant overlooking the bay in Port Kara.

'You look so beautiful, Eve.' It was down to Annie to utter the words that Max would once have said to her without fail when she entered the restaurant, and to envelope her into an embrace that left her smelling of the older woman's Chanel No.5 perfume.

'So do you, Annie.' Eve turned towards Max's father, who was already seated next to his son, smiling. 'And you don't scrub up too badly either, Nigel.'

'I know, I quite fancied myself when I caught sight of my reflection.' Nigel winked, but that didn't stop Max from rolling his eyes.

'Must be something wrong with your mirror, no one is going to fancy you with that many wrinkles.'

'Max, don't be so rude.' Annie's face had taken on a pinched look, and she was clearly worried that the shape of the day had already been determined, because it was Max's mood that would dictate whether or not they were able to have a nice time. He wasn't the only resident at Oakwood Park who had undergone a change in personality as a result of his head injury. One day, when Eve had gone to visit him, and he'd lashed out at her because her breathing sounded 'weird' and he'd shouted at her that she never thought about him or brought him anything nice, she hadn't been able to hold back the tears. She'd visited after a night shift from hell, without any sleep, because Annie had been at home in bed with the flu and for once wouldn't be coming in. Eve had been exhausted, but she'd driven ten miles out of her way before even arriving at Oakwood Park. Her first stop had been to the Asian foods supermarket, waiting outside until it opened, to get Max some of the matcha KitKats that had become his favourite on an holiday they'd taken to Japan two years before the assault. There were two types, one coated completely in matcha, and the other a combination of matcha and chocolate. She'd selected the wrong one and it had been enough to set Max off. As she'd stood in the corridor outside his room, one of the other residents, a man called Sammy, who was about the same age as Max, came up and stood next to her. She was furiously wiping away the tears, trying to stem more from coming, when Sammy had asked her a question in the gentlest of tones.

'Do you need a hug?' All she'd been able to do was nod, because she really did.

'Everything okay?' Jeanine, one of the carers had followed Sammy down the corridor, and he'd stepped back, releasing Eve.

'She just needed a hug, but she feels better now.' Sammy had smiled then and given them both a salute, as if to indicate his duty was done, before heading further down the corridor and disappearing into his own room.

'Are you really feeling better, because you don't look like you are?' Jeanine had reached out and squeezed her shoulder and the tears that Eve had desperately been trying to stem had begun to flow again.

'Max just seems to hate me most of the time, he's so angry and I don't know what to do to change that.'

'You can't do anything because it's Max who's changed.' It had been the first time anyone had been quite so honest about the situation, perhaps because Annie wasn't there to insist it was dressed up another way. 'It's common with head injuries like his to become more irritable and to no longer be able to comply with social norms.'

'But Sammy's really sweet, and when I spoke to his mum she said he'd sustained a very similar head injury to Max.' She hadn't meant to make the comparison, but she couldn't help it. If she couldn't have the old Max back, then why couldn't he at least be like Sammy?

'Even if they'd had identical injuries, it wouldn't mean it affected them in the same way. Sammy's mother told me he used to be really competitive in his job, even bordering on aggressive, when he was going after something he wanted before his accident. Now, he's a total sweetheart, but he's still not the same Sammy he was. The residents here almost always experience a change in behaviour because of the seriousness of their injuries and, as you know only too well, that can be one of the hardest things for loved ones to deal with. I know it's a struggle, but Max is so lucky to have so many people who love him unconditionally, especially you and his mum. Not all our residents get regular visitors and Max gets more than anyone else. Don't be hard on yourself if you find it tough some days, anyone would.'

Jeanine had hugged her then and it should have made Eve feel better, but all it did was bring forth a fresh crop of tears. It wasn't just the sympathy and understanding, it was the fact that Jeanine's words had made her feel more trapped than ever, because they seemed to come with the expectation that her visits would never stop, or even reduce. The thought of doing this for the rest of her life, made it feel like there was a hand pressed against her windpipe, with the weight of the world behind it, and suddenly it had seemed almost impossible to breathe. She'd known if she didn't get out she'd have a full-blown panic attack. So Eve had broken away from Jeanine and run out of Oakwood Park, not stopping until she'd got to her car.

It had taken her forty-five minutes to go back in and try again with Max; to take the photos of the two of them she would need to send to Annie to satisfy his mother that they were coping without her and that her son wasn't going without visits while she was unwell. If Eve hadn't done that, her phone would have rung constantly. It was easier just to do her duty and to try and power through, despite the love she'd once had for Max having died, not in one fell swoop, but by a thousand tiny cuts. She hated herself for not being able to love him like she used to, but she couldn't pretend any more, not even to herself. She did still love him, but it looked nothing like the love they'd once shared. The only pretence she maintained was with Annie, and she hated herself even more for lying to the woman who had done nothing but show her love, and had been the closest thing she'd had to a mum since she was fourteen years old.

As Eve looked across at Annie now, she could see in the older woman's face that the changes in Max hurt her every bit as much. She might be desperate to cling to the belief that this was all just temporary, but deep down she must have known that hope was futile. All Annie wanted was a nice family meal to celebrate Max's birthday and Eve would do whatever it took to make that happen.

'They've got fillet steak on the menu, Max.' When she spoke, Eve's voice had a sing-song tone she barely recognised as belonging to her, and she kept her smile in place despite the half-hearted shrug he gave in response. She resisted the urge to reminisce about the night they'd come to this same restaurant – his favourite anywhere in the world he'd told her – to celebrate their engagement, after his proposal at Halfmoon Cove, when they'd been down visiting his parents. He'd had steak that night and they'd drunk champagne and planned a whole life together, one they'd had so much certainty they were going to have that Eve had almost been able to reach out and touch it. Neither of them had known that a nightmare was just around the corner and that was something she was incredibly grateful for, because it remained the most perfect day of her entire life.

'Well, I'm going to have the fish.' Nigel was smiling now, too, both of them fighting hard to keep things upbeat. 'If I can't stop my face from wrinkling, I can at least feed my brain and stop that from shrivelling up as well!'

He laughed and the idea also seemed to amuse Max, making him join in. For a moment, as she listened to the sound, Eve allowed herself to believe that the old Max was back. It might have been his birthday, but that short-lived moment of make believe was her gift to herself.

* * *

After lunch, Annie had suggested that they drive to Port Agnes to take a walk around the harbour there, and Eve had hesitated. It was less than two miles from the restaurant and only three from the hospital, which was on the outskirts of Port Kara, which meant there was a very good chance of her bumping into someone she knew. As she'd admitted to Felix, she kept the part of her life that centred around Max a secret for her own sanity. It was hard enough having to play the role of his fiancée for Annie's sake, she didn't want people at work to start asking how he was, or probing deeper into how his head injury had changed things, and maybe even questioning what that meant for their long-term plans. She couldn't have answered that kind of question, because the one thing she wanted – for life to go back to the way it had been before the assault – was impossible.

But her second choice of walking away, was never going to be an option either. So for now all she could do was keep going and hope that fate, or the universe, or whatever it was that had let off the hand grenade in her life in the first place, would take charge again and map out the course of the rest of her life for her. In the meantime, her job allowed her to play make believe, and pretend that there were as many options for the next phase of her life as people with a valued profession like hers usually had at their fingertips. That's why her first thought when Annie had suggested going for a walk was to say it was too cold, but then she'd realised they could just as easily have been spotted in the restaurant and that no one seeing them together would assume she was in a relationship with Max anyway. The last time she'd tried to hold his hand he'd shoved it roughly away, and another tiny piece of her heart had broken off and floated into the distance forever.

Sometimes it felt as though she was the only person in the world experiencing this kind of pain and she'd spent countless hours, in the first year or so after Max's assault, searching for information about head injuries like his, to try and find grains of hope. That's when she'd found a Louis Theroux documentary, about a woman who'd sustained a head injury after a horse-riding accident and whose husband had described her as having lost all her 'squishy bits'; the soft and gentle side of her that had given and received physical and emotional affection. It had felt as though someone was telling hers and Max's story. It didn't make his rejection of her hurt any less, but she'd suddenly felt a tiny bit less alone.

'I'm seriously thinking about getting a boat this summer, you know.' Nigel made the comment as they approached the harbour. 'You'd love that wouldn't you, Max? The feel of the sun on your face and the wind in your hair. We could go fishing again, like we used to.'

'Fish stink.' Max wrinkled his nose and Eve could sense his twitchiness beside her. She knew that despite it being a beautiful crisp spring day, with a bright blue sky stretching endlessly above one of the most beautiful villages in the country, that Max wanted to be in his room, on his PlayStation or Xbox, lost in a world where he didn't have to interact in ways that required him to meet anyone else's expectations. He'd never been a gamer before the assault, at least not since his early teens according to Annie, but it had become his happy place since he'd moved to Oakwood Park.

'I think you should get a boat, Nigel. Imagine all the wonderful trips you could take Annie on around this stretch of coastline. I still remember the first boat trip I took when Max brought me down here and I couldn't believe that turquoise blue waters like that existed outside of an Instagram filter, let alone in the UK. That first glimpse of Dagger's Head, rising up out of the water like some kind of mythical sea creature, took my breath away.'

'Why can't you just say you thought it was nice, instead of all that flowery crap?' Max rolled his eyes.

'Don't be unkind, Eve is just trying to—' Before Annie could finish, Nigel cut her off.

'What Evie should do is write for the Cornish tourist board, or become a sales rep for the one of the boat building firms.' Nigel blew her a kiss. 'Either way you've sold me on buying one, Evie, I'm going to get a boat for the summer. It's time to seize the day, *carpe diem* and all that. It'll force Annie to take a bit more time to herself, too, if we're out on the boat together.'

Eve didn't miss the look of hope in Nigel's eyes and she knew he must miss the version of Annie his wife had been, before Max's assault, not to mention the relationship he'd had with his son. They'd all lost so much, but Annie was already shaking her head.

'If we're out on the boat it needs to be all of us together. As a family.' She said the last part forcefully, as if it was some kind of solemn vow, and Eve would have sworn she could actually feel her heart sinking. 'It will be lovely though and so good for us. All that sunshine and time outside is conducive to good mental health. We might even be able to use the boat for the wedding eventually. I saw a bride and groom here last year, arriving for their wedding at the church on the harbour, with a flotilla of other boats behind them carrying all the guests.'

'Well, we don't want Evie having to copy anyone else. When she gets married, it's going to be the unique and special day she deserves.' Nigel looked at Eve then, their eyes locking, and she knew without doubt that he understood. He wasn't talking about the fictional day that she and Max would get married and everything would go back to how it had been before. He was talking about a real event, something he wanted for her, and something he knew would never involve his son.

'Thank you.' She stepped towards him, allowing herself to be folded into his arms and he whispered words meant just for her.

'It'll all be okay. I promise.'

'God, this is so boring.' Max had adopted the petulant teenager tone he frequently used and he looked like one, too, as Eve turned around to face him. She might not be ready to put a stop to the full pretence yet, but Nigel's words had given her more hope than she could remember having in a very long time. She didn't want Max's mood to spoil that, so she decided to handle him the only way she knew how, by doing her best to give him what he wanted.

'It's your birthday. So you should get to pick what you do, Max.'

As he opened his mouth to respond, Max suddenly stopped and pointed in front of him. 'It's Felix.'

Eve spun round with much more haste than she probably should have done, to see Felix, Eden and Drew walking together side by side, with Teddie in his pushchair. She didn't want to acknowledge the quickening of her heart rate. If it had sped up it was just because she was nervous about Eden and Drew seeing her with Max and his family, and uncovering the parts of her life she'd worked so hard to keep separate. It couldn't be about Felix, that was a complication she wasn't going to allow herself to have.

'Fancy bumping into you guys.' Felix gave Max a fist bump, before hugging Annie and shaking hands with Nigel. He didn't make physical contact with Eve, something she was grateful for and yet somehow bereft all at the same time. After a quick round of introductions, where Felix tactfully left out the bit about Eve being Max's fiancée, he turned to look at Annie and Max. 'How are the birthday celebrations going?'

'It's so nice of you to remember.' Annie smiled, before being cut off again, this time by her son.

'Boring as shit.' Max shrugged and for a second Eve held her breath, wondering how everyone was going to react, but then Felix started to laugh and suddenly everyone else was joining in.

'I know the feeling, mate, I mean imagine being dragged along for a Sunday afternoon walk by your sister and her boyfriend, when you could be spending it getting to the next level on *Borderlands 4*.' Felix gave Annie an almost imperceptible nod, but Eve spotted it. He knew exactly how to handle Max, who was already laughing again.

'I just wish I'd blown the candles out on my cake so I could have made a wish to be back in my room playing that. What's the point of getting a new video game for your birthday and then having to wait all day doing other stuff before you can play it?'

'We'll take you back now, son, don't worry and before you ask the next bit, yes, you'll still get your cake.' Nigel put an arm around Max, who for once seemed genuinely happy at the show of affection.

'Eve deserves the biggest slice, she bought the cake and it looks gorgeous.' Annie beamed at her and Eve's heart dropped again. The thought of going back to Oakwood Park and carrying on the 'party', while Max was sitting with his headphones on gaming, filled her with dread.

'We can save her a big slice.' Nigel's tone was insistent, and he looked directly at Annie, clearly trying to cut off any protest she might make before she even had the chance. 'Evie's been working long shifts all week and she needs a bit of down time. Max just wants to get on with his game, so aside from the cake, I think we can safely say the celebrations are over.'

Annie opened her mouth and gulped a couple of times, like a fish out of water, but then Nigel took hold of her hand. 'Come on, we can FaceTime Lily when Max does the cake and we can sing the birthday song. It'll be just the four of us, like when the kids were little.'

Eve knew all about 'the birthday song', it was something Annie had made up to the tune of 'Happy Birthday to You', and the words were ingrained in her mind from all the times Max's family had sung it.

'We really love you, and you love us too. It's your birthday darling Maxie, you're the best son, it's true!'

The words were tweaked each time for Lily and eventually for Eve, which was how she first became known as Evie, so that it would fit the rhyme. Max had called her Evie most of the time before the assault, and his family had also used the pet name a lot. Nigel still did, but Max never called her Evie now and Annie seemed to have stopped as well. Eve suspected Annie was trying not to acknowledge that Max had changed in yet another way. If he'd been the only one not to use the pet name any more it would have marked him out from the rest of them.

In the past, Eve would undoubtedly have felt sad at Nigel's words about it being 'just the four of them, like the old days', but instead she was incredibly grateful to him, because Annie was nodding.

'Okay, if you're sure, Eve?' Annie turned to look at her.

'Absolutely.' She squeezed the older woman's hand.

'All right then, darling, but I'll save you the slice with the most icing on.' Annie folded her into another hug. Then, in a flurry of hasty goodbyes, with Max tugging at his mother's arm like an impatient toddler, they were gone. Leaving Eve standing with Felix and the others.

'I know you're probably exhausted from work.' Eden gave her a warm smile. 'But we're going back to Drew's place and we'd love you to come over for a bit if you've got time. We barely seem to get five minutes to catch up properly when we're on shift. No pressure at all. Although you would save my brother from being forced into spending the afternoon with just us. Which apparently is just about unbearable.'

'Don't come the wounded party with me, Eden Grainger, you know I was only playing along with Max.' Felix nudged his sister and she laughed.

'My feelings are deeply hurt, I'll have you know. I'm not sure I'll ever get over it.'

'Yeah, I can tell.' Felix looked directly at Eve, still smiling, and she should have made her excuses, because the attraction she felt towards him seemed to be getting stronger all the time, but she didn't. The truth was, even though she *was* really tired, she wanted to hang out with them all. The fact that Eden hadn't led with a string of questions about Eve's relationship to Max and his family just made her like Felix's sister even more. She trusted Felix when he'd said he hadn't told Eden about Max, so she must have been curious about the set up. Maybe she'd worked it out for herself, or maybe she was holding back on a string of burning questions because she'd sensed that Eve wouldn't want to answer them. Either way, Eden was respecting her privacy and ironically that was exactly what made Eve far more willing to let down the barrier she'd spent so long building up.

'I'd love to come over, thank you.' It was her turn to grin. 'Anything to help dilute Felix's presence, I know how tricky that must be to put up with!'

11

Felix hadn't enjoyed himself so much in a long time. When Eden had invited Eve back to Drew's place, he hadn't thought she would agree. When she had, he hadn't expected her to stay long. The four of them had spent the afternoon hanging out together in such an easy way that it had felt as if Eve had been a part of their circle for years. When he'd first met her, the attraction had been instant, but she'd seemed standoffish, maybe even a little cold, and one thing guaranteed to kill attraction for Felix was if someone wasn't warm. He just couldn't gel with people who had an aloof demeanour, whether it came to romantic or platonic relationships. It hadn't taken long to realise that Eve wasn't cold and as soon as he'd seen her at Oakwood Park, even before she'd explained more about the situation with Max, he'd known that what might appear to some to be detachment was just a way of trying to safeguard a heart that had already been badly broken.

Even if Felix had doubted his own judgement, he'd have got all the evidence he needed that Eve was a good person from the way Teddie had taken to her. His nephew was an impeccable judge of character and he only ever gravitated towards kind people, as if his autism gave him some kind of sixth sense. Eve had sat on the floor, patiently building towers out of stacking cups, just so that Teddie could demolish them, like a tiny, curly-haired Godzilla, flattening tower blocks in Tokyo.

Drew could often be quiet, his own high-functioning autism meaning that it had taken him a while to feel comfortable to be fully himself around Felix. He hadn't seemed to need that adjustment time around Eve and the four adults had chatted about all kinds of things, from the hospital and volunteering at Domusamare, to travel destinations they'd loved and others they longed to visit. Eve had said she had family living in California, who she'd love the chance to visit, but there'd been a wistful look in her eyes, as though she knew it would never happen. Even when Felix had told her about his own time living there and how flights could be picked up relatively cheaply if you timed it right, she'd shaken her head, seeming to dismiss the possibility without actually saying the words. They'd been at Drew's place for nearly three hours, when Eve suddenly made an admission that took Felix completely by surprise.

'Max is my fiancé.' To Eden and Drew's credit, there was no sharp intake of breath, but his sister was nobody's fool and Drew was a highly skilled pathologist. If they couldn't read between the lines and work out how deeply entrenched Eve was in Max's life, then nobody could. Eve closed her eyes for a moment, before opening them again and looking at Eden. 'At least he was, before he sustained the catastrophic head injury that has left him like a completely different person. He was training to be a surgeon and he was the most upbeat person I've ever met, now there's very little left from our old life that makes him happy, certainly not me. But I still feel like the worst person in the world for wanting to admit our relationship is over.'

Eden's eyes took on a glassy appearance as she looked at Eve.

'I can't imagine how hard that is, when you loved him as much as you must have done, and you don't want to hurt him.'

'It's not even about hurting Max.' Eve closed her eyes for a second time, swallowing so hard against the emotion that must have been bubbling up inside her that Felix heard it. 'I don't think he could care less if I told him I wasn't coming to see him any more, but it would kill his mum. Annie is still clinging to him somehow making a miraculous recovery, even though after almost two years, it's pretty clear the change in his personality is permanent, never mind anything else.'

'I take it you're close to Max's family?' Drew asked. 'I can't imagine they'd want you to put your life on hold indefinitely.'

'I don't have a family of my own to speak of and so they are my family, which means I'm not even acting selflessly, to protect Annie. I'm doing what I'm doing so I don't lose them, for my own sake. How bad is that?' Eve made herself sound like a master manipulator and Felix was about to protest, but his sister got in first.

'It doesn't sound bad at all. You love them and they love you, and you're all just doing what you can in a horrible situation. From the way you've described the kind of person Max was, it sounds like he'd have hated the way things are for you now. I know if anything like that happened to me, I wouldn't want Drew to put his life on hold forever.'

Eden had said more or less then same thing to Eve as Felix had done before, but she still seemed unable to believe that no one would judge her if she decided to end her engagement to Max. At least not anyone who understood or had witnessed first-hand the kind of impact of an injury like Max's. As medical professionals, all four of them knew there would be no amazing turnaround for Max. The only life Eve had any power to control was her own.

She'd changed the subject after that, and none of them had pushed her to talk about it any more. It had been huge enough for her to raise the subject at all, and Felix was just glad Eve now had the option of confiding in Eden further, if she wanted to. Loving someone who'd suffered an injury like Max's could feel desperately isolating, and the more support Eve had the better. Especially if an issue came up when she was at work.

When Drew suggested they get a takeaway, Eve had surprised Felix again by agreeing to stay. He'd offered to drive to Port Tremellien to pick up the Chinese they'd settled on, and Eve had said she'd go with him, while Drew and Eden put Teddie to bed. It wasn't a long drive, but Felix had something he wanted to get off his chest, in the hope it might help Eve realise that the choice about whether to stay engaged to Max didn't lie solely in her hands.

'I'm going to tell you something that not even Eden knows. You know I told you before that I understood a little bit of what it feels like to love someone who then seems to become another person in front of your eyes? Well, it happened to me when I was living in San Francisco. I shared my home and my life with a woman called Meredith for two years.' Felix kept his eyes on the road ahead as he spoke, grateful for the darkness in the car as he continued.

'Meredith was a therapist at the addiction clinic where I worked and she was a former addict herself. I couldn't tell Eden about Merri, because I'd begged her for years not to get involved with someone who had addiction issues, not even if they were in recovery. I knew we both had a bit of saviour complex, growing up with an alcoholic mum, and I wanted Eden to have an easy life. She ignored my advice and got involved with Teddie's biological father, but what she doesn't know is that I ignored my own advice too.'

'Sometimes love doesn't play by the rules. Oh God, sorry, that was so cheesy.' Eve laughed, breaking the tension for a moment. 'Just ignore me, please, and I promise I won't interrupt again.'

'Actually I kind of like your reasoning, it makes me feel a bit less of a hypocrite.' Felix breathed out slowly, bracing himself for recounting the rest of the story. Reliving it was never easy. 'Things went really well for the first year or so, and I was building up to tell my family about Meredith and even planning to bring her over to meet them, when she relapsed. I tried everything I could think of or knew about to get Merri well again, but nothing worked and her behaviour became more and more extreme. In the end she disappeared and cut all contact, not just with me but with everyone who cares about her. Occasionally she'll reach out and ask for money, but her family have begged me not to respond to that, and they aren't giving her anything either. They're working with a team who believe the best way of helping Merri is to allow her to reach rock bottom, when her only option will be to accept the help we've all been trying to give her. I know it's probably the right thing, but it's the toughest kind of love there is.'

'That must be incredibly difficult.'

'It is and I just couldn't stay in San Francisco and be certain I was strong enough to hold out. I'd been wanting to come home for a while, because of Eden and Teddie, and it just felt like the right time to leave. I thought it would be easier being thousands of miles away, but she got in contact recently and it took all I had not to just give her what she was asking for. Instead, I turned her away.'

'You didn't turn her away, you're doing what her family have asked and working with a strategy the experts think will give Meredith the best chance. No one could blame you for that.'

'I still feel like the worst person ever. I got in touch with her family, as well as one of the doctors at the rehab clinic where I used to work, and I've left it in their hands. Some people might see that as me abandoning Meredith and only the lowest of the low would turn their back on someone they loved, right?' He was taking a huge risk telling Eve all of this, because she might well agree with that assessment, but even in the darkness of the car he could see her shaking her head.

'It's crazy to think that. You wouldn't be helping her by giving her the money, that's not what she needs to get well. What she needs is the help you're trying to set up for her.'

'So you think that, even when you've loved someone and a part of you always will, sometimes it's okay to step away from their lives and let someone else help them in a way that nothing you do ever can?' He kept his voice low and steady, but Eve's response was sharp all the same.

'That's not fair, it's not the same situation.'

'You're right, it's not, but we've both tried everything we can think of and come to the conclusion that there's nothing we do can do to change the situation for Max or Meredith. If I'm not a bad person to draw a line in the sand about the extent of my involvement, then you certainly aren't.'

She didn't respond for a moment, but when she did the rawness of her emotions was spelled out in every syllable. 'Then why do I feel like the worst person alive every time I look at Annie?'

* * *

Felix wanted to believe that his motivation for telling Eve about Meredith had been entirely altruistic; an attempt to help her see that moving on from her engagement to Max wasn't the act of someone cruel or unkind, but he knew there was more to it than that. He'd wanted to tell someone about Meredith, and the decision he'd made to leave. He'd wanted that someone to tell him that he wasn't a heartless bastard for stepping away from Meredith, and allowing the hope that she might finally beat her addiction to rest in the hands of other people. There was also the fact that he liked Eve more and more, in a way that he had to admit wasn't entirely platonic, which made him question his motivations all over again. He shouldn't have pushed things so far and he probably shouldn't have told her about Meredith either, but it was done now. All he could do was back off and let her mull things over. If she decided she wanted to be straight with Annie, that had to be down to Eve. All of which was why he moved the conversation on to a far more neutral topic, as they walked from where they'd parked the car towards the Chinese restaurant.

'What was the first single you ever bought?' It was one of those kinds of icebreaker questions you might ask on a first date, but it seemed like the ideal way to lighten the mood, and he could tell as soon as he asked it that the answer was going to be interesting.

'Oh God, you're going to judge me. Especially when you find out I knew all the dance moves and used to lip-sync to it in my bedroom.' Eve pulled a face.

'Well, you didn't need to tell me that part, but now I really want to know!'

'All right, it was 'Don't Cha' by The Pussycat Dolls. I was thirteen and completely left to my own devices a lot of the time as my mum was really unwell and Dad was already starting to check out. It's probably a surprise that I didn't end up going down a very different path.' She grinned. 'Although I'm not the world's greatest dancer, so it probably had more comedy value than anything else. At the time I thought I could be in the next big girl band, though.'

'If you think that's embarrassing, you've got nothing on me. Mine was 'Rock Your Body' by Justin Timberlake. I was twelve and I recorded the video of him dancing on VHS tape, so I could perfect the moves.' Felix shook his hips and pouted in a way he knew for certain was more comical than sexy, but when Eve threw back her head and laughed, he wasn't sure he'd ever seen anything sexier in his entire life. He had to get the thought out of his head, otherwise she was going to pick up on it and she wouldn't want to be around him. She'd made it quite clear why she didn't even want to try moving on from her relationship with Max, so Felix making any kind of move on her, or even acting like he wanted to, would have been as unwelcome as it was inappropriate.

'I definitely don't feel quite as bad now.' Eve was struggling to stop laughing, as they turned into the street where the Chinese restaurant was, when he saw a figure out of the corner of his eye. The woman was staggering along the pavement opposite them, bouncing off the wall and against the lamp post, then back again like a ball bearing in a pinball machine.

'Is that Sophie?' He squinted, hoping his eyes and the darkness were deceiving him, and that it wouldn't turn out to be the woman he and Eve had helped get a place at Domusamare. Her face was half in shadow and he could so easily be wrong, but as he turned to look at Eve and saw her face fall, he knew he wasn't.

'I think it is.' She was already breaking into a run to cross the road and he followed suit, the two of them reaching the woman, who was now unmistakably Sophie, just before her legs gave way and she sank to the ground. Thankfully her descent was much slower than it would have been if they hadn't been holding onto her.

'Sophie, it's Felix and Eden, do you remember who we are?'

He spoke loudly and clearly, and she only gave a single word in response.

'Yes.'

'Have you been drinking or taken something?' It was Eve who asked the question this time, getting a similarly brief response.

'Yeah.'

'Can you tell us what you took?' The words were barely out of Felix's mouth before Sophie's head lolled back and she began to convulse, Eve's training immediately kicking in.

'Call an ambulance, I'll keep her head as still as possible until she stops convulsing and then get her into the recovery position. There's no way of knowing what she's taken, but whatever it was I bet she took a lot of it.' Eve's tone was urgent and she didn't even look up as she issued the instruction.

'Okay, but I might need to go back towards where the car's parked to get a signal, because it's notoriously patchy here. It might be quicker to ask the restaurant if I can use their phone. Is there anything in particular I should tell the ambulance service?'

'Go with your gut instinct and say whatever you think you need to, to get them to come out as quickly as possible. You'll get it right, I trust you.'

Felix broke into a run again, this time in the direction of the Chinese restaurant. He just hoped Eve was right about trusting him, because when it came to her, he wasn't even sure he trusted himself.

* * *

Thankfully the waiting time for the ambulance had been relatively short and within twenty minutes of Felix making the call, Eve and Sophie were on their way to St Piran's and he was following along in the car. He'd felt guilty at the idea of leaving

Eden and Drew without their dinner, but the thought of leaving Eve to face the situation alone had overridden everything else. So even before one of the restaurant staff had kindly offered to drive over and drop the food off at Drew's place, he'd already decided what decision he was going to make.

He'd made a call to the out-of-hours team at Domusamare on the way to St Piran's. They confirmed that Sophie was still staying at the hostel and that her son was living with foster carers. So at least they didn't need to worry about Carter's safety. Once Felix reached the hospital and parked the car, he headed straight into A&E, where Eve was waiting for him with an update.

'I found two empty packets of paracetamol and an almost empty bottle of vodka in her bag. There's no indication that she took anything else, but we can't be certain until we get the blood results back, or she becomes lucid enough to tell us. She's still out of it at the moment.'

'Thank God we found her when we did.' Felix couldn't bear the thought of what might have happened otherwise, but there was no look of relief on Eve's face.

'The trouble with paracetamol is that it can cause irreparable damage to the liver and sometimes the kidneys, even when a patient survives the initial overdose. We've got her on intravenous acetylcysteine, which is usually effective in preventing liver damage if it's administered within eight hours of the overdose, but there's no way of knowing when she took the tablets and then there's the risk of combining them with the alcohol. So she'll need an IV to top up her fluids too and regulate her blood sugar levels. The treatment will take about twelve hours and she'll have some blood tests afterwards to see if her liver has been permanently damaged.'

'Has she got anyone coming in to be with her?' Even before Eve shook her head, Felix was pretty sure he knew the answer.

'She wasn't making any sense, but when I looked on her phone, there was no one obvious; no contact tagged as mum or dad, but I think we already knew that would be the case from the last time she was bought in, didn't we?'

'I'll give the out-of-hours service at Domusamare a call and see if they can suggest anyone, or if they know what might have triggered this.'

'Thank you.' Eve reached for his hand and he tried not to think of it as anything more than a reflex action on her part, because allowing himself to believe she might like him as more than a friend was dangerous ground; territory he'd sworn to steer clear of less than an hour ago. It was almost a relief when two seconds later she dropped his hand, as if only just having realised what she'd done.

'I'll make the call right now.' He was already turning away. 'Are you going to wait with Sophie?'

'Yes, if she's got no one else, I don't want to leave her on her own. No one deserves to be left on their own at a time like this.' Eve's tone was light, but suddenly it felt like the comment could have been aimed at him and his decision not to help Meredith the last time she'd called. Eve had said she understood, but that had been before they'd found Sophie, in the grip of her own demons, and there was a good chance that had been enough to change Eve's opinion. He didn't have time to worry about that now. They needed to know if anyone at Domusamare could shed any light on the situation, because whatever Eve might feel about the way he'd handled things with Meredith, Felix's natural instinct was to be there for anyone who needed help, for as long as they were willing to accept it, and he was nowhere near ready to give up yet.

12

Eve had sat by Sophie's bedside while she waited for Felix to return from talking to the team at Domusamare. It had taken him almost half an hour and she'd spent the time watching the rise and fall of Sophie's chest, as her vital signs were monitored and the IV fluids and medication were pumped into her body in an attempt to wash out the toxins she'd flooded it with. Even before Felix had returned with an update, she'd known that Sophie's motivation was to numb herself from the reality of the life she was living; one that was just too painful for her to bear.

'Sorry it took so long.' There was a grave expression on Felix's face when he finally returned. 'The out-of-hours team wouldn't share anything with me because of client confidentiality, so I called Henry at home. I know him well enough for him to trust that I needed the information for Sophie's sake, and he told me that Pippa, Sophie's social worker, called to see her on Friday and said that visitation with Carter is being suspended until the CPS decide whether or not to proceed with the child neglect case. She'd assumed she would at least be allowed supervised contact, but apparently the contact centres are overloaded and there just isn't the capacity. Sophie became very distressed at the thought of not seeing Carter for an indefinite period, but her key worker supported her and thought the conversations she'd had with Sophie had helped her to see that the best thing she could do to overturn the decision was to prove she was determined to stay clean this time. But then she had an argument with another resident today, who told her she might as well forget she had a kid as she was never going to see him again and that's when Sophie left the centre. She's free to come and go as she wants, as long as she doesn't break the conditions of her bail, so they couldn't stop her. That must be when she bought the paracetamol and the vodka.'

'She just looks so exhausted. I know what happened to Carter was unforgiveable, but when she came in before, hearing about all the stuff she'd been through would have driven anyone to the edge. And she's so young, she can't have been more than a teenager herself when she had Carter.'

'I was fifteen.' Sophie's eyes shot open as she spoke and another wave of sadness washed over Eve. Sophie was barely more than a child herself, even now, but Eve knew how easy it was for people to slip through the safety net when they hit eighteen and all the systems that had been in place to support them when they'd been classified as a child suddenly dried up. She'd felt terrifyingly alone when her own mother had died, when Eve was only fourteen. She could still remember those last hours by her mum's bedside, watching the life drain out of the one person who'd always been able to make her feel loved and safe. Eve's father had provided a home in a practical sense, but the love had never been there to the same extent. When she'd left to go to university that had been it, as far as her father and stepmother were concerned; their duty done. Eve didn't want to think what might have become of her if she hadn't met Max, and had his family to go home to in the holidays. Sophie clearly hadn't found her safe haven, and when the safety net provided by the state had almost certainly been whipped away from her at the age of eighteen, she'd found herself at the mercy of an unscrupulous landlord and eventually sofa surfing just to keep a roof over hers and Carter's heads. It was heartbreaking and it was all Eve could do not to cry.

'Thank God you're awake, how are you feeling?' She took the other woman's hand, wanting to convey that someone cared, even though she knew it didn't feel that way to Sophie.

'Like shit.'

'That's probably to be expected.' Eve exchanged a look with Felix, and he seemed as relieved as she felt that Sophie appeared to be so lucid. 'Did you take anything apart from the paracetamol and vodka?'

'No, I didn't want to get high or wasted, I just didn't want to be here any more. I'm not a bad person.' Sophie's voice was raspy, no doubt as a result of the tube that had been inserted into her throat to pump her stomach, and there were dark smudges of mascara under her eyes, but agony was written all over her face too.

'I know and whatever you might have heard us saying, we weren't judging you, I promise. We just want to try and understand what drove you to this.'

'Carter's father was someone I met when I was staying out all night, finding a bed wherever I could, to avoid going home because of Mum's boyfriend.' Sophie shuddered. 'When she found out I was pregnant, she called me a slut and kicked me out. I wanted to do things so differently for Carter, and I was in a mother and baby foster placement for a bit, then in supported lodgings. I was happy because I had Carter and that was all that mattered. But when I got to eighteen, I had to find my own place to rent and that's when it all started to fall apart. The last year has been like hell, and I've just had enough of this life. I can't do it any more.'

'I know it feels like that's never going to change, but I promise you, it can. I've seen it lots of times before.' Felix moved closer to the bed as he spoke. 'I worked at an addiction crisis centre and I supported people who never believed they could get their lives back on track, repair their relationships with the people they cared about, or become full-time parents again, but I promise you all of those things are possible.'

'I've got no one. I wish I knew where to find my dad, but Mum made sure there was no chance of us ever having a relationship. There's not one person apart from Carter who cares if I live or die.'

'I do.' Eve grasped Sophie's hand all the tighter.

'So do I.' Felix stood at her other side, his voice firm but gentle at the same time. 'You thanked us last time we met and we said it was what we were here for, but we don't sit by the beside of just anyone. Neither of us are working today, but we're here because we both care about what happens to you, Sophie, and neither of us want you to give up. If Carter is worth fighting for, you've got to fight with all you've got.'

'I'd die for him.' Tears were rolling down Sophie's face and as Felix took a tissue from the stand by the side of the bed and gently wiped them away, the feelings that Eve had been trying to suppress for him rose even closer to the surface.

'Carter needs you alive. I know it must feel impossible right now, but there's lots of help and Domusamare is one of the best places to access that.' Felix's tone was warm and reassuring. 'You've just got to let them keep trying to help you, so that you can keep trying too. Eventually it won't feel impossible any more. It might never be easy, but nothing worth doing ever is.'

'Will they take me back?' Sophie's eyes were like two dark

pools, in the pallor of her face, her fear at how Felix might respond reflected in them.

'I've already spoken to Henry and he said there's a place for you, as soon as you're well enough to go back.'

'Thank you,' Sophie whispered and, as she closed her eyes again, Felix turned to look at Eve.

'You're amazing.' She mouthed the words to him, unable to keep them in, but he shook his head. Leaving her wondering if it was just the compliment he didn't feel able to accept, or whether the problem was that he didn't want to hear it from her.

* * *

It had been a huge relief to discover that Sophie wasn't showing any signs of sustaining lasting damage from the overdose. She'd been incredibly lucky that she'd got to the hospital so quickly. It had been a narrow escape and Eve hoped it really had been enough of a wake-up call for Sophie to accept the help that was being offered. For now, she'd been admitted for a further twenty-four-hour observation period and Eve finally felt able to leave her once she'd fallen asleep.

'You must be starving. I know I am.' Felix turned to her as they crossed the car park to where he'd abandoned his car the night before. 'We never got our Chinese and the crisps we bought from the vending machine just aren't cutting it any more. Although thank goodness it also sells toothbrushes and tooth-paste, otherwise after three packets of cheese and onion crisps, you might have insisted I drive with the windows open.'

'I would have done, although seeing as my flavour of choice was Thai sweet chilli, I'd hardly have had room to talk. Real food does sound good, but it's three o'clock in the morning. I don't think we're going to find anywhere open yet. Even that café in

Port Kara that opens for the fisherman doesn't start doing breakfast until five a.m.'

'Luckily for you, I know a place that does.' Felix grinned and a part of her wanted to say thanks but no thanks, after the way he'd reacted when she told him she thought he was amazing. The trouble was, an even bigger part of her wanted to talk to someone about the feelings that Sophie's overdose had brought up for her. The truth was she didn't just want to speak to *someone* about it, she wanted to speak to Felix.

'Okay, why not?' She shrugged and, on what turned out to be a very short journey, they talked about the hope they both shared that Sophie had turned a corner. Eve was just about to tell him about something Sophie had said that had really struck a chord with her, when he brought the car to a stop outside a set of six purpose-built apartments, on the edge of Port Kara, all of which had a view of the sea. 'Is this your place?'

'It is. I'm just renting at the moment, because I needed to find somewhere while the sale of my apartment in California was still going through, but the landlord has said he'd be willing to sell it to me, if the price is right. It's been a great opportunity to try before I buy and I love it.' He looked at her as she hesitated, seeming to pick up on the fact that she suddenly felt apprehensive about being alone with him, but probably not for the reasons he thought. 'It's all right, I promise my only intention is to cook you breakfast.'

More's the pity. The unwanted words were screaming in her head, but thank God she hadn't said them out loud. Although she still hadn't made a move to get out of the car either and he clearly felt the need to offer her further encouragement.

'I can guarantee you that the breakfast will be cracking, because growing up with a mother like mine, I became an expert at cooking for myself at a very young age.'

Eve finally managed to shake off the feeling that going into Felix's house for breakfast might be a mistake and she smiled. 'I'm sure you did, but I'm quite easy to cater for. A couple of slices of toast and I'm anyone's.'

What the hell was wrong with her? She had to turn away and open the passenger door, just so he wouldn't see her face turning beetroot, but that didn't mean she didn't hear his response.

'Good to know.'

As it turned out, Felix didn't serve up a couple of slices of toast and the mug of builder's strength tea that Eve would genuinely have been happy to settle for. He'd made delicious waffles and pancakes from scratch, with fresh berries and creamy yoghurt. He'd also served up the lightest and fluffiest scrambled eggs Eve had ever tasted, on toasted sourdough, with roasted vine tomatoes.

'That was lovely, thank you,' Eve said, as they sat at the table which in daylight would have had a direct view across the balcony and out to sea. In the darkness it was like looking out onto an expanse of black velvet covered in golden stars. Either way it was beautiful.

'I like cooking for someone other than myself. I miss that.' Felix sounded wistful and Eve turned to look at him, knowing that what had happened with Sophie must have triggered a lot of difficult feelings for him.

'It must have been hard seeing Sophie like that tonight.'

'It was.' Felix stared at the expanse of darkness beyond the glass doors. 'There were so many points when Meredith could have turned a corner and for a long time we both thought she had, but when she plummeted back into addiction there didn't seem to be anything strong enough to pull her out again. I just hope to God that Carter can give Sophie the motivation she needs to beat her addiction for good.'

'Me too.' Eve swallowed hard, wondering whether to continue, but she needed to get the thoughts out of her head. 'It's not quite the same and I know it probably sounds weird, but there were things about Sophie that reminded me of what happened with Annie and Max's sister. After Max's assault Annie became incredibly tightly strung and she put so much pressure on Max's sister, Lily, that it led to her becoming horribly depressed and she just couldn't cope any more. I was terrified about what might happen to her, but she decided to move to America to try and save her mental health. Annie spiralled even further after that, eventually having what I can only describe as a breakdown. I did what I could to help and when she was beginning to recover again, she told me that in the darkest days of it all she'd considered ending her life and that she might well have done if it hadn't been for me. She said how grateful she was knowing I'll never leave—'

'That's a hell of a lot of pressure to put on you.' Felix looked directly at her and she nodded.

'It is, but I understand it and the truth is, I won't leave. Not because I'm some kind of saint, but because I'm terrified if I do, that I could end up like Sophie, feeling like there's no one who cares if I'm around or not.'

'I care.' Felix held her gaze for a moment and Eve's heart hammered against her chest. She should turn away, change the subject, or make light of his comment, but she didn't want to. She wanted him to kiss her and, as he started to close the gap between them, she found herself mirroring the action and closing the gap on her side, until their lips met. It was a tentative kiss at first, as if Felix was waiting for her to stop it, but she'd wanted this from almost the first time Eden had introduced them, before he'd even started work at the hospital. Suddenly she was the one dictating the pace, kissing him back with a passion that had lain dormant for so long she'd wondered if it was gone forever. When she finally pulled away she was breathless, flushed with a mixture of desire and guilt that left her desperately wanting to take one course of action, but knowing with a sinking feeling in the pit of her stomach that she had to take the other.

* * *

Felix had refused to allow Eve to head home in the dark, even when she called an abrupt and awkward end to their time together. He must have thought she'd hated the kiss, but the truth was she'd enjoyed it far more than she'd ever have imagined possible despite how incredibly attractive she found him. Maybe she'd secretly hoped the kiss would put an end to that attraction, but if she had, that idea had seriously backfired, because the connection between them had gone beyond just the physical.

On the drive back to her place, Eve had kept up inane chatter about Felix's interior design choices, including the beautiful dark green sofa and how he must tell her where he got it from, anything to avoid acknowledging the elephant in the room. To his credit, Felix had joined in the conversation like it was the most natural thing in the world, but then he probably hadn't wanted an awkward silence either. It would be far better if they both just forgot the kiss had even happened, but Eve already knew she wasn't going to be able to.

'I'll see you at work then,' he'd said when they arrived at her place.

'Yeah, see you at work and thanks again for breakfast.' This time she'd leapt out of the car so fast her seat might as well have been on fire, and she hadn't turned and waved, or watched him drive away, instead going straight indoors and shutting the door firmly behind her.

Eve should probably have gone straight to bed, she was certainly tired enough, but she couldn't settle. Her mind was racing and to her surprise there was only one place she wanted to be: Oakwood Park. She needed to be close to Max to remind herself why it would be so wrong to give into her feelings for Felix.

Visiting times in the residential unit were very open ended, but no one was allowed to arrive before 8 a.m. without special permission. So Eve took a long hot shower, dried her hair and got ready, before spending another couple of hours poring over old photographs of her and Max. She was at Oakwood Park for 8 a.m. on the dot and she knew that although Annie would almost certainly be going in at some point, she was highly unlikely to arrive before 10 a.m. It would give her a chance to be alone with Max for a bit.

'Morning, Jean.' Eve greeted the mother of another one of the other residents with a kiss on both cheeks. Jean visited her son, Michael, who'd sustained a head injury in a car crash decades earlier, every single weekend without fail. She was an absolutely devoted mother, just like Annie, and although Michael's siblings visited whenever they could, more often than not Jean would come on her own, seeming far more able than Annie to cope with that.

'Morning, Eve, you're here bright and early today.'

'I couldn't sleep.'

'Ah, you should have come and kept Michael company. He's been so excited since his birthday last week and he doesn't seem to have come back down to earth yet. He always gets like that when he sees his brothers, and his nieces and nephews. Throw birthday cake and presents into the mix and it's his idea of heaven.'

'I think it would be most people's and I'm so glad you all had a lovely time, you both really deserve it. I'll see you later, Jean. Have a great day with Michael and give him a hug from me.' Eve managed a smile, because Jean was so kind and she didn't want to feel envious that Michael still seemed to find such joy in being around the people he loved, even after his head injury had changed so much. Maybe she just needed to find a way to reconnect with Max. It wouldn't be presents and cake for him, but there might be something else that worked.

'See you later, my love.' Jean gave Eve's arm a squeeze, before the two women turned and walked in opposite directions along the corridor.

'Gaming already?' Eve said as she walked into Max's room. He was sitting on the two-seater sofa, the controller in his hand and his focus firmly fixed on the screen in front of him rendering her question redundant.

'Yes.' He barely looked up at her, instead reaching for the slice of toast sitting on the table beside him and taking a bite.

'Can I play too?' This time Max's head shot up in response to her question.

'Do you want to?' He couldn't have sounded more surprised if she'd said she wanted to paint herself green.

'Yes, I do.'

'Okay then.' He got up and pulled a second controller out of drawer, before adjusting the settings on the game to go into two player mode.

'I might not be very good at this.' Eve was almost certain that statement would turn out to be true.

'That's okay. I can teach you.' When Max smiled, it felt like the most genuine one she'd received from him in months, maybe even since before the assault. Eve swallowed against the emotion that was suddenly threatening to spill over. She wanted to cry because of the hint of affection in his tone that was so rare these days, and because of the wave of guilt that had followed. She'd kissed Felix; betraying not just Max but his entire family, and she found herself blinking hard to stop the tears from coming. It would just annoy Max and ruin what felt like a precious moment between them, so she had to shake the guilt and sadness off.

The next two hours passed quickly, despite Eve struggling to get to grips with the game. There'd been occasional flashes of impatience from Max, but on the whole he'd seemed to enjoy the fact that she was sharing in his passion. If Eve concentrated really hard at blocking out all the things that had changed, there'd even been a couple of moments where it had felt almost like the old days, sitting side by side with him on the sofa. Eventually the events of the night before had begun to catch up with her and as her eyes had got heavier, her reflexes had slowed down further and she'd been even less able to keep up with the game.

'I think I might just watch you for a bit now, to see if I can pick up some tips.'

'Good idea.' Max had patted her hand then and it had been all Eve could do not to give in to the tears that had threatened earlier. Instead she'd allowed her eyes to close, as she curled up next to him on the sofa and he continued his game. The next thing she was aware of was the sound of Annie whispering, but she didn't open her eyes.

'Look at them, Nigel, it's almost like nothing has changed.' Eve could hear the sound of Max softly snoring beside her. She had no idea how much time had passed, but he must have dropped off for a nap as well. It was no surprise, given that he often stayed up for most of the night gaming and then slept on and off during the day. It was a habit the staff at Oakwood Park were trying to break before he moved to semi-independence, but they weren't there yet.

'It really does look like that.' Nigel's voice cracked with

emotion and Eve decided against opening her eyes. Max's father struggled with visiting Oakwood Park and if this moment was giving him some comfort, she didn't want to be the one to shatter his illusions.

'I'm going to cover them up with a blanket.' Annie was still whispering. 'We can come back later.'

'I'm so glad Eve stayed. I was scared we were going to lose her too after what happened to Max.' It was the first time Eve had ever heard Nigel talk like that, and she'd had no idea he felt the same way as Annie. Her love for them both felt almost over-whelming in that moment and she struggled to swallow back the emotion rising in her chest.

'So did I, and I don't know how I'd cope if she ever decided she didn't want to do this any more.' Annie pulled the blanket over Eve and Max as she spoke, before she and Nigel quietly left the room, shutting the door slowly behind them.

If there'd ever been a question in Eve's mind about whether she could walk away from Max and his family, she knew for certain now that she never could. It didn't matter how much she liked Felix, or how good it felt to be wanted again. This was the life she had chosen and she loved the people in it too much to ever give it up.

13

'This is boring as shit.' Max's favourite pronouncement was one he'd made during their last OT session, when Felix had been trying some techniques to help him improve his coordination and balance, something that had undoubtedly been affected by his head injury.

Felix had been forced to suppress a smile and instead trot out the line: 'Yes, it might be boring, but it's really going to help. You just need to be consistent.' Max had told him where he could stick his consistency, but not in an aggressive way, it had been more like a bit of a joke between friends and Felix had felt over the past two or three sessions that they were getting closer. The difficult part was that the NHS-funded sessions would be ending soon, just as they seemed to be making some progress. Annie had already taken Felix to one side and told him that she and Nigel would be more than happy to pay him to continue working with Max once the funding ran out. Felix had no idea if that would be allowed and he'd told Annie that he'd need to check his contract with the hospital before he could commit. Usually he wouldn't even have considered it, because he had a full-time job that was already full-on, not to mention the volunteering at Domusamare, but this was Max and that changed everything.

Felix and Max were the same age and he'd been on plenty of nights out with friends that had been very much like Max's stag do. When Felix thought about Max, it was one of those 'there but for the grace of God type moments' that made him realise a twist of fate could so easily have put him in Max's shoes. It wasn't like Max had driven drunk, or overdosed on drugs to end up where he was. Felix did his best not to judge anyone, but it was easier to stay a step removed from patients who ended up needing his support because of a stupid risk they'd chosen to take. With patients like Max it was much harder not to feel a personal commitment to them, as well as a professional one. These were people who'd been living their everyday lives one minute, and then some small decision or twist of fate had changed everything.

His commitment to Max went even further, though. Max belonged to Eve and that made Felix want to go way above the norm. The strangest thing was witnessing Max's interactions with other people. He'd begun to open up to Felix and make a joke or a deadpan comment, and he did the same with some of the staff and other residents from Oakwood Park. But when it came to Annie and most of all to Eve, Max was at his most prickly and difficult. Felix suspected it was because he knew how much they loved him and he could take his frustrations out on them while trusting that it wouldn't change how they felt. Felix also suspected that seeing them hammered home how different Max's life had become and that things were never going to be the same again. Felix could understand it, but he'd also seen the hurt in both women's eyes and that made him even more determined than ever to keep helping Max move forward. He just wasn't sure that agreeing to work with him on a private basis would be doable. Then it had struck him that perhaps they could have a more informal arrangement. Something where Max could continue to develop both his social skills and his balance and coordination, without it providing a conflict of interest once Felix had finished delivering the NHS-funded sessions.

Waves 4 Everyone was a local charity that made surfing accessible for people with both physical and intellectual disabilities, running sessions from all the beaches across the Three Ports area. What was even better was that one of Felix's friends was heavily involved with the charity. He'd first met Nathan Lark when he was twenty, after Felix had taken a job in his summer break from university working as a labourer for the building firm that Nathan ran with his brother, Will. Despite there being more than a five-year age gap between him and the brothers, they'd all got on brilliantly from the start. Up until he'd left for San Francisco, Felix had still helped the Lark brothers out when he could, if they were short-handed, and he'd learnt some skills he was grateful for in all areas of his life, including his job.

Nathan had begun volunteering with Waves 4 Everyone, after his nephew, Leo, had been diagnosed with muscular dystrophy. So he'd been the perfect person to talk to about whether surfing sessions might be beneficial to Max. Nathan had listed a whole host of potential benefits, not least the sense of freedom and the adrenaline rush it might give Max, when so many of the things that would have previously provided that to him had been taken away. Then there were the physical benefits, the meeting new people and socialising. April had brought sunny days that could easily have passed for summer, and Nathan had explained that if they wore all the right equipment there was no reason why they couldn't have a surf lesson. All it had needed then was for Felix to persuade Max.

'Can we get dirty fries from Bayside Café after we've finished surfing?' Of all the questions Max could have asked, that had been the last one Felix was expecting. Admittedly, the café that overlooked the bay in Port Tremellien was famous for the chips it served, which were loaded with barbecued pulled pork, cheese and sour cream, but Felix had thought Max's biggest concern might be about falling in. So it had been an easy question to answer.

'Of course we can, mate, and whoever falls off the surfboard the most is buying.' Felix had grinned and Max had roared with laughter, in a way he'd never heard him do before.

'Fancy making a bet with a patient with brain damage,' Max retorted. Even though Max's response hadn't been that funny, it had made him laugh even more and Felix hadn't been able to stop himself from joining in. It had felt really good to play some small part in making him laugh like that.

* * *

Now they were on the beach, side by side on surfboards, and Max's laughter was ringing out again.

'Your arse was where your head was supposed to be on that last wave.' Max could hardly get the words out he was laughing so much.

'What you don't realise is it's all part of my cunning plan to make you fall off your board because you're laughing so much at my attempts to stand up.'

Max shook his head and shouted: 'No chance, loser,' before paddling his board away as though he'd been doing it his whole life. It was funny to think that, in other circumstances, Felix and Max could so easily have become good friends, instead of having a relationship based on their roles as patient and occupational therapist. There was a big part of him that wished Eve could see Max now, to help her realise that aspects of the man she'd fallen in love with were still there. But he felt a stab of something uncomfortably like envy when he thought of that, and he hated himself for the part that was glad Eve wasn't there. It was stupid given the way she'd reacted after their kiss, when she couldn't seem to get away quickly enough, and how muted her responses to his messages had been since then. None of that changed the fact that he liked her far more than he probably should and there didn't seem to be anything much he could do about it.

* * *

Eve took one look at the young boy sobbing in his mother's arms and the very sheepish face of his sister, looking pale and remorseful by their mother's side, and she could have guessed that a spat between siblings has caused his injury. Both sets of the boy's teeth had gone through his bottom lip, falling just short of meeting in the middle and severing the whole thing.

'She shoved me.' Despite the fact that his bottom lip was so swollen that it must have been painful to get the words out, somehow the little boy, whose name was Rufus managed it.

'You punched me first.' His sister might feel guilty, but she clearly wasn't ready to shoulder all of the blame.

'Stop arguing over whose fault this is.' Their mother's voice was sharp and she looked exhausted.

Rufus was definitely going to need stitches and Eve would have to consult with the plastic surgery team to see whether he might need a more refined approach to minimise the risk of scarring.

'They were playing outside on the trampoline and I should have known it was too good to be true.' Rufus's mum sighed. 'Next minute a fight broke out and when Rufus fell off—'

'I didn't *fall*, I was pushed.' He clearly wasn't going to let this one go.

'Okay, when Rufus was pushed off, he bit down on his lip when he hit the ground and there was blood everywhere.' His mother shuddered. 'I'm hoping it looks worse than it is.'

'That's almost certainly the case with these things, so let's get you through and take a proper look.' Eve glanced at Rufus's sister and gave her what she hoped was a reassuring smile. For all the little girl's bravado, it was obvious she was scared.

Eve carried out an initial assessment, cleaning the wound to remove dirt and debris, and checking Rufus's teeth to ensure there were no tooth fragments in the lip. Having done so, she called the plastic surgery team and one of the consultants came down to see Rufus, before announcing that she was certain Eve could handle the repair.

'Will the stitches hurt?' Rufus who had been incredibly brave so far, looked on the verge of tears, but his sister responded before Eve could even try to reassure him.

'The medicine will make sure it doesn't hurt. Do you remember when I had my appendix out?' She hauled up her jumper to show him the scar as a visual reminder. 'That didn't even hurt.'

'Thanks, Ellie.' Rufus tried to smile, but it made him wince.

'Why can't you two always be this lovely to each other?' Their mum might have been gently chiding them, but she was squeezing both their hands, as she looked up at Eve. 'I'm an only child and I never had any of this sibling stuff. Sometimes I've wondered if I was crazy to have two kids only eighteen months apart, but I know they love one other really and they'll always have each other, won't they? That's something I wish I had.'

'Me too.' Eve hadn't meant to say it, but the words had just come out. The fact it felt as though the only family she had was hanging by a thread definitely wasn't something she wanted to discuss with a complete stranger though. Instead she ploughed on with the job in hand before Rufus's mum could even respond. 'Ellie is right, I promise it won't hurt and if you look at your mum and sister the absolute most you'll feel is a bit of tugging.'

Eve had been grateful of the need to concentrate, so that her mind couldn't linger on how much it hurt that she didn't have anyone linked to her by birth who she could call upon, or reminisce about old times with, the way Rufus and Ellie one day could. She treasured the photographs she had in the album her mother had put together for her before she'd died, it was more precious to her than any other possession could ever be, but it couldn't make up for no longer having a parent who cared about her, or a sibling she could laugh with about their childhoods. It hadn't felt nearly this raw when she'd been planning to marry Max and had assumed she'd always have a role in his family. That felt so much more precarious now and the thought of losing them was so unbearable she couldn't dwell on it for too long.

'Right, you're all done.' Eve touched Rufus's arm lightly after she'd finished the stiches. 'You've been an absolute star.'

'You were really brave, Roof.' Ellie sounded almost in awe of her brother, and Eve turned towards their mum.

'I'm going to send Rufus home with some painkillers and antibiotics, just to make sure we head off the potential of any infection, because teeth can carry a lot of bacteria. The stitches are dissolvable, but I'll also make a follow-up appointment for you with the outpatients department, just so we can check that everything is healing okay.'

'Thank you so much and hopefully it'll be a lesson for these two that however much they might get on each other's nerves, there's nothing more important than family!' Rufus's mum gave a hearty laugh and Eve nodded and smiled, not trusting herself to speak. It was stupid to feel so emotional over something as everyday as an exchange like this, but for some reason it had hit her really hard. Thank God it was at the end of her shift, because she needed to clear her head and get herself back on an even keel before she was going to be of any use to anyone.

* * *

Eve wanted a walk on the beach, but the last thing she needed right now was to bump into anyone she knew, so she'd decided to head out of Port Kara. Her stomach had been rumbling like a washing machine on the drive over to Port Tremellien and she wanted a huge portion of dirty fries from the Bayview Café, a place Max had introduced her to on their first trip to Cornwall after they got together. Getting out of her car, she took a huge breath, letting the fresh air fill her lungs and trying to release the negativity with the exhale. She repeated the process as she walked towards the sea and it didn't take long before it felt like it was working. The sky was bright blue and there was only a very light breeze carrying the seagulls that dipped and soared overhead, calling out in that familiar way that would have told Eve where she was even if she'd been blindfolded. She could taste salt on her lips and feel the sun warming her skin, the aroma of the delicious food served at the Bayview Café drifting on that same breeze, as a handful of surfers braved the water in the distance. It felt good to be here and, although she and Max had visited plenty of times, it was less bound up with him than either Port Kara or Port Agnes. Here, it was easier to appreciate just being by the water and allowing her mind and body to slow down and live in the moment. Just for a moment she allowed herself to briefly close her eyes, but then they flew open again in response to what she'd been almost sure was Max's voice. Except it couldn't have been him.

'You owe me lunch.' The voice that sounded so much like Max's called out insistently, and she stared ahead, trying to work out whether both her eyes and her ears were deceiving her.

'Okay, you've got me, I definitely fell off the surfboard more than you did, but that might be because until your mum turned up, I had no idea that you used spend most of the summer surfing when you were a kid.' Felix laughed as he gently nudged Max; the two of them standing close together, still wearing their wet suits, like old friends who joked easily with one another. Neither of them had spotted her yet and nor had Annie, who was too busy wrapping her son in the Dryrobe that another man in a wetsuit had handed her. Eve ducked back between two beach huts, where she could still see them but it would far harder for them to spot her. The Dryrobes were emblazoned with the Waves 4 Everyone logo, a charity that Eve had seen advertised on some of the hospital noticeboards. She'd never have believed Max would agree to go to one of their sessions and she knew it must be Felix's doing.

'Lunch is on me.' Annie was beaming as she spoke. 'For everyone! You'll join us won't you, Nathan?'

She was talking to the man who'd passed her the Dryrobe, who said something in response that Eve couldn't quite hear, triggering more laughter, including from Max. She wasn't sure she'd seen him laugh as much as he had in the last couple of minutes since before the assault. She certainly couldn't make him laugh like that any more, most of the time she could barely even raise a smile these days. She knew that if she stepped out from her hiding place, or called out to Annie, she'd be welcomed with open arms and invited along for lunch, but she also knew with just as much certainty that Max wouldn't want her there. An uncomfortable thought joined the maelstrom of emotions already racing around inside her head. She wanted to be able to walk along the beach next to Felix and to discover whether their mind-blowing kiss was a one-off, or whether the connection they seemed to have could lead to something more. But that wasn't an option she could pursue, not without risking everything that already felt as though it might slip through her fingers at any moment.

She had to find a way of reaching Max that would remind him of why she'd been such an important part of his life instead. They were never going to be a couple again, but she desperately wanted them to be family. It was something she couldn't give up, not even to see where things with Felix might go. It would have be far too big a risk for something that might fizzle out before it even began. She'd just have to push her feelings for Felix back down again. She was sure she could do it, if she was careful and avoided spending time with him as much as possible. It all sounded so easy in her head, but the reality was never quite that simple.

14

The spring ball was yet another fundraising initiative conjured up by the force of nature that was Gwen Jones.

'We're all going,' Meg had insisted three weeks before the event, when Eve had pulled a face about the prospect of attending. 'At least those of us not rostered to work that night.'

'I'd be more than happy to do a swap with someone who wants to go instead.' It had seemed like the perfect solution to Eve, but Meg shook her head, her tone suddenly much firmer.

'You and I need to make the effort to attend this more than anyone. It's a fundraiser for the Friends of St Piran's, and if we want to make friends here, *proper friends*, who'll give us the fresh start we're both looking for, then this is exactly the sort of event we should be attending.'

Eve had stared at Meg for what felt like an eternity, even though it could only have been a matter of seconds. She'd wanted to ask her how she knew that Eve had been craving a fresh start more and more lately, and to correct her assumption that the move to Cornwall had been about finding that. She'd come to Max's home county because of ties to their past and to his family, not for a shiny new start. But she didn't say any of that, and she didn't ask the questions that were burning in her throat either, about why Meg was here and what it was she'd chosen to leave behind, because she'd known that any confidences Meg shared might need to be reciprocated. Instead she'd tried to come up with some other excuse not to go to the ball.

'Isn't the whole point to go with a partner, so you've got someone to dance with? I mean I'm quite happy to dance with you, but we'll have to agree beforehand who's going to lead.'

Meg laughed. 'You're a good six inches taller than me and I've got two left feet and the rhythm of a robot, so I think we both know who's going to have to lead.'

'Should I get myself a tux?'

'No need to go that far. There'll be plenty of us who are going stag. I think that's what they call it and, who knows, you might even find yourself more than a friend.'

'Now that I can confidently say I do not need.' Eve had offered up no further explanation. Despite the temptation she'd felt to confide in Meg on more than one occasion, she still valued the escape of life at the hospital too much to tell her about Max. Eden, Drew and Felix all knew of course, but she trusted them to keep it to themselves and allow her to continue pretending that her life was far simpler than it was.

'Please come, Eve. Everyone else has known each other for so much longer and I'd feel much less like a spare part if you were there.' Meg had given her a pleading look then and even though she still didn't know what had brought her friend to Cornwall, Eve could see in her eyes that Meg was carrying some trauma of her own. Suddenly it hadn't felt like nearly such a big deal to say yes.

'Okay then,' she'd agreed, already trying not to wonder if Felix would be there and, if he was, whether or not he would be going on his own. It shouldn't matter – it *didn't* matter – she'd told herself that again and again, because she and Felix could never be anything more than friends. She tried to pretend that the prospect of him going to the ball hadn't crossed her mind when she'd gone to Truro to find a dress, settling on rust-coloured silk that brought out the amber in her eyes. Later, when Felix had told her he was going and had mentioned that there was a spot free on his table, she hadn't allowed herself to picture him in a tuxedo, because if she did that it would be even more difficult to think of him as simply a friend. Now, as she smoothed down her dress and took one last look in the mirror, she readied herself for coming face to face with him, and practised the enigmatic smile she hoped would disguise all the emotions that were bubbling just below the surface.

* * *

Eve had been avoiding Felix since they'd kissed, that much had been obvious. He'd considered the possibility that she'd thought it was awful, but he found that difficult to believe given how fantastic it had felt from his perspective. She'd kissed him back in a way that suggested she felt the same. He suspected the real reason she'd backed off had been guilt about Max. He understood it; technically she was still engaged, even if Max was doing his best to push her away. He also knew how close she was to Max's parents, and how much she'd have hated to hurt them. Eve was beautiful, with long dark hair that shone as if it had been polished, and eyes the colour of amber, flecked with highlights of gold, but what made her even more beautiful was the goodness in her that went right to the core. He'd seen in her interactions with patients and her volunteering at Domusamare that she had an almost unbelievable capacity for kindness. Perhaps it might seem odd to some people, given what she'd told him about her own upbringing and how little kindness she'd been shown by the people who should have loved her the most. But he had a strong suspicion that was what drove her kindness to others; wanting them to feel there was someone who cared for them, because of the very fact that there'd been times when Eve had believed no one had cared for her.

Felix had considered asking Eve to the ball, but had known she'd almost certainly turn him down if she thought it was meant to be a date. He'd tried to play it off as casual, saying that he'd be sharing a table with Eden and Drew, and some of the others and that there was a space if she wanted to join them. He wasn't like it was an actual date, but she'd still turned him down and he could have guessed the outcome of her text long before it arrived.

> Thanks Felix, but I can't. If it got back to Annie, she might read something into it that isn't there. I'm going with Meg, so I'll see you there anyway, and I really hope we can go back to being friends.

There were no kisses on the text and she'd made it abundantly clear there'd be no more kisses in real life either. At least it was honest and upfront, not a hint of the game playing there had been in so many of his exchanges with Meredith. He knew where he stood with Eve. He might wish things were different, but he liked her directness – he liked everything about her – and if they had to remain just friends, that was still something to cherish.

To his relief, the ball wasn't all waltzes and couples twirling their partners around the dance floor. There was an excellent band, playing a mixture of upbeat music and slow dance songs, spanning the last five decades. Eve was on the dance floor now, with Eden, Aidan, Isla and Meg, singing and dancing along to 'I

Have Nothing', with the kind of air grabs that would have made Whitney Houston proud. He smiled, enjoying seeing her having such a wonderful time and looking, for a few moments at least, as if she didn't have a care in the world.

'Another beer, Drew?' He turned to the man he was incredibly grateful had come into his sister's life. He'd never known Eden as happy as she was lately and she deserved it more than anyone, after what both their mother and her ex-partner had put her through. It gave him hope that moving on from a life with an addict was possible. He didn't ever want to stop helping people, but he wanted it to be on a professional basis, not slap bang in the middle of his personal life. There might always be blurred lines, but he never wanted something like that to consume his whole life again.

'Another drink sounds great. I've promised Eden I'll dance with her later.' Drew looked like he'd rather pull his own teeth out. 'And I'm going to need to loosen up a bit, otherwise, it'll look like she's pushing a wardrobe around the dance floor.'

'She won't want you to do anything you don't want to do, Drew. Trust me, you don't have to pretend to be anything you're not for Eden's sake. She likes you just the way you are.'

'I know and that's exactly what makes me want to push myself out of my comfort zone. It's not that I *have* to, it's that I *want* to. For her.' Drew shrugged and Felix nodded. They were going to go the distance, these two; he just knew it. He had no idea what gave him such confidence in making the prediction, after all he'd been convinced at one stage that he and Meredith would make it. This time he was certain, though, and he just hoped that next time he found someone willing to take a chance on him, he'd be half as good at working out the chances of success as he was when it came to his sister's relationship.

Felix was still waiting at the bar when his phone started to ring. It was Karl, his friend and former colleague from San Francisco who'd promised to keep an eye on Meredith and who was doing his level best to track her down after her recent phone call. It was seven hours behind in San Francisco, which meant it would be one thirty there and Karl would probably be on his lunch break at the clinic. It was probably nothing, just a quick call to let Felix know there were no updates and to offer reassurance that Karl was still trying. Felix considered letting it go to voicemail, but there were still quite a few people in front of him in the queue for the bar and it was far enough away from the music to be able to make himself heard without having to shout, so he pressed the button to answer instead.

'Hi, Karl.' Felix wasn't sure the call had even connected for a moment because it seemed to be silent, and then he heard his friend take a deep breath.

'Hey, Felix.' The melancholy in Karl's tone was as obvious as it would have been if they'd been standing face to face, instead of thousands of miles apart and it felt as if Felix's blood was rushing in his ears.

'What's wrong. Is it Merri?' Another pause, followed by what was quite possibly the deepest sigh Felix had ever heard.

'I'm so sorry, buddy, there's no easy way to tell you this, but she's dead.'

* * *

Eve came off the dance floor still laughing and struggling to catch her breath. She hadn't had this much fun in a long time and it was all the more wonderful for how unexpected it had been. Singing along to a medley of classic songs hadn't been what she'd thought the fundraising ball would be like, but she should have known better than to expect any event organised by

Gwen to be boring. Her throat was sore from a mixture of shouting out the 'tune' – a somewhat generous description of what they'd done to the songs – and from laughing at just how into the performance Aidan had got, flinging his arms out wide as if he really was Whitney, on stage, giving her all for an audience of adoring fans. His lip-syncing had been so flawless that it couldn't possibly have been the first time he'd done it. Desperate for some ice-cold sparkling water, she'd offered to get the others a drink as well and was heading towards the bar when she caught sight of Felix.

He looked every bit as gorgeous in his tuxedo as she'd expected him to. He was tall with broad shoulders, his dark hair a tiny bit longer than might be considered 'appropriate' to pair with such formal attire, but the slightly just-got-out-of-bed look made him all the more appealing as far as Eve was concerned. He was on the phone, and as she got closer she could see this was no ordinary call. The colour seemed to have drained from his face and she realised he was pacing, like a caged animal. As he turned, his back faced towards her for a moment, the tension visible in the ramrod straight set of his shoulders. When he took another couple of paces and turned to face her again, their eyes meeting, she knew without a shadow of a doubt that the call had brought him bad news.

'You okay?' Eve mouthed, anticipating the answer before Felix shook his head, and she was close enough now to hear his conversation.

'Thanks, Karl. I'll let you know as soon as I can work out when I can get there… Okay, yeah, you too.' He ended the call and held Eve's gaze, still not speaking.

'Do you want to talk about it?' She broke the silence and he nodded, before finally uttering four words.

'Yes, but not here.'

*　*　*

They headed outside, despite the fact that even in spring it was cold by this time of night. When Eve had given an involuntary shiver, Felix had insisted on removing his jacket and putting it around her, the scent of his aftershave taking her back to the night they'd kissed and making her long to do it again. She hated herself for even thinking that, and not just because of Max this time. Felix had been given bad news and her role, as his *friend*, was to listen and comfort him. Not stand there imagining what it would be like to kiss him again.

'Meredith has died. She overdosed again and this time it killed her.'

'Oh God, Felix, I'm so sorry.' Her hand flew to her mouth and she kept it there, hoping it would help her resist the urge to reach out to him.

'I feel like it's my fault.' He screwed his eyes shut for a moment. 'Maybe if I'd sent her the money she asked for, she'd have been okay.'

Eve was already shaking her head, no longer fighting the desire to reach for him, and she took his hand. 'If someone is hell-bent on self-destruction, nothing anyone else does will change that. The only change can come from them and, if you had sent Meredith the money, she's far more likely to have spent it on drugs than anything else.'

'I know logically that you're right.' There was so much pain in his eyes that it twisted something in Eve's chest. 'But I'll never know that for certain.'

'You won't and it's the what-ifs that always hit the hardest at times like this.' She was still holding his hand, her thumb now gently stroking his palm in a gesture that was far more intimate than she had a right to be. But in that moment it felt as though they had a connection with one another that no one else quite did. 'When Max was assaulted, I drove myself mad with what-ifs. What if I'd arranged to pick him up earlier, so that he wouldn't have been walking back down that precise road at that precise moment? What if I'd suggested he did something else for his stag do, or swapped shifts with someone so he ended up choosing another night? None of those thoughts could have changed the outcome, all they did was torture me. What's done is done and sometimes I think facing that reality is the hardest part of it all.'

'I need someone to blame and, if not me, then who the hell can I pin it on, so that I can believe it wasn't because I didn't do enough?' Felix's eyes searched her face, desperate for her to give him an answer that would offer some comfort.

'Sometimes there isn't anyone to blame, it's just circumstances and bad luck; an accident that could have happened to anyone. I know that's not the same for Meredith and it definitely wasn't the same for Max. I've got someone to blame, the guy who hit him and you can try and find someone to blame as well. Maybe it's the person who sold Meredith the drugs that killed her, or whoever helped get her hooked in the first place. But it doesn't help nearly as much as you might think.' Eve swallowed hard, knowing that what she was about to say was a conversation she should have with Max's mother, too, but suspected she never would. 'Annie is obsessed with getting revenge on Brandon Moorcroft and I get it, I really do, but what she doesn't seem to realise is that increasing his sentence won't undo what's happened to Max. He'll still be living with the consequences of a severe brain injury and Annie won't be happy in the way she thinks she will.' Eve paused for a moment, shaking her head, before continuing.

'She's obsessed with it and I'm terrified of what it might do to her if she doesn't get what she wants, or even if she does and she realises her heart is still broken. I think her anger and bitterness is stopping her from acknowledging the pain and I'm scared of what will happen when she has to move on from the idea of revenge, one way or another. I think trying to find someone to blame and pouring all your emotions into that can be every bit as self-destructive as blaming yourself. It's just a way of staving off the grief, but you can't bypass that, no matter how much you might want to. You have to let yourself feel it.'

Felix looked exhausted as he nodded in response. 'I left San Francisco because I didn't want to have to hurt for Merri any more. I thought leaving would enable me to forget what she was doing to herself and the fact that I hadn't been able to help her stop.'

His eyes were glassy and Eve finally let go of his hand, putting her arms around Felix instead and holding him close. 'You can't run away from caring when you love someone. It doesn't matter how far you travel.'

She was vaguely aware that she was partly speaking to herself now, acknowledging that it would have been impossible to outrun the pain of what had happened to Max and all the plans they'd had for their future, no matter how tempting it had sometimes felt to want to try.

'Do you know the worst thing about Meredith's death?' Felix pulled away slightly, their eyes locking as she shook her head again. 'It's that a part of me is relieved. I think I always knew this day was coming and I was waiting for it and dreading it, but now it's happened, I'm finally free. Whatever you might have thought in the past, you must admit that makes me the worst person in the world.'

'I refuse to believe that.' Tears had filled her eyes now too. 'Because if the idea of wanting to be free earns you that title, then you're going to have to share it with me.'

15

After Felix had told Eve about Meredith's death, he hadn't been able to face going back into the ball and she'd promised to explain the situation to Eden and Drew.

'I had no idea he even had a serious girlfriend out in San Francisco.' Eden had looked like she was struggling to process it all after Eve had recounted the story, including the background to his relationship with Meredith, which Felix had given her permission to share. 'Let alone that he was with someone struggling with addiction. I feel awful that he didn't think he could confide in me.'

'It wasn't that, he just didn't want to give you anything else to worry about.' Eve hoped her tone had been reassuring, but it was Drew's arm around Eden's shoulders that had seemed to give Felix's sister the most comfort, and the wise words he'd imparted next had also clearly helped.

'Sometimes it's easier to confide in someone you don't have all that shared history with. Felix would have known you'd worry about him, the same way he worried about you when you met Jesse, because of what happened with your mum.'

'I suppose.' Eden had nodded and turned back to Eve. 'But it looks like the two of you have got pretty close, quite quickly.'

Her tone had been hopeful rather than accusatory and a huge part of Eve had wanted to be honest with her new friend, but that would have involved revealing far too many of her own secrets. Instead she'd shrugged as casually as she could manage.

'I was just in the right place at the right time, that's all, and I think because we've worked together at Domusamare, he knew I'd understand the sort of problems Meredith was facing.' She'd hesitated then, not sure whether to tell Felix's sister just how worried she was about him, but unable to stop herself. 'What I think you'll understand far better than I ever can is the guilt he's feeling about not being able to save her.'

Felix hadn't expressly given her permission to share that part of the story, but he hadn't asked her to gloss over it either. Her decision to tell Eden how he was feeling wasn't because she wanted to gossip, she'd been genuinely concerned that he wouldn't be able to shake off the idea that he was somehow to blame. She'd known from personal experience that children often blamed themselves for their parents' behaviour. She'd done it often enough herself, believing that something she'd done had caused her father's cold indifference, or her stepmother's outright dislike. It meant Eve knew there was a good chance that growing up both Felix and Eden would have felt responsible for their mother's actions, and that the desire to save her was probably what had influenced them choosing partners like Jesse and Meredith. The cycle seemed to be broken for Eden, but she was worried that Felix wouldn't be able to stop blaming himself and his sister was the probably the only one who could pull him out of that.

'I couldn't save Jesse either, but I had to give him the space to decide whether or not to save himself. None of this is Felix's fault.'

Eden's words had proven to Eve that she'd been right. If anyone could make Felix see that he wasn't responsible for Meredith's death, it was his sister.

'Will you speak to him and make sure he's okay?' She hadn't been able to keep the concern out of her voice and Eden had nodded, before narrowing her eyes.

'Of course, but are you sure there's not something you aren't telling me?' She'd cocked her head on one side then, her eyes never leaving Eve's face. 'I think there's more between you and Felix than just the fact that you were in the right place at the right time.'

'I really like him and maybe if we'd met at a different time...' It had been more than Eve had meant to say, and she'd found herself with no way of ending the conversation without at least trying to give a reason why things couldn't go any further between her and Felix. 'The last thing he needs is another relationship and you know that things for me are... complicated. You will keep an eye on him, won't you?'

'Of course I will, but you know, sometimes, when a person dies, it's a reminder of just how short life can be.' Eden had locked eyes with her and she hadn't needed to spell out the message; she thought Eve should act on the feelings that had developed between her and Felix. She could understand why her friend might think that was the obvious choice, but Eden had never been completely alone, in the way Eve had been before Max's family had taken her in, so she'd couldn't ever comprehend just how much was at stake.

* * *

Now, three days had passed since the ball and Eve still hadn't seen Felix, although they'd continued to exchange texts. He'd thanked her for being there in the wake of the news and she'd said she was around any time he needed to talk. His response had been typical of Felix, not wanting to put a burden on anyone else.

> It's so kind of you to offer, Eve, but the last thing you need is me bending your ear when you've already got so much on your plate.

She'd fired off a response before she had time to rethink it.

> It's the least I can do, when you've done so much for Max. I really am happy to listen, any time.

He hadn't taken her up on her offer and when she'd arrived at Oakwood Park to find him there, she'd almost turned around and gone back out again, feeling embarrassed at having put herself out there. It was stupid to think his reaction had anything to do with her personally, though, especially given the real problems they both had in their lives. So she'd painted on a smile, as she stopped in the reception area to talk to him.

'How are you doing?'

'Okay.' The smile he'd attempted to mirror hers with didn't fool Eve. She could see he was still wrestling with his emotions. 'I'm just trying to fit in some extra sessions with a few of the residents here, because I'm taking a week off to fly out to San Francisco for the funeral.'

'You've decided to go then?' It was a stupid question, given the fact that she'd overheard him telling his friend, Karl, on the night of the fundraiser that he was planning to go out there, and she couldn't have justified why the thought bothered her so much. She wanted to tell herself it was because she thought facing the stark reality of Meredith's death might not be good for him, and that it could exacerbate his feelings of guilt. That was true, but there was more to it. What she didn't want to acknowledge, even to herself, was that she would miss him and that she couldn't shake off the nagging fear that he might decide not to come back.

'I wasn't sure if I should. But what is it they call it? Closure?' He attempted another half smile. 'Although I think I might call it acceptance, and I need to go there and say goodbye, before I can get that.'

'I hope you find it.' Lowering her voice she leant closer to him. 'Maybe I should get you to take Annie. That's where Lily lives and I know she's desperate to see her mum. It would do Annie the world of good to see Lily, too, but it's like they're at an impasse, both of them digging their heels in.'

On the day of Sophie's overdose, Eve had shared more of Lily's story with Felix than she'd told anyone else. Even her closest friends back in Leeds only knew a tiny potted version of all the things that had happened since Eve had moved to Cornwall. Yet she'd told Felix how scared she'd been for Lily, after Max's sister had confided in her that sometimes she went to bed and wished that she wouldn't wake up. After Max's head injury, Lily had admitted to feeling like she was drowning in her mother's expectations. When her boyfriend, Scott, had told her he'd be returning to the US for work, it had been the final straw and Lily's withdrawal into herself had been terrifying. He'd wanted her to go with him, but at first Lily hadn't seen any possibility of that being able to happen. But there was one thing Eve hadn't even told Felix yet.

'It was me who told her to go with Scott.' She met his gaze and took another deep breath before continuing. 'She told me she couldn't go, that there was no way she could leave Annie, but I told her she had to, because I didn't want to lose her as well and I promised I'd make sure that her mum was okay.'

'You're pretty amazing, do you know that?'

'I'm no saint. They're my family and I only did what anyone would do for family, especially after everything they did to welcome me in when I met Max. Lily knew her mum wouldn't take it well, and we both knew there was a good chance it might permanently affect their relationship, but she had to get away. Otherwise I really do think I could have lost her.' Eve tucked a stray strand of hair behind her ear. 'Annie took it even harder than we thought and she told Lily if she left that she was choosing Scott over her family at a time when they needed her most. I tried to reason with Annie, but Lily begged me not to tell her it was my idea for her to go, or about the promise I'd made to be there for Annie. She said if I did that Annie would turn against me too and then there'd be no one to keep an eye on her mother.'

'You were both in such an impossible position and I suspect Annie wasn't in the right frame of mind to listen to any kind of reason, so Lily was probably right.'

'I think she was and I'm so grateful that things have thawed a bit between them. At least there are text messages and calls now, and even the odd FaceTime.' Eve closed her eyes for a moment, swallowing hard before she continued. 'They've both had mental health crises since the assault and they're both still incredibly fragile, but I'm sure spending time together would make a huge difference. No matter how hard I try I can't persuade Annie to leave Max to go out for a visit, and I think Lily is still scared to come home, in case she can't leave again. I don't know what to do to help any more. All I know is that I miss Lily loads, she's like my little sister as well as Max's.'

'Why can't you go to see her?'

'I can't leave Max either.'

Felix looked at her for a long moment. 'Do you really think he'd care if you didn't visit for a week?'

'Harsh.' She laughed then, but it was brittle and far more

humourless than it should have been. 'You're probably right, but Annie would. She'd be scared that I'd do the same as Lily and never come back.'

'You're not the sort to run away, surely she must realise that.' Felix made it sound so certain and Eve wasn't sure whether to take it as a compliment or an insult.

'Maybe not, but I really do wish I could go out there.' Eve's honesty had shocked her, and Felix looked surprised too.

'So why don't you? We could travel together, I know I could use a friend.' He made it sound so easy, but he was being ridiculous. She couldn't just up and leave and fly half way across the world on a whim. Except she was about to start a week's leave and if she could tack a day or two on the end, it might technically be possible. Although just because something was *possible*, actually making it happen was very different.

'I'd be worried about Annie, she'd be super stressed the whole time, thinking that I either wouldn't come back, or that something would happen to me out there. She's already got every news app on her phone set up for alerts about San Francisco, in case something happens to Lily.' Eve could picture the older woman's face if she told her she was jetting off to California for a week. It would be like Edvard Munch's painting of *The Scream* come to life.

'Tell her you want to see Lily and check how she's doing. It's not a lie and I'm sure Annie will welcome someone checking in on her daughter and, who knows, maybe once you've visited it will open up the pathway of Lily coming home for a visit next time, or even of Annie going out there for a break eventually?'

'Even if I thought it might have that effect, I can't just book a flight last minute and go to California.'

'Yes, you can; in my opinion that sort of thing is what the internet was invented for and it would save me sitting next to someone who snores like as walrus for the entire eleven hour flight.' He raised his eyebrows, a genuine smile on his face for the first time.

'How do you know I don't snore like a walrus?' She mirrored his expression and he shrugged.

'Just a hunch, but I'd like to have the chance to find out for definite.' As he spoke two bright spots of heat coloured her cheeks and she tried not to think about all the things she'd love to discover about Felix. She should have shut it down, told him he was being absolutely ridiculous to think that she could finally take Lily up on her offer to go and visit, but to her shock she found herself nodding. Maybe the fact that she'd already arranged leave was a sign of the universe telling her to do it.

'Okay, I'll talk to Annie and if she can cope with me going, I'll speak to Lily to see if it's a possibility. For all I know, Lily might be away herself, or not have the space for visitors right now.' Dropping her hand to her side, Eve found herself crossing her fingers, but she wasn't sure what she was hoping for. If Annie or Lily put the brakes on her visiting San Francisco, there was far less chance that she might cross the boundary between friendship and something else with Felix. After their kiss, she'd firmly drawn that line in the sand, or she'd thought she had. At least this way she was leaving it up to fate to decide. If the universe decreed that she should make the visit, then who was she to argue? *It* would also have to take responsibility for the consequences, because when she looked at Felix, it definitely wasn't just friendship on her mind.

* * *

Even on the short flight from Exeter to Heathrow, Felix had been expecting Eve to change her mind and tell him she was getting off there, turning around and heading straight back home again, instead of sharing a flight with him across the Atlantic. But she hadn't.

'I'm doing this for Annie.' She said for at least the fifteenth time as they waited at the boarding gate at Heathrow to be called forward to take their seats on the flight.

'I know you are.' If it helped her to hear it, he was more than happy to give her the affirmation she needed, even if he hoped it wasn't entirely true. He hoped that at least a tiny part of her was here because she wanted to spend time with him. It was terrible for him to want that, especially given the nature of his own visit to San Francisco, but he'd have been lying if having her company hadn't made the prospect of the trip a million times more appealing.

'I'm just worried about how much hope she's pinning on me being able to persuade Lily to come home.' Eve turned to look at him. 'I don't want to let Annie down, but I don't want to force Lily into that either. No one deserves to feel trapped by obligation. We only get one life.'

'We do, indeed.' Felix couldn't help wondering if Eve could hear the irony in her own words. Duty had made her restrict her life for almost two years and he had a horrible feeling it might determine the course of the rest of her life. She deserved so much more than that, but she had to see that for herself. No one could tell her that, because she wasn't ready to listen. He just hoped that maybe, when she reflected on the conversations she was going to have with Lily in the next few days, she'd be able to apply them to her own life too. In the meantime, he wanted to do his best to reassure her. 'Whatever happens, you won't let Annie down, she's incredibly grateful for everything you do, not just for Max but for all of them. I've heard her saying that to anyone who'll listen.'

'I owe her and Nigel so much.'

'You don't have to repay love like a debt, not when you've given it as freely as you have.' He was looking straight at her and for a moment he thought she might close the gap between them again, just as she had on the day they'd kissed, but then she laughed.

'You should put that on a plaque and sell it in the souvenir shops in Port Kara. It would outsell *"Live, Laugh, Love,"* and *"Dance Like No one's Watching"* for sure!'

He tried for a look of mock outrage, but it was soon replaced by a grin. 'Sometimes I've got no idea why I like you.'

'But you do.' She laughed again and he whispered his response under his breath, so that not even she could hear him.

'More than you'll ever know.'

When they were called forward to board the plane a few minutes later, Felix could tell she was worried. He didn't know whether it was because she was still concerned about letting Annie down, or because she was a nervous flyer. But then, as the plane taxied down the runway, she clasped his hand.

'Sorry, but take offs and landings really get to me.'

'It's okay, you can hold onto my hand for as long as you need to. I'm just grateful I'm not a surgeon, because with a grip like that you could jeopardise my career.' It was his turn to laugh and she rolled her eyes calling him a drama queen before relaxing her grip just a little bit. But she didn't let go, not even when the plane climbed into the sky and levelled out, the drama of the take off over. It wasn't until her eyes grew heavy from the early start, more than half an hour after they'd taxied down the runway, and she gave into sleep, that she finally released her grip on his hand. And from the moment she let go, he missed it.

16

Eve had known that Felix would almost certainly turn down her offer to attend Meredith's funeral with him, the day after they'd landed in San Francisco, but she'd wanted to make the offer anyway.

'Thank you.' He'd looked at her with those intense blue eyes of his, wearing the expression that had a way of making her forget there was anyone else in the world who had anything she wanted to hear. Before she'd met Felix, she'd have laughed if someone had said they could get lost in another person's eyes, but now she understood. Maybe it was because just lately she wanted to get lost, to forget that anyone else existed. Whatever the reason his eyes were beautiful, like the sea on the sunniest of days in Cornwall, the realisation making her feel a tiny bit homesick. It was silly, because when she thought about all the things she loved about her adopted home, she had to admit that Felix was never at the top of that list and he was in California with her; a living, breathing reminder of 'home'.

'As much as I'd love the company, I need to be with the people who meant something to Merri and who might actually feel the loss of her in this world.' He'd sighed deeply then, taking another sip of his coffee, before setting it down. 'When I met her, she so desperately wanted her life to mean something. She thought all the stuff she'd been through with addiction might have been because she was supposed to use that to help others and create some kind of legacy. Instead she fell back into it, and I just wish I could think of something that would mean it wasn't all in vain.'

'Isn't she the reason why you volunteer at Domusamare?' Eve had asked, and he'd nodded slowly.

'I might not have been able to fix Meredith, but I know she'd have wanted me to keep trying to help other people who were fighting the same demons.'

'Then that's her legacy. I've seen the difference you make there, to people like Sophie. They're all Meredith to you, and you might not be able to save all of them, but for every one that you help, you're making a difference in her name.'

'I know I've said it before, but I'm going to have to say it again. You're amazing. Do you know that?' Felix had reached across the table, knitting their fingers together and she'd wanted his hand to stay there. She wasn't amazing, she wasn't even loyal enough to Max and his family to be able to keep her feelings for Felix in check. The only reason she was supposed to be here was to persuade Lily to come home, but she'd known before she even got on the plane that she wasn't even going to try. Eve had encouraged Max's sister to leave in order to save her sanity and she'd never ask Lily to change her mind, no matter how much she might long to have her home. All Eve could do was hope that seeing her might pave the way for Lily to visit her family, but pressurising her to do that was out of the question. It meant she already knew she'd be letting down the family she loved even more badly than she had already. And the guilt that had kept her up the night before, when not even jet lag could summon the blissful oblivion of sleep, was destined to be her travelling companion, no matter where she went.

* * *

Meredith's funeral was being held on her birthday, at the insistence of her sister, Ashleigh.

'I want the number of days when I have to remember how much it hurts to lose her to be minimised and, at least this way, there might be some good memories of this day – from when we were kids – mixed in with the bad ones.' Ashleigh's argument had some logic to it. Not that it was a strategy Felix would have gone for, but he'd given up the right to have any say in what happened when he'd split with Meredith. Despite all the conversations they'd had in the past about the best way to try and help Meredith, he'd wondered if her family would hold her death against him. He wouldn't have been surprised if they'd tried to pin some of the blame for what had happened onto him, the way he'd done to himself. But when he'd called to give his condolences, that hadn't been how it had gone.

'Thank you for trying to help her for so long and for playing such a big part in giving her the part of her life when she was the happiest I'd ever seen her. It was such a bonus after we thought we'd lost her to addiction the first time.' Ashleigh had sniffed hard then, unable to continue for a moment and Felix had given a shuddering sigh.

'She fought so hard during that time and everything she achieved, she did herself. It was nothing to do with me. I'm just glad she was happy back then.' Felix swallowed down the emotion that had been rising in his throat.

'Me too.' Ashleigh had started to sob then, and he'd felt incredibly helpless. It might not have made any difference to

Meredith whether or not he was there to say his goodbyes, but it mattered to him and he knew it would matter to Ashleigh and her parents. They'd all done what they could to rescue Meredith, but over the years she'd damaged every relationship she'd had and rejected every offer of help.

The whole thing had started with alcohol and then it had escalated after a fairly minor car accident when she'd been in college. She'd been prescribed strong painkillers for an injury to her back. It had led to an addiction to pain meds, that had spiralled into something far more extreme and it had been the start of a cycle of addiction and attempts at recovery that had eventually killed her. Now Ashleigh had lost her sister, and their parents had lost their daughter. He knew they felt as if they'd lost her once already, when she'd been in the grip of addiction before, but this time there was no coming back. Meredith had used up her final chance, and nothing he or her family had done had been enough to change that. Maybe there would be people at the funeral who'd blame all of them for failing her, and he suspected a part of him would always wonder if he could have done more, but whatever anyone thought, he still wanted to be there, to prove that Meredith's life had meant something to a lot of people, himself included.

* * *

On the morning of the funeral, Felix could feel Eve watching him from across the table as they met for breakfast in their hotel in downtown San Francisco.

'I can't eat my pancakes if I know you're watching me like that.' He looked up and caught her in the act, and she gave an apologetic shrug. He had no appetite anyway. He just wanted today to be over and for Meredith to finally be at peace. Eve had insisted that he try and eat, though, so he'd put some pancakes on his plate to humour her, thinking he could push them around a bit and fool her into thinking he'd eaten some, but she was watching him like a hawk.

'Sorry, I was just trying to see if you're okay. I know you keep saying you are, but I just wanted to make sure. It's not too late for me to come with you. I know I'd want someone to lean on for support, and God knows you've been there often enough for me lately.'

'Thanks, but I need to do this alone.' Part of him really wanted to take Eve up on her offer, but he wasn't sure Meredith's family would have understood him bringing a total stranger to her funeral, just so he had someone to lean on, and he really did need to do this alone. He had to face up to the fact that he'd walked away from Meredith and see if he could forgive himself for it. It didn't matter what Eve said to him, or even what Meredith's family had said. He had to decide for himself if *he* could be okay with what he'd done. Having Eve there would only muddy the waters, because she would be desperate to convince him that he deserved forgiveness and he was nowhere near sure that it was true.

Not wanting her there with him today didn't change how glad he was that Eve had agreed to come on the trip. They might only have three full days in the city he'd once called home before they had to fly back again, but he was determined to make it count. She needed a break far more than she seemed to realise. 'Honestly, Eve, you've already done more than you'll ever know by agreeing to come out here at the same time as me. Knowing I can talk to you about everything when I get back from the funeral tonight means a lot. If you're still up for meeting for dinner, that is?'

'Absolutely. I'll make sure I don't eat too much when I meet

Lily for lunch. You've got to pace yourself over here, you know? And if you're not going to eat any of those pancakes, they could probably be donated to feed a family of five.'

He raised his eyebrows. 'All this talk of pacing yourself from the girl who made the taxi driver stop off for fried chicken on the way from the airport.'

'That meal on the plane looked like something that belongs in a kidney bowl at work.' She shuddered. 'But Lily said she knows the best diner, three blocks from Fisherman's Wharf, and apparently the sandwiches are *When Harry Met Sally* level, if you know what I mean.'

'Don't go having an experience like that without me.' As soon as the words were out of Felix's mouth, he wished he could take them back. He didn't want Eve to think he was being creepy, or thinking about her *like that*, when she'd made it clear they could only ever be friends. Ever since the kiss, it had been almost impossible not to think of her in that way, but he had to try, because he'd rather have her as a friend than not have her in his life at all. 'I just meant, you know, if you're going to have a sandwich that amazing, the experience would be enhanced by being able to reminisce about it with a friend.'

'If it's as great as Lily claims it's going to be, I'll take you back there before we go home.'

'It's a date.' He was doing it again, saying things that made the situation unnecessarily awkward. It was time for a change of subject. 'Are you apprehensive about seeing Lily?'

'Now that I'm here, I'm not sure what I'm even doing.' Eve's attempt at a smile didn't even make it halfway. 'I miss Lily so much, and I know how much Annie and Nigel miss her. They think I'm here to try and persuade her to come home, but I couldn't be honest with them about that and I don't know if I'm going to be able to be honest with Lily either. I don't want her to come home if it means she goes back to that dark place she was in before she left, but the truth is, I don't want to be the one trying to hold Annie together all by myself any more either. I don't really know what I'm hoping for, except maybe that Annie will wish she was here instead of me, seeing Lily and spending time with her, and she'll realise it's okay to step away from Max for long enough to come and see her daughter. If she does it might allow her to see that it's okay for me to step back from Max every now and then as well. So the truth is, I'm not just here for Annie and Nigel's sake, or even because of how desperately I miss Lily. I'm far more selfish than that. I'm a horrible person, aren't I?'

'You're about as far from being a horrible person as anyone I know.' He hesitated, knowing he probably shouldn't say what he was about to, but he did it anyway. 'And whatever you end up saying to Lily, I'm really glad you decided to come out here.'

'I only did it because you promised to show me the sights, don't forget. A whistle-stop tour of San Francisco like no other, I seem to remember you promising me.' Her smile was genuine this time and he would have given anything for them to be here for different reasons. He wished they'd met at the hospital, without any of the baggage that was dragging them both down, and that he'd brought her to see the city he'd adopted as home for several years. He wished their kiss could have gone somewhere and that they could have dated like any other normal couple, but he understood better than anyone the ties that bound you to the past. He just hoped that whatever Max's sister decided to do, Eve would find her own passport to a new life at some point soon. It wasn't just because he would love the chance to get to know her even better than he already did, it was because she so clearly deserved it. But putting herself first didn't come naturally to Eve, and he was worried it never would. The least he could do was make sure she had the best possible time in San Francisco.

'I promise you'll get to see all the big highlights and I'll also show you a few places that only locals know about. Alcatraz, the Pier 39 sea lions and the Golden Gate Bridge are all amazing, but there's a place I know that does a chowder that blows all the tourist offerings out of the water.'

'That sounds amazing. Do you think we might be a bit too obsessed with food?' She laughed and he held up his hands in response, grateful that she didn't seem to have realised he still hadn't taken a single bite of the breakfast she'd insisted he have.

'Maybe, but I think that's where you find the heart of a place, in the food. However good this sandwich Lily is talking about turns out to be, I promise you my diner is where you'll find the real San Francisco.'

'I look forward to it.' She leant forward, as if to emphasise her words, and he knew she wasn't just saying it, but then she glanced at her watch. 'You'd better go soon, if the service starts at ten.'

'God, yeah, you're right.' Pushing the plate away, he got to his feet. 'I'll see you tonight, then?'

'Uh huh.' Reaching out she took his hand. 'I wanted to say that I hope it all goes okay, but it sounds so crass. You know what I mean, though.'

'I do.' He nodded, wishing once again that things were different, and that she wasn't about to let go of his hand. The best Felix could hope for was that today would bring some closure, and that he could finally move on from the pain of losing Meredith to her demons. Although in that moment he'd have settled for never getting closure, as long as Eve found some of her own. It was what he was silently praying for as he finally turned away from her, and headed out of the hotel to the funeral.

* * *

Lily ran across the road, seemingly oblivious of the tram coming down the tracks in her direction. Thank God she easily made it across in time and flung her arms around Eve with so much force she almost knocked her over.

'I'm so glad you finally made it out here.' Eve couldn't help smiling as she detected the slightest twang of an accent in Lily's voice.

'Me too. I've missed you so much.' She hadn't known just how much until she saw Lily again, having tried so hard to push those feelings down inside her, but it hadn't worked. Lily was the closest thing she'd ever had to a sister and they'd got on brilliantly from the outset.

The first time they'd met, Lily had hooked her arm into Eve's and told her she was just the sort of girl she'd hoped Max would end up with. They'd both teased him about his insistence on pronouncing *paella* the Spanish way, in the restaurant they'd met up in, and the laughter that had been the soundtrack of that night had bonded them from the start and set the seal on a friendship that had become an integral part of Eve's life. Now, with her arms around Lily, Eve realised that was something she'd missed almost as much as she missed the old Max. She just hadn't allowed herself to admit it, until now.

'Please tell me you weren't serious when you said you were only staying for four days.' Lily pulled away, trying and failing to blink back the tears that had filled her eyes.

'I already had some time booked off work when my friend said he was coming over for a funeral and that he could use some company on the trip. I didn't want to miss an opportunity like that, but I couldn't extend my leave. There were too many people already booked with time off and—'

'And you had all that time off when Mum got ill last year.' Lily sighed. 'Part of me wants to be insulted that you're only here because your friend was coming over, but I know you, and I know it would have taken someone else needing you even more than Mum does to get you here. So as sorry as I am that he's flown over for a funeral, I'm just glad that it brought you here.'

'I really have wanted to come and see you before now, it's just...' She couldn't finish the sentence, but she didn't need to. They both knew why she hadn't visited, and why Lily hadn't been home for a visit either.

'How is Mum doing? All I get from her when I call is updates about the appeal against Brandon Moorcroft's sentence. Or videos of Max, followed by her asking me if I can see how much progress he's making and wanting me to tell her she's right about him having turned a corner.'

'That pretty much sums up how she's doing.' Eve forced a smile. Right up until the moment she'd seen Lily, she'd wondered if she could really ask her to consider not just coming back home for a visit, but coming home for good. But as soon as she'd set eyes on Max's sister, she'd immediately had her answer. Lily was happy, she'd gone from looking like a young woman with the weight of the world on her shoulders, to someone who could see the possibilities in life again. It was obvious in the way she'd smiled from across the street, and the enthusiasm of her embrace. As soon as Lily had begun talking about Annie, that *joie de vivre* had slowly drained out of her, and Eve wasn't going to be responsible for making that a permanent thing. Maybe she'd be failing Annie and Nigel again, but nothing she did could change the situation with Max, and she knew in her heart that the old Max would have wanted her to save his sister instead. She wasn't going to try to persuade her to come home, not even for a visit if Lily didn't want to, she was just going to enjoy whatever time she could with the woman who'd become one of her best friends, and who she'd always wish she'd had the chance to call family in a way that no one could dispute.

It was Eve who looped her arm through Lily's this time. 'Let's not talk about any of that, I want to know how you are doing.'

Lily smiled, her face lighting up again. 'Well, that's one question Mum never asks me, but I have to say I'm doing great. Scott is amazing and work is going brilliantly.' Lily took a deep breath and turned to face her. 'There's something else, too. If all goes according to plan. In eight months' time, you're going to be an auntie!'

'Oh, Lily, oh my God, really?' Eve crushed her into another hug, laughing and crying all at the same time. 'Sorry, sorry, I know I probably shouldn't hug you quite so tightly, but that's amazing. It's the best news ever in fact.'

'It really does feel like it, I just wish...' This was another unfinished sentence that needed no words, Eve knew exactly what Lily was wishing for. She wished Max could share in the excitement, and that Annie could be as thrilled as she should be about the impending arrival of her first grandchild, but it was never going to be the most important focus in their lives, not even temporarily, and a bit of Eve's heart broke for Lily. She couldn't do anything to change that either, all she could do was make sure that Lily knew just how happy she was for her.

'It truly is the best news I've had in forever and we're going to go out now, to have a slap-up, pregnancy-friendly lunch on me to celebrate. I want all the details. How you found out, where you were, how you told Scott.'

'As long as I don't have to recount the conception, because it was after too much tequila at our favourite Mexican restaurant and the details of that night don't cover either of us in a lot of glory.' Lily laughed. 'I'm really glad, though, it's the happiest accident ever, because I don't think I could have ever planned for this, with the way things are with Max, and everyone else I love being on the other side of the Atlantic. But this feels like a new beginning.'

'It really does.' Eve hugged again her and swallowed back the surge of panic that lodged itself in her throat, at the realisation that there might never be a new beginning for her. But she wasn't going to give in to that thought, not today, when there was something truly wonderful to celebrate for the first time in a very long while.

17

The funeral had been strangely cathartic, especially given that Felix had been to more funerals for people who had lost their battles with addiction than he wanted to recall. Often there was a tendency to whitewash over the truth and talk about the person as though they'd been some kind of saint. Ashleigh and her parents didn't do that. There was no sugar coating the reality of all the things that Meredith had been, and the eulogy Ashleigh delivered had said it all.

'What can I say about my big sister?' She'd turned and put a hand on the coffin, taking a steadying breath before looking out at the congregation in front of her again. 'Merri was everything. She could be the best company in the world, or the hardest person to be around. She was joy and laughter, and pain and sorrow. Ever since we were kids, she had her own way of seeing the world and reacting to the things around her.

'She loved being the centre of attention, and she thrived when the spotlight was on her. She could dance and sing anyone else off the stage, and drink anyone else under the table. She was my biggest champion and my most loyal supporter, but she was also my harshest critic. Merri was by my side when I married my beautiful wife, Alicia, and I think the ears of the man standing outside city hall when we were having our photo taken – who made the mistake of saying it was an abomination that two women had got married – are probably still ringing!

'She'd fight for me to the death, but she'd probably fight with me to the death too. Never more so than when I tried to intervene and persuade her to change the lifestyle we could all see was killing her. She was a mass of contradictions and I'm mad as hell at her for checking out before she got to meet these two.'

Ashleigh had paused for a moment, then, running a hand over her very pregnant belly. There were still three months to go until she'd be full term with the twins, but she already looked nine months pregnant. When Felix had met Meredith, she'd told him that one of her biggest motivations for 'getting clean' first time around was because she wanted a family. She was never going to have that now, or see her beloved younger sister become a mum and, in that moment, Felix was certain he'd been able to feel his heart physically contract. It was such a futile loss and he just couldn't shake off the sensation that he might have been able to do something to change it. But Ashleigh hadn't finished yet.

'We all tried so hard to turn things around for Merri. I can't count the number of times Mom and Dad went to her aid, or I drove to some terrifying location in the early hours of the morning to pick her up from a bar she'd been thrown out of, or sent her money because she'd got herself in trouble for not paying a dealer. Then she surprised us all by getting herself clean.'

Ashleigh had paused again then and turned towards Felix. 'She even trained as a therapist and started working as a peer counsellor for the clinic that had spent years trying to help her. She met the most amazing man. It was what we'd prayed for and we couldn't have asked for anyone better than Felix and neither could she, but it still wasn't enough. He tried to help her every bit as much as the rest of the family did, but Merri had demons that none of us could defeat. In the end they lured her back to the life we hoped with all our hearts she'd left behind.

'We couldn't reach her after that. She stole from us and abused us, and rejected our offers of help, time and time again. We had to step back and hope to God she'd find the will to come back to us and ask for the help that would have been hers the moment she was ready to accept it, but it never happened. Sometimes Merri was incredibly difficult to love, but none of us ever stopped, and the only comfort I have is that I'm sure she always knew that. If Merri touched your life, and I'm sure if you're here today that she did, try to hold onto that and the good memories you have of her. Remember her at her best, not her worst, and please try not to question if there was anything you could have done, because believe me we tried everything. Merri wouldn't want anyone to blame themselves, at least not the Merri she was when her demons were at bay. She'd want us all to live our lives to the fullest, the way she never quite could.'

Turning towards the coffin one final time, Ashleigh had laid her hand upon the lid again, her final words choking in her throat. 'Love you, sis, fly high and free at last.'

Nothing anyone else said could top that and it had taken until the end of the service for Felix to be able to swallow down his emotions enough to be able to speak.

* * *

Now that he was at the wake, both Ashleigh and her parents had thanked him for all that he'd done to try and help Meredith.

When he attempted to object and tell them he wished he could have done more, her father, Don, held up his hand.

'No, you couldn't. We all wanted to find the thing that could have prevented this outcome, but I think it was somehow written in her DNA from the start. This was always going to happen, no matter what we did. Beating ourselves up about it won't change that. The only comfort we can take is knowing that Merri's battle is over at last. She was exhausted from fighting for so long, but now she's finally at peace.'

Felix nodded. 'I thought the same thing. She tried so hard for so long.'

'She did.' Don's eyed filled with tears. 'I couldn't imagine ever wanting her to give in and just let go, but her torture is over and, in some ways, so is ours, because we know where she is now and that no one is hurting her. I try to take some comfort from that, even though in another way the torture is just beginning. The chances are we've got decades ahead without our baby girl, and Ashleigh has to face the rest of her life without the big sister who was by her side from day one. I'm just so grateful we've got Ash and Alicia, and that the babies will be here soon. If we hadn't had them, I think I'd have lost it completely, and I'm not sure I could have found the strength to carry on.'

'I know for sure I couldn't.' Ashleigh's mum, Deanna, dropped her head onto her other daughter's shoulder as she spoke, snaking a hand around her waist, and despite their obvious pain, the heaviness in Felix's heart lifted a little. When families suffered a loss like this it could widen the chasms that already existed, or it could bond those left behind all the more tightly. It was clear which way it was going to go for Meredith's family and that was something else to be thankful for.

For the next twenty minutes, Felix stayed talking to them and remembering the good memories he had of Meredith before they shared another round of hugs, more tears, and promises to stay in touch.

'I'd love you to come and meet the twins when they arrive,' Ashleigh said, after she'd hugged him. 'But I only want you to do that when you've moved on with your life. If I think you're still holding on to any negative thoughts, because you're labouring under the misapprehension that you could have done more for Merri, I'm going to kick your ass so hard you won't be able to sit down for a month.'

'Is this an insight into your parenting style?' Felix laughed and she grinned in response.

'I've got twins coming, so I'll be doing whatever it takes!' They hugged again then and she held him so tightly for a moment that it was a struggle to breathe, but it felt as if the weight of the world had been lifted from his shoulders, when she whispered one last bit of advice to him.

'Grab all the life you can, Felix. We've got to live ours twice as big now, and twice as hard, for Merri. We've got to take the second chance she turned her back on.'

'I will.' Even as he said the words, he hadn't been able to stop himself thinking about Eve. And when a text came through from her, as he walked back towards his hire car, Ashleigh's words were still fresh in his mind. Eve's message asked if he'd mind Max's sister and her boyfriend joining them for dinner, and he didn't hesitate to reply, telling her that he'd love to meet them. He knew Eve could never let go of the life she'd shared with Max and he didn't want her to. All he wanted was the chance to be part of it and he hoped tonight might be the start of that. The kind of connection he felt with Eve didn't just come along all the time and he wasn't going to walk away from the opportunity to discover where this could go, otherwise, he'd already be breaking the promise he'd only just made to Ashleigh.

* * *

Lily and Scott had taken them to dinner in Sausalito, on the opposite side of the bay from San Francisco, a beautiful little town stretched out along two miles of shoreline. They ate at a seafood restaurant in the harbour, watching the sunset give way to the twinkling lights of downtown San Francisco, as they began to light up the skyline. It was a romantic destination without a doubt, and Lily and Scott were in the sort of loved-up bubble that sometimes accompanied impending parenthood. Eve watched as Lily rested her head on Scott's shoulder, and he placed a hand over hers, where it rested on her non-existent bump. She'd admitted to Eve during their lunch together that she had no intention of telling Annie or Nigel about the baby until she was as certain as she could be that nothing could possibly go wrong. Eve didn't need to ask why she'd decided to keep quiet. Annie couldn't take one more blow, and Lily couldn't become responsible for her happiness again either. So for now, it was a secret Eve was only too happy to keep.

The meal had been wonderful and the company even more so, with easy conversation and lots of laughter between the four of them. Scott had commented that he hadn't known before coming to the UK that there were so many different accents in such a small country. Felix had made them all laugh, and taken Eve completely by surprise, by being able to do every accent that Scott had been able to name, taking in all four countries of the UK and at least six different regional English accents. He seemed to have an endless capacity to surprise her, and it felt so lovely having the chance to get to know him even better, away from all the pressures of home.

'Felix is great.' Lily looked at Eve's reflection now, as they stood side by side in the restroom at the restaurant. 'Max would have loved him.'

'Max *does* love him.' She paused from re-applying her lipstick and met Lily's eyes in the mirror. 'Felix is Max's occupational therapist.'

'I know he is, but I meant the old Max.' Lily bit her lip, clearly struggling not to give into the emotion that was never far away when they talked about Max, and Eve reached across and squeezed her hand.

'I think he would have too.'

'Felix must be incredibly patient doing a job like that and, if he's built up enough of a relationship for Max to love him, he must be a bit of a miracle worker. Not to mention having a very thick skin.' Lily glanced down, focusing on her hands for a moment, before looking at Eve's reflection again. 'He hasn't seemed to like anyone or anything all that much since the assault.'

'Things are settling down a bit and Max definitely has good days if he's allowed to spend time doing the things that make him happy, they just don't look anything like his good days used to look. He has his favourites amongst the staff at Oakwood Park, and the medical professionals who work with him, but maybe love was the wrong word. He really likes Felix, though, and that's helped him make a lot of progress recently.' Eve shook her head. 'I know your mum's a bit worried about how Max might react when the funding for OT with Felix runs out, but we're working on a plan. In the meantime, one thing Max definitely does love is his gaming. It's mostly me he seems to find infuriating.'

Once again, Eve hadn't meant to be that honest. She'd been so determined not to say anything that might make Lily feel guilty, but it had felt so good to talk to someone who accepted that the old Max was gone forever.

'I think you remind him of what he's lost and that must be so hard.' It was Lily's turn to squeeze her hand this time. 'You're such a kind person, Eve, and you've done so much to support Mum and Dad, but I'm not sure whether it's good for Max to still have you around all the time if seeing you makes it harder for him to feel content with the way things are now. And it's definitely not good for you.'

'I can't just walk away.' Eve wanted to cram the words back down her throat, the moment she saw the hurt on Lily's face. It hadn't been an accusation, or a comparison between them, and the last thing she'd wanted was to make Lily feel bad. So she had to try and explain. 'Your family have been the only family I've known since my mum died. Max might not want me around any more, but I don't want to lose any of you.'

'You wouldn't, and maybe you just need to give Max enough space to miss you, in this new version of your relationship, but you'll never lose me whatever happens.' The tension had left Lily's face and she squeezed Eve's hand again. 'I'm certain Mum and Dad wouldn't want to lose you either.'

'It's a risk though, isn't it? If I'm no longer Max's fiancé, I've got no claim to be a part of your family.'

'You don't need a title when you've got history.' Lily turned to face her. 'And everything in life is a risk. I could spend my whole life feeling terrified that something might happen to Scott, after what happened to Max. Or that something is going to happen to either one of us, or both, now that we're going to be having a baby. But what's the alternative? To stop taking chances, to not fall in love, or start any new adventures? Or do I try to build a life that makes all the risk worthwhile? The old Max would be as mad as hell if he thought he'd played any part in you deciding to live your life in a way that means you can avoid all the risk, but miss out on all of the rewards as well. And so would I.'

'You're supposed to be the little sister.' Eve smiled. 'How did you suddenly get so wise?'

'It must be the hormones.' Lily laughed and pulled her into a hug. 'Just promise me you'll start taking some risks again and living your life, and that you'll start with Felix.'

'Okay, I'll take a risk. I might even have the peanut butter brownie instead of the cheesecake.' It was Eve's turn to laugh, as Lily tightened her embrace.

'I'm going to squeeze you like a tube of toothpaste if you don't make me that promise.'

'How can I promise you that, if I don't even know whether it's what Felix wants?' Eve was glad Lily couldn't see her face, because she'd gone hot just talking like this. Lily was the last person she should be confiding in, but the truth was she really wasn't sure if Felix saw her as more than a friend any more. She'd pushed him away and they'd agreed to focus on friendship instead, and being there for one another at a difficult time. He'd just lost the woman he'd been in love with for years, and he was Max's occupational therapist. There was so many reasons why they should maintain the status quo, and she was nowhere near as sure as she had been that discussing it was still what he wanted. Suddenly Lily pulled away from her and waved a hand in front of her face, making Eve blink.

'Ah, so you're not blind, then?' Lily raised her eyebrows. 'I thought you must be, if you can't see for yourself that Felix is interested. It's obvious. Just like I can see it written all over your face every time you look at him. Now stop playing for time and do something about it. Otherwise I'm not going to let you be godmother to this baby, and then you'll never be an official part of this family in a way that being a godparent would definitely qualify you to be.'

'Oh my God, really?' Eve could feel the huge smile that had broken out on her face, all the way down to her toes.

'Really, but only if you start living again.'

'How can I say no to that?' Eve couldn't stop smiling, even when she thought about the prospect of putting herself out there and telling Felix she'd had a change of heart. After all, what was the worst that could happen? She'd already been to hell and back since Max's assault, and even the humiliation of getting turned down flat could never come anywhere close to that.

* * *

Felix had delivered on his whistle-stop tour of San Francisco. They'd hired electric bikes and he'd taken her all over the city, including across the Golden Gate Bridge in cross winds so strong that she'd thought they might end up in the water. It had made her feel alive, having the kind of new experiences she'd put on hold since Max's head injury. They'd been joined for a second night in a row by Lily and Scott on a night tour of Alcatraz, and Felix had recounted some of the myths and legends about the prison. He was a natural storyteller, making use of his talent for accents and the sort of comic timing that had made Eve throw her head back in laughter, in a way she couldn't remember doing in years.

'If you don't ask him out, I will.' Scott had whispered to her, when they were on the boat back over to San Francisco and she'd laughed again. Surprising herself that she wasn't cross with Lily for talking to Scott about her feelings for Felix. Maybe it was because being here – thousands of miles away from Port Kara – made if feel like they were in a bubble that nothing else could touch. There'd been several times she'd wanted to tell Felix that she'd changed her mind and that if he still wanted more than friendship, then she did, too, but something had stopped her each time. She wanted to pick the right moment, so that he'd feel like he could be honest with her if he didn't feel the same way.

On their last full day they'd spent the morning in Muir Woods, a few miles outside of the city, where the huge redwood trees had taken Eve's breath away. She'd walked side by side with Felix, her fingers so close to brushing against his that it had felt as though electricity was pulsing between them. Yet somehow she still couldn't bring herself to tell him how she felt. There were too many people around and she didn't want to just blurt it out while he was driving the hire car back over the bridge to the city. Now they were back in San Francisco, and as he parked the car it felt as if time was running out.

'What do you fancy doing with our last few hours, we could go to the—' Felix suddenly stopped talking, his head turning sharply to the left, and when Eve followed the direction of his gaze she could see why. There was what looked like a body lying in an empty parking space, where a vehicle could pull in at any moment.

'Do you think he's dead?' Eve couldn't keep the horror out of her voice, but Felix shook his head.

'I can see his chest moving.' He breathed out slowly. 'I've picked up fentanyl addicts from this parking lot before when I worked at the clinic. I'm going to need to try and get him some help, even if he doesn't want it.'

'Is there anything I can do?'

'Come with me to the clinic. That's if they agree to take him in and he agrees to go.' Felix turned to look at her. 'I haven't been back there since everything with Meredith and I'm not sure I can face it on my own.'

'Of course.' Eve could see the pain etched on his face and it was a reminder of what losing Meredith had done to him. Going back to the clinic was going to be so tough on him, but Felix clearly wasn't thinking about himself as he got out of the car and strode over to the man, and that just made her like him even more.

* * *

'That wasn't quite the way I'd have chosen for you to spend your last afternoon in San Francisco, and this wasn't quite the last dinner I'd have planned for us either.' Felix set down the pizza he'd bought, and she handed him one of the beers she'd just taken from the mini fridge in her hotel room.

'I don't know, this feels very authentic. Takeaway pizza and beers, with American football on the TV.' They were watching a re-run of the most recent Superbowl and she wanted to tell him that she was just glad to be spending the evening with him, whatever that looked like. It had been a long day and their visit to the clinic had been an eye-opener. It had been heartbreaking to see the people waiting in the drop-in centre, begging for a hit of something to tide them over until they could score again. There were all kinds of addictions amongst those waiting, but the fentanyl addicts looked by far the most tortured of all the desperate souls. They needed to be numbed from reality so badly that they were willing to anaesthetise themselves, rather than feel anything at all, and it had suddenly struck Eve that, in a way, she'd been doing the same thing. She buried herself in work and her duty to Max and his mother so that she didn't have to feel the pain of losing what they'd had together, or be forced to admit that she wanted more from life than she had now. But she didn't want to keep pretending any more.

Max had shown her around the clinic, after the care of the man they'd found in the parking lot had been handed over to some of his former colleagues, who'd assessed the patient to see what they could do to help.

As well as the drop-in centre, the clinic had in-patient facilities and the difference between those going through the various stages of recovery was startling. There were new admissions who were so painfully thin they were almost skeletal, with clumps of hair missing and skin so grey Eve would have sworn they were already dead if she hadn't known better. Then there were those further down the line in their recovery, who had the life back in their eyes again, and all kinds of improvements to their physical appearance. There were none who didn't appear physically scarred in some way by their experiences, though, and some of the recovering addicts had a condition called 'fentanyl fold'. It was caused by the drug depressing the central nervous system, which stopped the brain from sending messages telling the body to stand upright. For some long-term users, it had led to chronic muscle weakness, as a result of spending prolonged periods bent over, and it was one of the things Felix had focused on as an OT.

Eve had been so impressed by the work being done and what Felix's former colleagues had said about him, which had just solidified everything she'd already thought about him. Felix Grainger was a very special man and she knew now, with 100 per cent certainty, that he was worth taking a risk on.

'If we were here for longer and it was the right time of year, I'd have taken you to a proper game.' Felix flipped open the lid of the pizza box and handed it to her. They were sitting side by side on the sofa in her hotel room and there were nerves bubbling in the pit of her stomach, because she knew it was now or never.

'I'd have no idea what was going on.'

'Even after all the time I spent living here, I still don't really know, but it's the whole atmosphere that's brilliant. Although, I've got to admit that baseball is my favourite and the season's just got underway.'

'That's like rounders, right?'

Felix laughed. 'Whatever you do, don't let any Americans hear you make that comparison.'

'Okay, so is it like cricket? Because to be honest, I'd rather watch paint dry.'

He laughed again. 'Talk like that will get you deported.'

'I kind of wish we didn't have to go home at all.' It was something else Eve hadn't meant to say out loud. 'At least not yet.'

'So do I.' He looked at her and the frisson of nerves in her stomach went into free fall.

'It's like we're in a bubble here, isn't it? Almost as if nothing back home exists.' She held her breath, waiting for him to answer and when he did his voice was low.

'But it does and we will be going back there, so I don't want you to regret anything.'

'Didn't someone wise once say that the only things you regret in life are the things you don't do?' Her heart was thudding in her ears now, and her stomach did another flip as Felix smiled.

'Wise or stupid, I'm not quite sure, but I want you to be. Sure, that is.'

'Does this convince you?' She set the pizza box down on the floor and leant forward, pressing her lips against his, her hands sliding inside the back of his T-shirt as she pulled him towards her. He kissed her back in a way that made it obvious Lily had been right, he wanted this every bit as much as she did. The kiss left her breathless when he finally pulled away.

'Pretty convincing.' Felix smiled that gorgeous slow smile of his, that had hooked her on the first day they'd met. 'But I think we better try it again, just to make sure.'

'Okay, if you insist.' She grinned, before leaning towards him again, suddenly as certain of where this was going as she was of how much she wanted it to happen.

18

Post-shift drinks with members of the team had become one of Eve's favourite things about working at St Piran's. It didn't matter if it was a glass of red at one of the wine bars in Port Kara or Port Agnes, or a coffee outside the hospital shop. It was just so nice to feel she'd begun to build relationships that were making some of her colleagues feel like friends. She hadn't even been sure at first whether she'd wanted to let people get close enough to know the details of her personal life, or if she wanted to risk letting new people in who she might also end up losing. Not to mention that between work, visiting Max and being there for Annie, she hadn't thought she'd have time for friends.

Somehow they'd come along anyway, and as she carried the drinks to the table, outside the hospital shop, she made a decision. She wanted to tell Isla and Meg the truth about Max, and to let them and Eden in on the news that she and Felix had become a little bit more than friends.

'So, come on then, how exactly was your trip to San Francisco?' Eden narrowed her eyes as she asked the question. 'I've barely had a chance to speak to you since you got back and all I get from Felix when I ask him is a big smile.'

'Well, it doesn't take a brain surgeon to work it out then.' Isla shook her head. 'If you decided to take a trip like that with someone, it's because you like them. A lot.'

'I just went to see an old friend and the timing worked because Felix was going out there for a funeral, and it was nice to have someone to do the journey with.' Eve was so used to trotting out the line, more or less the same story she'd given Annie and Nigel, she forgot for a moment that she'd decided to confide in her friends.

'Hmm.' Meg looked doubtful. 'The photos you showed me didn't look like you were on two parallel trips to the same place. You look very enmeshed.'

'Is that what they're calling it these days? We just used to call it having the hots for someone.' Gwen suddenly appeared from nowhere and Eve realised it was just as well she'd decided to come clean, because she seemed to be having a coffee at a Miss Marple convention, the amount of amateur sleuthing that was going on. Gwen certainly wasn't holding back from the conclusions she'd reached. 'For what it's worth, Eve, I think you'll make a great couple. You've both got everything going for you. Great jobs, shared values and you're both pretty easy on the eye too.'

'Thanks.' Eve laughed and she was about to admit she definitely couldn't argue with that last part when it came to Felix, but then Eden screwed up her face.

'Eurgh, Gwen, please don't describe my brother as being easy on the eye and definitely don't talk about anyone having the hots for him.'

'Oh, but he is,' Meg shrugged, 'and there's no awful ex-wife still lurking around, ready to stalk you on social media or spray an obscene message about you on the wall of the hospital car park.' It was something Meg had been through herself in the past few weeks, after going on a couple of dates with another doctor who had just finalised a very acrimonious divorce. 'A man with no baggage of any kind is a bit of a unicorn, and you can both go into a relationship with a clean slate. That's not an easy thing to achieve when you get into your thirties, trust me.'

'It's not quite as simple as that.' Eve ran a hand through her long dark hair, her eye catching Eden's.

'You do like him, don't you?' Concern clouded her friend's face. 'If you don't, you need to be straight with him, because I know he *really* likes you and, as much as he might always be my annoying big brother, I can't bear the thought of him getting hurt.'

'I do like him, well, more than that.' She wasn't ready to call it love, but it certainly felt as if it had the prospect to become something that big. She wished it was as easy as allowing things to just play out, and see where they went, but there was such a huge price to play for going all in with Felix. She could lose everything else that mattered to her. Lily had promised her that wouldn't happen, but she couldn't know for sure how Annie and Nigel were going to react. Yet putting her life on hold was making her so unhappy, and she knew that closing the door on the potential of a relationship with Felix would make that even worse, so sooner or later she was going to have to jump and see where she landed. Eden already knew there were complications, but she was always going to root for Eve to take a chance on her brother. She needed to tell the others what the problem was and see if that helped. 'Felix might not have any baggage, but I have.'

'Are you about to tell us that you've got three kids we know nothing about?' Isla widened her eyes, and they were all looking in her direction. It was now or never.

'No, but I have got a fiancé.'

Meg lost her grip on her coffee cup and it hit the table, sending forth a spray of liquid that just added to the shocked expression on the faces of most of Eve's friends.

'Does Felix know?' Gwen's voice was dangerously quiet. She might be all for people living the best life they possibly could, but Eve had a feeling from the expression on her face that one thing she would never condone was infidelity.

'Yes.'

'And did you know?' Meg looked at Eden, who nodded slowly.

'Okay, I've got no idea what's going on and you're going to have to explain it to me like I'm ten years old, because I can't imagine you or Felix doing the dirty on someone like that, let alone Eden being okay with you dating her brother when you're supposed to be marrying someone else.' Meg shook her head. 'I just can't believe it, or that you've got a fiancé you've said nothing about.'

'Max, my fiancé, lives at Oakwood Park and he's one of Felix's patients.' Eve took a deep breath, deliberately not making eye contact with the others. She had to get the whole story out. 'He was assaulted over two years ago and he suffered a very serious head injury, affecting his frontal lobe, which impacted everything from cognition to language processing skills, but more than anything it completely changed his entire personality. We were weeks away from getting married and he was training to be a surgeon; we had our whole lives mapped out. Now it's like I don't even recognise the version of Max that's still here, because the old him definitely isn't, and he can hardly even bear to be in the same room as me.'

'Oh, Eve, I'm so sorry.' Isla wrapped an arm around her shoulders. 'My dad had Huntington's disease and it affected his personality in the end. It's agony.'

'Isla's so right.' Gwen had moved to the other side of her. 'I lost my mum to aphasia and I know that's not the same as someone living with a head injury, but the impact on who they are can be equally catastrophic.'

'I've known about Max for a while, but I still can't imagine how that feels.' Eden reached across the table and touched Eve's hand, the look of concern she'd worn earlier back on her face. 'What I don't understand is why you're still engaged, not when everything's changed and you said Max doesn't even want you around. What happened is unbelievably awful, but you can't give up your chance of being happy again.'

'I don't want to.' Eve's voice was so quiet now that it was barely audible. 'And I know Max – the old Max – wouldn't want that. These days I don't think he even thinks of me that way.'

'What's the problem then, if Max doesn't want you around? You can still be there for him, as much as he'll let you, just not as his fiancée.' Meg furrowed her brow.

'It's Max's family that's stopping you, isn't it?' Eden's eyes searched her face and she nodded.

'It's like I told you before, they're *my* family as well. I've wanted to do what Meg said and be there for Max in a different kind of way, ever since I realised he's never going to come back from this, but his mum still can't accept there isn't going to be a miracle. She tells everyone we're engaged and talks about our wedding as if it's actually going to happen.'

'As hard as it is, you've got to be honest with her.' Gwen's tone was insistent. 'Take it from someone on the wrong side of seventy that life is far too bloody short not to take the chance of happiness when it comes your way. You can only live your life for yourself. If I'd lived mine according to what everyone else thought I should do, I'd be at home now with my knitting, not heading off to belly dance at the Old Town Hall in Port Tremellien, and I wouldn't have done paragliding, had my own magic act, or been a nude life model at the art college. We only get one go at this thing, Eve, don't waste it.'

'Would you have done any of those things if you thought it might cost you your family?' Eden turned to look at Gwen.

'My family just want me to be happy and they know the more weird and wacky things I can pack into my life, the happier I'll be. You're just asking for the chance to fall in love again and I can't believe anyone would begrudge you that.'

'Max's family mean more to me than I could ever explain and it's going to break his mum's heart if I tell her that Max and I are never going to be a couple again. Having me around will just remind her of how much she's lost and she's not going to want that.' Eve let go of a shuddering sigh. 'If I want to give things a proper go with Felix, I've got to be honest, but if it doesn't work out, I'll have lost everything for nothing.'

'Your freedom isn't nothing, Eve, it's everything.' Gwen grasped her wrist, as if she was worried that Eve might suddenly make a bolt for the door, before she'd heard everything the older woman wanted to say. 'There's no way of knowing if things will work out with Felix, I get that, but you can't spend the rest of your life playing it safe. That really would be a waste. If you're honest and it costs you your relationship with Max's family, I know that's going to hurt like hell, but even if things don't go anywhere with Felix, you'll have the freedom to try again and one day you'll meet someone who makes all that sacrifice feel like it's worth it.'

'Yeah and you won't be on your own anyway, you've got your St Piran's family now.' Meg gave her a gentle nudge and tears pricked Eve's eyes. There were people sitting around this table who cared for her and would continue to care for her, whether or not she stayed engaged to Max. That was the deciding factor; she was going to take a leap of faith to allow herself to make a fresh start, she just had to decide when.

* * *

'Did you have a bath in that aftershave?' Max pinched the end of his nose. 'Because it smells like you did.'

'Last time I was here you said I smelt of hospitals and I know you hate that.' Felix smiled. The funding for Max's OT sessions had been extended in light of the progress he'd made, and the fact that he was now so close to being ready to move to semi-independence. But there was still a lot of work to do and once Max moved into the bungalow, he'd no longer receive the same kind of intensive therapy, which meant they had to make the most of every visit. Felix and Max were approaching the end of a session where they'd been working on life skills together in one of the communal kitchens at Oakwood Park, and now they were back in Max's room. Felix raised his hands in mock surrender as he continued. 'I can't win with you sometimes, can I?'

'Not when you smell like an explosion in a factory that makes air freshener for Poundland.' Max had a cuttingly dry sense of humour when he felt like it and Felix couldn't help wondering how much of it was a legacy from before the assault, or if that was something else that had changed. 'I just hope you haven't put it on for the benefit of a woman, because unless she's lost her sense of smell, you're going to be out of luck.'

'So what would your advice be if I find someone attractive and I want them to notice me?'

Max's eyes widened in response. 'Before I answer, can I just get one thing straight? You're not talking about me, are you?'

Felix laughed. 'No, you're quite safe, Max. I just want your advice that's all.' Maybe it was wrong of him to ask a question like that, especially when the person he was talking about was the other man's fiancée, but he'd seen the two of them together, and it couldn't have been more obvious that Max no longer felt the same way about Eve. He seemed to get angrier and more upset around her than anyone else. Maybe it was because she was such a reminder of how different his life had been before the assault, or because having her around made him feel more pressure to try and be the person he no longer was. Whatever the case, it was clear her presence was a trigger.

'Umm.' Max looked thoughtful for a moment. 'Just tell her you like her? I don't know why people can't just say what they mean, it would make life a lot easier.'

'I guess it would.' Just as Felix responded, the door to the bedroom was pushed open and Max clearly wasn't happy to see the new arrival.

'For Christ's sake. I've told you before, this is MY room and you've got to knock so I can decide if I want you to come in or not.'

'I don't think I need you to tell me that, it's pretty obvious.' Eve attempted a smile, but Felix could see the hurt in her eyes and he desperately wanted to give her a hug, even though he knew he couldn't. On the flight home from San Francisco, she'd made it clear that she wanted to take things slowly and he'd known what that meant; that she didn't want Max or his parents to find out what was going on between them, at least for now. He could understand that and he was happy to move at her pace. It was just hard when he wanted to be there for her and he had to keep up the pretence that they were nothing more than friends.

'Not everything's about you, Eve, the whole world doesn't revolve around you.' The irony of Max's words seemed to afford her a genuine smile and Felix couldn't help thinking how beautiful she was.

'Sometimes I do forget that.' She grinned again as she exchanged a look with Felix and the desire to kiss her was almost too much, forcing him to look down at the notes he'd taken.

'We've had a good session today, haven't we, Max? Lots of progress towards being ready for semi-independent living, the sky's the limit after that.'

'Yeah, I thought maybe brain surgery. How many years do you think it will take before I'm ready to start my training. One?' Max held up his middle finger in a gesture that was obviously designed to convey his feelings about Felix's comment, before switching to a two-fingered V sign. 'Or two.'

'As long as all your patients are unconscious and they don't have to talk to you, I think you should be fine,' Eve said, before sticking out her tongue and for a few seconds Max stared at her, before starting to laugh.

'Okay, that was good.' Sitting down heavily on the sofa in his room, he picked up the games console that Felix had been forced to more or less wrestle from his grasp when he'd arrived for their session. 'But why are you here? You only came in yesterday.'

'Your mum's got a migraine, so she asked if I could pop in and see if you needed anything.'

'You could have phoned.' Max was already loading the game.

'I could.' Eve breathed out slowly, before taking two steps closer to Max. 'So do you need anything?'

'An upgrade to my PlayStation.'

'You know your mum wants to get you that next Christmas.'

'Yeah and she should know I'm not a bloody ten-year-old. I'm a grown man and if I want a new PlayStation, I shouldn't have to save up for it with my Christmas money like a little kid.'

Eve was wearing an expression that suggested she might agree with Max, but she didn't say so. In all the times Felix had interacted with the family, and even when he'd spoken to Eve on her own, he'd never once heard her say anything to challenge Annie's opinion.

'Why don't you talk to her again?' Eve's tone was reasonable.

'But in the meantime, is there anything I can get for you *now*? What's on the menu for dinner? I can go and pick up a takeaway for you if you don't like what's on offer.'

'Yeah, I'll have a McDonald's.'

'Are you just asking for that because you know the nearest one means I'll be out of your hair for forty-five minutes?'

'That's just a bonus.' Max didn't even look up.

'The usual?' Eve asked. 'A Big Mac meal with a strawberry milkshake?'

'Yep.'

'Right, see you in forty-five minutes, then.' She turned to look at Felix and he wanted to tell her that it didn't have to be like this. She didn't have to keep doing this when it clearly hurt her as much as it did, but he knew his words would be futile.

'I'll walk out with you,' he said instead. 'See you again on Tuesday, Max.'

'Yeah, okay, shut the door on the way out. I don't want to hear that old woman next door watching the *Yorkshire Auction House* on bloody volume fifty all night long.'

When they got out into the corridor, Eve was the first to speak. 'I wish you'd known Max before all of this.'

'He's quite the character and his sense of humour is still sharp, so I can only imagine.' As Felix replied, he tapped in the code to release the door to the reception area.

'It used to be sharp, but now it's mostly vicious.' Eve sighed. 'It's like the sight of me brings out the worst in him and I'm at the point where I think trying to carry on like we are is bad for us both.' She turned to face him after they'd walked through another set of double doors into the car park. 'I told Eden and some of the others about us.'

'Did you?' He smiled, but her face clouded again in response.

'Yes. Should I have asked you first?'

'Not at all, I'd tell that guy getting into his car over there if I thought he'd listen. I want us to be able to go out and be open with our friends and my family about all of it, but I know it's not as straightforward for you and the last thing I want is to put any kind of pressure on you.'

'Being with you,' Eve slipped her arms around his waist, 'is the part of my life that has the least pressure. It feels easy and right. It's all this stuff that feels hard, but if I thought Max got something out of it, I'd battle on. Except I've realised I'm not doing this for him, any more, I'm doing it for Annie and I don't think that's helping her. So I've decided I'm going to tell them. I just need to pick the right moment.'

'That's really great.' He couldn't keep the smile off his face, but he needed her to know he wasn't going to force her hand in any way. 'Although if you change your mind, I'll understand.'

'That's exactly why I won't change my mind.' She kissed him, seeming as reluctant to let him go as he was to leave. But he was going to dinner with his parents, and Eden and Drew, to celebrate his dad's birthday. Introducing Eve to the rest of his family might be a step too far, too soon, even if she hadn't promised to go on a lengthy errand for Max.

'I'll see you tomorrow, then?' He held her hand as he spoke and she nodded, before finally pulling away.

'See you tomorrow.'

He watched her for a moment as she climbed into her car and then turned back towards his own, just as a text message pinged through. It was from Ashleigh.

> Just wanted to let you know that Dad had a
> stroke the day after the funeral. It was scary as
> hell, but they're pretty sure he'll make a full
> recovery. I'm certain it was the stress of losing
> Merri, but he told me the thought of the twins
> carried him through and that he's determined to
> get better for them. We're all trying to look
> forward to the future and we want you to do the
> same, I know Merri would. Take care, Felix, and
> come visit us soon xx

Felix hit the reply button and typed out his response, wishing Don a speedy recovery and telling Ashleigh he was only ever at the end of the phone if she needed someone to talk to. Meredith's family had been through so much and yet they were still focusing on what the future could bring them. He hoped for Eve's sake that Annie and Nigel would be able to do the same, because if anyone deserved to move on from the past it was her.

19

Eve had planned to tell Annie about Felix the next time they got together, but Annie had been even more highly strung than normal. The verdict was due in from the Court of Appeal about Brandon Moorcroft's sentencing. It had taken over a year for the case to come to court in the first place, so that reports could be compiled on the extent of Max's injuries, and the doctors had needed to be certain that they'd reached a finite point in his recovery. Annie had appealed to the Attorney General's Office against the leniency of the sentence straightaway, her job meaning she was well aware of the twenty-eight day window open to the family to do so. She'd pinned all her hopes on the case being referred to the Court of Appeal and while they were waiting for the outcome she'd made herself ill again, barely sleeping and not eating at all.

Now that the Court of Appeal were about to give their decision, Annie was back to being like a cat on a hot tin roof, displaying some of the same behaviours she had just after Brandon Moorcroft was sentenced and Lily moved away. Eve couldn't bear the thought of her spiralling down to rock bottom again, so she was doing everything she could to prevent it.

'Have you eaten anything today?' she'd found herself asking Annie as the two of them crossed the car park together on their way in to see Max.

'I can't seem to face anything, my stomach's like a washing machine.' Annie had thrummed with nervous energy, tapping her fingers against her thighs almost as if she had an involuntary twitch.

'You've got to eat something, otherwise you're going to make yourself poorly again.'

'I'll be okay once this week's over and we get the verdict.' She'd looked at Eve, then, her eyes like two dark pools, contrasting sharply with the pallor of her face. 'I might even manage to make it through the night without waking up in a cold sweat thinking about the prospect of Moorcroft being released from prison.'

Eve had wanted to ask her what would happen if the sentence was upheld, but she'd already known the answer. Annie would go into the kind of apocalyptic meltdown that would almost certainly lead to another crisis. But it wouldn't matter what Eve said or what she did, she wouldn't be able to prevent that because Annie was pinning all her hopes on the sentence being extended. All any of them could do was hope that the Court of Appeal revised the sentence sufficiently to avoid triggering a complete breakdown in Annie's mental health, although in truth no sentence they could impose would ever be enough for her. Eve was almost as worried about what might happen when Annie's energies were no longer being poured into trying to get Moorcroft's sentence increased; when she no longer had that as a focus, she might finally have to face up to the reality of never getting the old Max back and, when she did, Eve had a horrible feeling that it would trigger an even bigger crisis.

Whatever the next week brought, she knew one thing for sure, now wasn't the time to tell Annie about Felix. She was glad to have work to focus on, even on days like today, when it seemed to be one high-octane emergency after another.

'There's an RTA on the way in. The patient has bullseye'd the windscreen and there's a suspected spinal injury. ETA five minutes.' Aidan summarised the outcome of the call that had just come through on the red phone and the team swung into action to prepare resus for the latest patient's arrival. The first priority would be to stabilise them and then get a CT scan to check the extent of the injuries, before deciding which specialist teams to involve. Eve just hoped that stabilisation would turn out to be possible, whatever injuries the patient might have. RTAs were one of the biggest causes of fatalities coming into the emergency department, and Eve had seen far more deaths than she wanted to remember. She'd also seen life-changing injuries, sometimes ones so catastrophic that patients had told her they wished they'd died.

When Eve and Max had got together, they'd talked about all kinds of scenarios; hardly surprising given their occupation. He'd told her that if he ever got an injury that left him too disabled to do his job, or live the life he wanted, he'd rather not survive. She'd challenged him back then, about all the people who'd adjusted to their new normal after a serious injury, sometimes achieving the most amazing things. He'd accepted that was true, but had still insisted that if he couldn't be a surgeon he would never be truly happy. She'd wondered in the early days after the assault, when they hadn't been certain whether he'd live or die, what she should pray for. But the thought had only ever been fleeting, and she'd begged every deity that might exist to save him, no matter what the cost. Max had been saved, but it had quickly become clear that his life would never be the same again and she'd found herself wondering something else; whether he still wished he hadn't survived. He'd never said so, but after the assault he'd been a different person, with different views about almost everything to those the old Max had held.

Now, whenever Eve got a call to say a seriously injured patient was on the way in, she found herself praying that they'd be able to take the first steps to ensuring the person made a full recovery, but if they couldn't, the patient would get the outcome they would have wanted, even if that meant not making it. She'd never admitted that to anyone, and had never done less than everything possible to save a life. She just had to hope that the cost of that was never more than that person would have been willing to pay.

Right now though, she had a job to do and as Jeff and Julia, two of the paramedics, rushed the patient into resus, Eve caught her breath at the amount of blood caking the woman's face. Her hair looked blonde, but it was so matted with dried blood that it was impossible to know for sure.

Jeff gave a rundown of the painkillers administered at the scene and the checks on her vital signs that had been carried out en route to the hospital. The patient had regained consciousness at the scene, but had been hysterical and incoherent, resisting attempts to move her from the vehicle, and they'd been forced to sedate her for her own safety and theirs. The outcome of the checks suggested the injuries weren't life threatening, but there was no way of knowing yet whether they might be life-changing. Jeff turned to look at Eve. 'Unfortunately, we haven't got a name, because there was no ID in the car, no handbag and not even a phone.'

'The sedation should wear off soon and hopefully she'll be able to tell us who she is.' Eve turned to look at Meg as she spoke. 'But I'm worried about the extent of her facial injuries and whether that might affect her ability to talk, as well as what else might be going on internally. Given her agitation on scene, I think it might be best to maintain sedation until the scan, bearing in mind that she's stable. What do you think?'

Before Meg could even answer, the doors to resus burst open and Eve caught her breath. Nigel was suddenly framed in the doorway. Aidan right behind him, urging him to stop.

'I've told you, you can't go in there. You need to wait outside and I promise to find out if your wife has been admitted.'

Nigel lurched forward, pushing Aidan out of the way as he tried to block his path. Eve blinked hard. This couldn't be happening. It had to be a nightmare, one she'd wake up from at any moment.

'Eve, it's her, isn't it? It's Annie.' The fear in his eyes made her shiver and she tried to speak, to tell him that he was wrong and it wasn't his wife lying on the bed in front of her, covered in so much blood that she was unrecognisable, but the words wouldn't come out. Instead she turned back towards the patient and glanced down at her hand, spotting the distinctive sapphire engagement ring, circled by petal-shaped diamonds, like an exotic flower. Eve had only ever seen one like that before and it had been on Annie's hand.

* * *

Felix had been looking forward to finishing work all day. It wasn't because he didn't love his job or because he was the sort of person who watched the clock from the moment he arrived, waiting for it to be time to leave. The reason he hadn't been able to wait on this particular Tuesday, was because he had a date to go to the cinema with Eve. It might have sounded pretty dull to anyone else. But it was the routine nature of it that appealed to him most. He really liked her, more than he probably should this early in their relationship, but then Felix had never been one to play games, and he wasn't really the sort of person to date for the sake of it – at least not now he was in his mid-thirties. He was dating with a view to the long term and the hope that this might have the potential to go the distance. He wanted someone he could do the ordinary things with, as well as embark on big adventures.

Going to the cinema was something couples did all the time and the fact that Eve had agreed to such a public date, in the cinema at Port Tremellien, where anyone could see them, felt like a milestone. She might still be waiting for the right moment to tell Annie and Nigel that she was seeing Felix, but she wasn't trying to hide it from them or anyone else either. It was proof that she'd meant what she said, and she liked him enough to risk the consequences of their reaction. That in itself felt huge and, if he hadn't like her as much as he did, he might have been the one urging her to proceed with caution. The last thing he would have wanted if he wasn't sure about Eve, was for her to put her relationship with Annie and Nigel on the line, but he *was* sure about Eve. He'd been 99 per cent certain before San Francisco, but afterwards there'd been no question in his mind.

Felix had been relieved when Eve had told him she'd spoken to Eden about him, and it had meant he felt able to confide in Drew and admit just how much he liked Eve.

'Do you think I should try and play it a bit cool?' He'd posed the question to his sister's boyfriend when they met for lunch and Drew had laughed.

'You're asking the wrong person if you want advice on how to be cool.'

'Oh, I don't know, whatever you did worked on Eden, and my sister can be a hard nut to crack.'

'I just won Teddie over first.' Drew had shrugged, a smile quickly spreading across his face. 'Maybe that's the answer, find someone she loves and get them on side first.'

'I think I might already have done that. I'm the only OT Max will cooperate with, but it's not him Eve is worried about upsetting by dating me, and I don't think anything would make that okay with his parents. Eve is the biggest link to who Max was before the assault, and if I break that link in any way they'll be forced to face up to the fact that things are never going to go back to the way they were.'

'They're never going to do that anyway.' Drew had shrugged for a second time, his brilliantly straightforward response quite possibly a by-product of his high-functioning autism. 'I think what Eden appreciated was that I didn't mess her around, I said what I meant and I meant what I said. It might just be because of the way I'm wired, but I think all relationships should operate on that basis. Don't try and play it cool if you like Eve as much as I think you do, be honest with her, so that she's got the confidence to be honest with Max's parents too. That way, everyone knows where they stand and they can decide if they're in or they're out.'

'Has anyone told you you're a genius?'

'Not nearly as often as they should do.' Drew had laughed again and Felix had decided to follow his advice. You couldn't go far wrong by being honest, and Meredith had proved just how much harm lies could do. She'd lied to everyone, including herself, about just how out of control her addiction had become. Eve couldn't have been more different to Meredith, and she'd already decided she wanted to be honest with Annie and Nigel.

Felix couldn't imagine them turning their back on her, but he also understood why she wanted to make it as painfree for them as possible, when they learned that she was moving on. He wasn't going to put any pressure on her to have that conversation with Max's parents; it was enough to know she wanted to. If she could put so much of her life on the line to see where their relationship might go, the least he could do was tell her just how much she meant to him and he had every intention of doing that tonight.

He'd arranged to meet her in the emergency department, once his shift ended. She was due to finish before him, but she'd told him she was more than happy to have the chance to catch up on some paperwork and an online training course she'd been putting off for weeks. Felix had expected her to be ready and waiting when he got to the department, but she was nowhere to be seen.

'You don't know where Eve is, do you?' Aidan stopped in his tracks as Felix called out to him, a pained expression on his face.

'She's with her in-laws.' It was an innocent enough remark, but somehow it felt like a stab to the gut and he wanted to correct Aidan. He knew it was stupid and there's no way he'd actually have done it, but he didn't get the chance anyway, because Aidan wasn't finished. 'I didn't even know she had a fiancé until Isla told me last week. She's a dark horse our Eve, isn't she? And so are you come to that!'

Felix opened his mouth to respond, but once again Aidan didn't give him the chance. 'Max's mum was in a car accident and his dad is in a right state. I think he'd have lost it completely if Eve hadn't been there.'

Felix shivered, suddenly experiencing an almost overwhelming sense of déjà vu that for a moment he couldn't identify, but then it hit him. It was what Meredith's father, Don, had said about losing her; that he'd have lost it completely if he hadn't had

Ashleigh and her babies giving him a reason to carry on. What would Nigel have if he lost Annie, after already going through so much with Max? Lily was thousands of miles away with no intention of coming home, and Eve had been the rock for everyone through all of that. But if Felix took her away, who would Nigel have to lean on?

'Does Max know what's happened?'

'I don't think so.' Aidan furrowed his brow. 'You know him quite well, don't you?'

'Yes, I've been working with him since I started here.' Felix was surprised at just how much Eve had shared with her friends over the past few days, having decided to stop keeping secrets. But she could never have predicted what would happen to Annie and he couldn't help wondering if she wished now that she'd kept quiet. 'I need to talk to Eve and see if there's anything I can do. If she wants me to speak to Max, or if he needs to come in and see his mum...'

Felix didn't want to ask how bad things were, because part of him didn't want to know. He couldn't bear the thought that Max and his family might have to face even more trauma. He also knew there was only so much Aidan could say without breaking patient confidentiality and in truth he'd probably already overstepped the mark.

'I'll go and find her.' Almost before the words were out of Aidan's mouth, Eve came along the corridor, side by side with Nigel, who had his arm around her. They were both drained of colour, united in their love for Annie. They were a family, that much would have been apparent even if Felix hadn't known anything about them. And he understood as well as anyone just how priceless family was in moments like this. He couldn't be the one to take that away from Eve, not when it was the only family she had. It would put too far much pressure on their relationship, when he was in no position to offer her any of the same guarantees of support, or the shared history that her bond with Max's family gave her.

'I'm so sorry to hear what happened. How's Annie?' Felix kept his eyes fixed on Nigel, it was his only hope of fighting the desire to reach out and try to comfort Eve.

'Her face is badly messed up and they've sent her for a scan. I'm just terrified that she might be—' He shook his head and looked towards Felix. 'What if she's got an injury like Max's, or something even worse?'

'It's going to be okay.' Eve turned towards him. 'We've got to believe that.'

'I've wanted to believe that things are going to be okay for the past two years. I kept trying to convince myself that Max would recover eventually, because Annie wouldn't even consider another outcome, but I know now that he won't. Not fully. I told myself that Lily would come home eventually, when she'd had enough space to think things through, but I don't think that's true either. Now I want more than anything to believe that Annie's going to be okay, but even if there's no lasting damage from the accident, I know she's changed forever. The Court of Appeal have upheld Brandon Moorcroft's sentence and I'm scared that all the fight that was keeping Annie going will have disappeared, and that she's going to want to give up on life. You know how low she got when Lily left and I think the outcome from the court was one blow too many. She just can't take any more.'

'We can get her through this. We've got through everything else together these past two years and I promise you I'll do whatever it takes to help you get Annie well again.' Eve said wrapping her arms around Nigel. The realisation hit Felix that Max's family were her priority, exactly as they should be right now, and he liked her far too much to add to her burden by making her feel even a moment's guilt for choosing them over him. He was going to back off and give her all the space she needed for as long as it took, even if that cost them the chance to see where things might have gone between them. He'd had to walk away from Meredith in order to save himself, but he couldn't put himself first again and risk Eve losing the family she loved, because even if she could forgive him for that, he'd never be able to forgive himself.

20

The scans revealed that Annie hadn't suffered a head injury, news that made both Eve and Nigel weak with relief. She had some deep lacerations to her face, extensive bruising and swelling, as well as a broken nose and fractured jaw.

'Will they be able to make her look like she did before?' Nigel's eyes searched Eve's face as he waited for her answer and she knew she couldn't lie to him, because he'd be able to see the truth in her expression.

'They're going to realign the bones and use small metal plates to stabilise the fractures in her jaw while they are healing, which will probably remain there permanently. They'll repair the deeper laceration and, once the swelling has gone down, we should get a far clearer picture, but it will be a long time before Annie looks like herself again.'

That was as close to honest as Eve was prepared to go. She had no way of knowing just how long-lasting the impact of her injuries would be. Annie was having an open reduction and internal fixation surgery and whilst it was undoubtedly the best option for her, there was no guarantee that it would restore her face to exactly the same shape it had been before. Some patients could suffer permanent changes in appearance and if Annie got an infection after the operation that could be catastrophic to the chances of recovering her previous appearance. Nigel didn't need to hear that when he was already terrified, so Eve didn't mention any of those possibilities; reinforcing the positives instead.

'The main thing is that she's stable and there are no life-threatening concerns. All of Annie's injuries are fixable.'

'I know and I'm incredibly grateful to whoever or whatever it was that answered my prayers.' Nigel pressed his hands together, as if he was going to start praying again. 'But I know the first thing she's going to want to do when she's well enough is to see Max and you know what he's like... He's not going to hold back.'

'I know.' Eve put a hand on Nigel's shoulder. 'But let's not worry about that for now.'

'Okay.' He placed his hand on top of hers. 'Thanks, Evie. I don't know what I would have done without you. I don't know what any of us would have done without you these past couple of years.'

'I don't know what I would have done without all of you either.' When losing Annie had seemed like a possibility, and no one had known the true extent of her injuries, Eve had been every bit as terrified as Nigel. Annie was the closest thing she had to a mother and the thought of losing her had been devastating. It had brought home once more, just how much Max's family meant to her and suddenly her decision to tell Annie and Nigel about Felix didn't seem nearly so clear.

There'd been other difficult decisions to make in the wake of Annie's accident. Nigel had wanted to call Lily and let her know what had happened, but Eve's first thought had been how news like that might affect Lily's pregnancy. She was in the early stages and, even though Eve knew it was rare for shock to trigger a miscarriage, it suddenly felt like a risk they didn't need to take. In any case, the journey back to the UK in a state of heightened anxiety wouldn't be good for her or the baby. She'd figured it would be much better if they waited until they could tell Lily that her mum was going to be okay, but if she didn't tell Nigel that his daughter was pregnant, he'd never understand why Eve wanted to hold off. So she'd decided to break the news to him that Lily was expecting a baby and he'd wept like a newborn, a mixture of joy, sadness and fear all rolled into one.

'I just hope all of this isn't for nothing,' he'd said eventually, when he'd finally managed to regain some composure. 'I hope to God that this accident makes Annie realise that she can't spend any more time fighting against things she can't change and that she can find a way to enjoy all the things we have still got and look forward to all the good things that are still to come.'

'Me too.' Eve had never agreed with a sentiment more, but she had no idea if Annie's accident would be a catalyst for some kind of positive change, or if it would entrench her even further into the bitterness she'd been stuck in since Max's assault. Only time would tell.

Now, as Eve sat by Annie's bedside, having ordered Nigel to go home and get some rest, she was still waiting and watching for signs that she was coming round from the surgery and that they could all start to work towards a brighter future.

'How's she doing?' Eve jumped at the sound of Felix's voice, having not seen him come into the ward.

'She's still pretty much out of it, but the operation went well.' Eve smiled, feeling touched that he'd made the effort to come up and check on Annie.

'And how about you, how are you coping with it all?' He was asking the right things, but there was an awkwardness about him, a sort of over-the-top formality, that was so at odds with the way he'd always acted around her before. Maybe it was because he'd offered to go and speak to Max about what had happened and Nigel had insisted that it should be 'one of the family'. Felix hadn't seemed in the least bit offended, but perhaps it had been a reminder of her bond with Max's family and Eve had to admit that she might have found it hard to know how to navigate the situation if their roles had been reversed. She was probably just reading too much into something that wasn't really anything. Exhaustion and stress were triggers for that kind of thing, after all.

'I'm okay. Much better now that I know the surgery went so well. It's all been incredibly worrying.' A sudden thought entered her head. 'Oh God, I was supposed to be helping out with the food bank at Domusamare tonight, but I'm definitely not going to be able to make it, and I might have to take a break from volunteering until Annie is back on her feet. Nigel is worried about how Max might react to her injuries, so I'll probably have to do the majority of visits until she's strong enough to go, and to deal with any comments he might make about the way she looks.'

'Of course, no one would expect you to do anything other than prioritise your family at a time like this.' The oddly formal tone was still there and Felix seemed colder somehow, almost as if they were strangers. Was he regretting their relationship suddenly? He hadn't pushed her to tell Max's family about them, saying it needed to be Eve's decision. But maybe he'd never wanted her to come clean, and it had been the clandestine nature of being with her that had appealed. There'd been no expectations of any future when it was something they had to keep to themselves and maybe he'd liked it that way. What he said next did nothing to reassure her. 'I'm sure if you wanted to quit altogether, everyone would understand.'

Was that what he wanted, to sever one of the bonds that had

brought them together in the first place? She shook herself, determined not to go down a rabbit hole trying to guess what Felix was thinking. She'd be better off just asking him straight.

'I don't want to quit.' Eve glanced at Annie and then looked back towards Felix. 'Are you okay? You seem a bit strained.'

'I'm just worried about you and Max, I suppose, and how all of this might affect him.'

'Max will be okay.' Eve sighed, wishing what she was about to say wasn't true, because it was a horrible reminder of just how much the man she had adored had changed. 'If things don't affect Max personally, he's okay with pretty much anything. So as long as one of us buys the stuff he wants and takes it in to him, picks up his takeaways and makes sure he can access his streaming services, it won't stress him out all that much. As you know, sadly his empathy was one of the things he seemed to lose after the injury, so he won't be worrying about how much pain Annie is in, only how much her absence might affect him. As long as Nigel and I can minimise that, he'll be fine.'

'He's lucky to have you, they all are.' For the first time there was genuine warmth in Felix's voice and she desperately wanted him to take a step towards her, to come and hold her and tell her it was all going to be okay. But instead he took a step away.

'Okay, I'll leave you to it then, but if there's anything I can do to support Max while Annie is out of action, I'm happy to help.'

'Thank you.' Eve's voice was small and it felt as if her heart had constricted to a hundredth of its size. Felix suddenly felt like a stranger, at a time when she desperately needed someone to lean on. She should have played it safe and kept his friendship, because now she had a horrible feeling she'd lost that too and she needed a friend right now, almost more than she ever had before.

* * *

It had taken a sleepless night before the realisation had hit Eve that she was still surrounded by friends, even if she had lost Felix. Word had spread quickly about Annie's accident, and when Eve had eventually given up trying to sleep and got up at 5 a.m.; there'd been texts from Eden, Drew, Isla, Meg, Aidan, Gwen, Esther and Danni. At just after ten a huge bunch of flowers had arrived from the whole team, and Danni had called to tell her to take as much time off as she needed. Eve had been incredibly grateful for the offer, but Nigel had decided to stay off work until Annie was released from hospital. So Eve had told Danni she wanted to come in for her late shift as usual, in case Annie ended up needing more support when she went home and Eve had to take time off then instead.

She'd gone to see Max on the way into work and had explained what had happened. His first question had been whether he'd still be getting the pods for the coffee machine in his room that he'd asked Annie to order, and she'd had to fight the urge to take hold of his shoulders and shake him. She knew Max couldn't help the way he was, but he was so far removed from the kind, loving, and generous person he'd been before the assault. Now he was completely self-interested, barely seeming to register anyone else's problems, even when they were spelled out to him, much in the way that a narcissist might react. All that mattered to Max was whether it would affect what that person usually did for him. It was almost as if his frontal lobe had never developed at all, rather than having been catastrophically damaged during the assault.

Eve had always known that the brain was an incredibly complex and fragile structure, her awareness of that having been heightened during her medical training, but nothing had brought that home as powerfully as Max's injuries. Other residents of Oakwood Park who had suffered similar levels of brain damage had been affected in vastly different ways to Max, when it came to changes in their personalities, and amongst them were some of the kindest and sweetest souls Eve had ever met. That included Tasha, who presented Eve with a beautiful blanket she'd crocheted, almost every time Eve saw her. Tasha made the blankets for the babies delivered at St Piran's who would never make it home and Eve knew just how much that small gesture had meant to some of the bereaved parents. Of course there were other residents who displayed far less positive behaviours and, deep down, Eve knew that Max's behaviour only seemed extreme to her because she'd known and loved the old version of him with all of her heart. This new version wasn't anywhere near as easy to love, especially when she was still grieving so hard for *her* Max, the way he used to be.

After reassuring him that she'd bought in the coffee pods he'd asked for, she hadn't stayed long and had arrived at work forty-five minutes before the start of her shift.

'Good, we've got time to go for a coffee before we start,' Meg had said, having also been at work early, almost as if she was lying in wait for Eve to arrive. They'd gone to the Friends of St Piran's Shop and almost as soon as Eve had sat down at one of the tables outside it, Gwen had bought over a huge piece of coffee and walnut cake.

'I made it especially for you,' she announced, setting it down on the table. 'I guessed you wouldn't have got much sleep last night and I also had a bet with myself that you'd turn up for your shift as usual, so I got up early and whipped it up before work. I figured you could use the caffeine to help you make it through until hometime.'

'Will you be my mum?' Eve had meant it as a joke, but the words suddenly caught in her throat and a sob escaped before she could stop it.

'Hey, hey, hey.' Gwen moved to sit in the chair next to Eve, opposite where Meg was already sitting, and wrapped an arm around her shoulders. 'Is this about the car accident or something else?'

'It's everything.' Eve was still trying not to cry, but she didn't seem able to stop.

'Oh, Eve, you shouldn't be here. This is all too much, I'll give Danni a call and get her to arrange some cover.' Meg was already pulling the phone out of her pocket when Eve surprised herself by shouting.

'No!' She shook her head, in case the word needed even more emphasis. 'I don't want to be at home on my own, thinking about all of this. I already feel like I'm suffocating and the last thing I need is to be indoors, alone, feeling like the four walls are closing in on me too.'

'Do you want to talk about it?' Gwen still had an arm around her shoulders as she spoke and it felt comforting rather than weird.

'I'm just tired, that's all.' Eve tried to smile but it went all wobbly. 'You don't want to listen to my problems. Even if I had a mum, she'd probably be fed up with hearing about them by now.'

'I'm more than happy to be a stand-in mum for you, but I also make a great agony aunt, and all advice comes with an extra slice of cake.'

'Gwen's advice is legendary, and her cake is officially better than sex.' Meg gave Eve a meaningful look, and Gwen's eyes widened in surprise.

'I do make great coffee cake, but Meg, my love, you're doing sex all wrong if that's your conclusion. I could always start with some advice on how to change that, if Eve doesn't want to talk about what's on her mind.'

Gwen looked over the top of her glasses and Eve found

herself smiling at their attempts to cheer her up, as Meg clasped her hand.

'Please, Eve, save me from another sex talk. I'm still not over the one my mum gave me when I was ten and I realised that she and my dad had done *that* at least twice!'

'You're opening up a whole can of worms there, my girl.' Gwen shook her head and Meg squeezed Eve's hand even tighter.

'Eve, you're my friend. Save me, please!'

'Okay.' Eve's smiled deepened, her heart already feeling much lighter than it had before, and Meg sighed with relief.

'Thank you!'

'So, come on then, lovely girl. What's going on?' Gwen waited for a beat, but when Eve didn't respond she continued. 'You don't have to tell us anything you don't want to, but I'd bet my last pound on you feeling better about whatever's worrying you, once you've shared it with someone.'

'Maybe you're right, even if you can't do anything to change it.' Eve squared her shoulders and took a deep breath. It had helped when she'd told Felix about how difficult things had got for Lily before she left. Maybe this would help as well and she had nothing to lose by confiding in Gwen and Meg. 'As you know I've been seeing Felix and things got quite serious, or at least I thought they did.'

'You can't possibly doubt how much he likes you?' Meg furrowed her brow. 'The way he looks at you, no one could miss it.'

'I thought he did at first, but I think it was more the thrill of the chase. When we started to get close, I told him nothing could happen because of Max, but after San Francisco...' Heat flooded her face at the memory of how certain she'd been that things were going to change, because of the way *she* felt about Felix – the way she'd thought they felt about one another – but she'd clearly been wrong. 'I realised that all the advice you guys gave me was right and that I couldn't live like this any more – going along with Annie's fantasy that one day Max would be back to his old self and we could carry on with all the plans we made before he got hurt. I didn't realise how suffocated and trapped I felt by all of that until Felix came along. I still love Max, but not in the way I used to, and I love his family as well, but Felix made me realise I want more than that. I want the chance to be able to create a family of my own one day, but I don't think Felix was ever on the same page. He's gone cold on me, and now I don't know if I can tell Annie and Nigel the truth and risk losing them too.'

'This isn't about Felix.' Gwen's tone was firm. 'Whatever he is or isn't thinking, or does or doesn't want, he's allowed you to be honest with yourself about what *you* want.'

'Gwen's right,' Meg said, earning her an *'of course I am'* kind of look from the older woman, before she continued. 'Forget about Felix, it's his loss if he can't see how amazing you are, although I still think you're wrong about that. Either way he's made you realise you can't put your life on hold forever because of what happened to Max.'

'I've just spent so long being scared of being on my own again. I know it was wrong of me to cling to Annie and Nigel because of it, but it wasn't until I met Felix that I started to believe there really could be another life out there for me, if I had the courage to go for it. I want to move on and I feel like I've made a life for myself here, at the hospital, that goes beyond Max's family and even Felix, but what if I've read that wrong? Where would that leave me?'

'Of course you haven't read that wrong, everyone at the hospital thinks you're bloody amazing.' Eve had never seen Meg so resolute, and Gwen was nodding along enthusiastically.

'I think I might have got myself an apprentice.' Gwen grinned for a moment, but then her expression grew more serious. 'Any change can be scary and I know putting yourself out there to make connections with new people probably felt like a huge risk, but you can't go through life afraid to take risks. Maybe Felix was only meant to be the catalyst for change, but like you said, look at all the other relationships you've built since starting at St Piran's. There's a whole world out there, Eve, and you need to grab it by the short and curlies. Otherwise, one day, you'll turn around and find yourself in your eighties, wondering what could have been and there's no way me or Meg, or any of your friends are going to let that happen.'

Gwen held her gaze for a moment and Eve found herself nodding slowly, the other woman's words echoing what Lily had already said about finding the courage to make a new start. Her friends were right about Felix, though. This wasn't about him, not really. This was about the chance for life to begin again, a new kind of life. That didn't mean it couldn't include Max and his family, and she really wanted it to, but it did mean the roles they all played would have to be different. She was going to make a fresh start, whatever the cost of that might be. Even though there was a part of her heart still aching because that wouldn't necessarily include Felix, she knew she'd survive. After all, she'd already survived far worse.

21

Annie had been released from hospital and was recovering at home. She was going to be on a diet of liquid and soft foods for the next six to eight weeks, which Eve knew was going to be pretty miserable. She'd put together a big box of all the things she could think of that might make that more bearable including milkshakes, smoothies, Madagascan vanilla custard and even some sweet potato soup that Eve had made from scratch. Annie would gradually be able to build up to a wider diet, but the important thing was to take it slow. She couldn't afford to lose more weight, the last two years having already taken their toll on her appetite and her ability to prioritise her own needs. Eve wanted to do all she could to help out, and she was still visiting Max every day, so that Annie could get some proper rest. One of the few positives was that Annie seemed to be focusing on her recovery, so that she could get back to seeing Max as quickly as possible, rather than dwelling on the fact that Brandon Moorcroft's sentence had been upheld.

Max hadn't asked after his mother when Eve had dropped in, but that hadn't been a surprise. The visit had been good nonetheless, because for once Max had seemed far more engaged in talking to her; as long as it focused on his new favourite subject – getting a dog.

'Did you know that dogs have a third eyelid?' He'd looked up at her as she came into the room, after going to make them both some toast in the communal kitchen at the end of the corridor. She was supposed to encourage Max to do more of that sort of thing himself, but the truth was she still liked finding small ways to make him happy, and one of his greatest pleasures in life was peanut butter on toast. Although woe betide anyone who used crunchy peanut butter, it absolutely had to be smooth. He'd once thrown a plate out of the window – toast and all – when one of the staff members had tried to insist that using crunchy peanut butter made no difference and had refused to make it again with the smooth variety. Eve knew that trying to have a debate with Max was pointless. These days, once his mind was made up, it was made up forever. Being able to do the little things, like making him a plate of toast, allowed her to feel that she was still showing Max she loved him, even if the shape of that love had changed. He was never going to be the person she'd imagined building a life with, but she still cared about him and wanted him to be happy.

'No, I had no idea that dogs had three eyelids.' It made Eve smile to see the look of excitement on his face. 'What do they need a third eyelid for?'

'It helps keep their eyes moist and protects them. They also have a nose print that's as unique as our fingerprints, so even if you had a whole bunch of dogs you'd never have to guess which one had left a dirty mark on the window from pressing its face up against the glass. It would be as plain as the nose on its face.' Max laughed and it made Eve laugh, too, but he was nowhere near finished with his new favourite subject. 'I still can't decide what sort of dog I want, but there's a breed they have in Norway that has six toes on each paw. That would take some beating.'

'It would. So is that the big goal then, to get a dog?' Max had talked about it a lot over the past few months, but this past couple of weeks his interest in dogs had become his main focus, and he was spending far more time researching different breeds online than he was gaming, which Eve thought had to be a good thing.

'I always wanted one but Mum's allergic.' He rolled his eyes. 'Sounds like an even better reason to get one, once I get out of here. Then she might give me a bit more peace, instead of visiting every bloody day.'

'I can see why you might want a bit more space and time to yourself.' The revelation hit Eve like a thunderbolt and she felt ridiculous for never having thought about it that way before. Max might have a head injury, but he was still a grown man with the right to make his own choices and live the life he wanted. None of them had ever asked him if he wanted a visit every day, they'd just assumed he had. Maybe the reason he sometimes lashed out and could be rude and disengaged wasn't all down to the impact of his personality changing, maybe he was just sick of the sight of them. No one had ever sought his opinion, they'd all just assumed they knew best. It was time for that to change.

'Let's have this toast and you can tell me which dogs are at the top of your shortlist, then I'll get out of your hair and let you get on.' Eve settled back as Max launched into a comparison of the pros and cons of Labradors over spaniels, a renewed determination settling upon her. They all needed to start talking and being honest about what they wanted, and she was going to begin the process by telling Nigel the truth about what had gone on with Felix. Not at some arbitrary point in the future, but as soon as she saw him, later that day. She just had to hope that the shape of the love between her and Max's family could also adapt and re-form.

Either way the change was coming, and it wasn't a moment too soon.

* * *

Annie was asleep when Eve got to the house and Nigel ushered her inside. April showers had continued into May and she'd got soaked on the short dash from the car to the front door.

'Oh, sweetheart, you're wet through.' Nigel sighed. 'You'll catch your death like that, there are some of Annie's things in the wardrobe in the spare room. I'm sure you'll find something in there.'

'I'll dry off in a bit, I don't want to take anything that Annie might need.'

'Nonsense, that woman has enough clothes to open a department store. And I can't be worrying about another one of my girls, when the other two are already giving me sleepless nights. I just hope Lily's not having as hard a time with her pregnancy as her mum did with her, poor old Annie was sick almost every day.'

'Lily seems to be doing brilliantly and she's got a date for her first scan. She told me when she's had it done, she's going to tell you and Annie the news. Just remember you've got to act surprised!'

'I will, but I might have to get practising.' Nigel smiled. 'It's bad enough reading through every message I send trying to make sure I don't give the game away about what I know. I've just been sending her the usual photos I take when I'm out walking, to help remind her of all the great things about Cornwall, so she might get a bit homesick and want to come home for a visit. I know that's terrible, but I can't help it, I miss her so much.'

'She misses you, too, all of you, and I think she'll want to bring the baby over here for a visit when she can, especially if you guys can't make it over there.' Eve shivered, but it was only partly because of the damp that seemed to have seeped into her bones. She just hoped she'd still be included in any family get-togethers that might happen once she'd told Nigel what she needed to say.

'Will you go upstairs and get changed for goodness' sake.' His chiding was gentle, just the sort of fatherly show of affection she'd always longed for and had eventually found in Max's dad rather than her own. 'You're making me cold just looking at you.'

'I need to tell you something first.' She locked eyes with him and his face fell.

'It's not Max, is it?'

'No... well, yes, in a way I suppose it is.' She looked at the floor for a moment, needing to get this out all in one go and not wanting to see anything in his expression that made her hesitate or doubt her decision. 'I love Max and I always will, but there's never going to be a me and Max in the way there used to be. He's changed so much and he doesn't want that, but the truth is, neither do I. I still want to be a part of his life and his family, but I can't be his fiancée any more and I think we need to let him dictate how much involvement he wants me or any of us to have in his life. It must feel like all his free will was taken away after the assault and, to be honest, it has felt like mine was too.'

'Eve, you don't need to—'

She cut off his response, desperate now to get everything off her chest. 'I'm sorry, Nigel, but please can you just let me finish what I need to say and then we can talk about it? Because if I don't do it now, I might never do it and I don't think I can carry on like this.'

'Sorry, yes, of course, go on.' She still didn't look at him, instead focusing on a family photograph in pride of place on the wall of the hallway. It had been taken three Christmases ago, when Max had still been Max and she'd been by his side, at the centre of his lovely family.

'I need to allow myself a fresh start, a new life that still has Max in it, but just in a very different way. I met someone I really liked, I thought... *hoped* it would be something serious and I finally found the courage to admit to myself that I wanted that again, to love someone and be loved in the way that I used to have with Max. It hasn't worked out, but it's opened my eyes to what I really want, the chance to start over. I know it won't upset Max, he doesn't see me the way he used to, and I think he'll be relieved not to have that pressure on him. What scares me is the thought of losing the rest of you. This family has been the only family I've really known since Mum died and you mean the world to me, you really do. I know if I'm no longer Max's fiancée then I'll never really be family, but I hope that doesn't mean—'

'Sorry, but no. I can't even listen to this.' It was Nigel's turn to interrupt and his tone was sharp, her stomach sinking like a stone as she finally looked up at him and saw the expression that had clouded his face. 'I have never heard anything so ludicrous in my life and I can't believe you'd think for one moment that we'd ever want to turn our backs on you.'

It took a moment for Eve to process his words and relief flooded through her body as he held out his arms, pulling her towards him, not seeming to care a bit that she still resembled a wet dog. 'Of course you're family and you always will be. You've done more for us than we could have expected of anyone, even if you had been our daughter. I know it was you who saved Lily when she was at a point where she didn't know which way to turn, and it was you who was there for Annie when she hit her lowest point and I had to work. I can't believe you even have to question that and, if it was an option, I'd bloody well adopt you now if I could. Whatever it takes to make you realise you're a part of this family for good, I'll do it. And I'm pleased as punch that you met someone who helped you see you needed to have a life of your own, even though Felix must be a complete idiot not to want to hang onto you until his dying day.'

Shock that Nigel had picked up on the situation already, rooted Eve to the spot and as the tears streamed down her face and burned in her throat, she couldn't seem to find her voice. She wasn't sure she'd ever felt as unconditionally loved as she did in that moment, but there were so many emotions racing through her head and she was struggling to process them all. The utter joy that Nigel had reacted this way, the fear of what Annie might think still lingering, and the sadness of all that she'd lost with Max and now with Felix. But when she finally managed to speak, there was one thing she had to find out.

'How did you know I was talking about Felix?'

'Because anyone with eyes could see it and I find it impossible to believe that the way he acted around you wasn't real. The only time I've ever looked at a woman the way Felix looks at you, is when I'm with Annie, and I'd walk through fire for that woman. God knows over the last couple of years it feels like I have.'

'Oh, Nigel, I know how hard it's been for you, but you're amazing. The rock that holds the whole family together.' Eve couldn't think about Felix right now, or what Nigel had said about him. It was too much for her. Maybe he'd only ever been meant to be the catalyst for change, just as Gwen has said, but she couldn't focus on the prospect of him not being a part of her life any more. Her sadness about that would just muddy the waters, when right now she'd to keep going with what she had started; finding a way for life to begin again, without losing everything she valued about her old life. 'How do you think Annie's going to take it, me moving on?'

'It'll be an adjustment, but she'll get there, I promise.' Nigel pulled back from her slightly. 'I don't want you to worry about that, because when she's feeling better, I'm going to be giving Annie a few home truths of her own to think about. She can't destroy the rest of her life focusing on hating Brandon Moorcroft and losing out on a relationship with you, or Lily and our grand-child, because her bitterness is stopping her from seeing the good that's still all around her. I read that article you sent me about the restorative justice and I want to see if we can go ahead with it, whether Annie wants to be a part of it or not. We all need to find a way to move on and be as happy as we can be. You're right about Max, too, he needs to have a say in what that looks like for him.'

'You're the best dad he could ever have asked for, you know that, don't you?' She managed to smile through her tears and he nodded, a broad grin suddenly lighting up his face.

'Yeah, I know, I'm absolutely awesome.' He laughed. 'Just don't forget it, because I'm also the best bloody dad *you* could have asked for, and I'm not going anywhere. You're never getting rid of me.'

'Thank you.' It was all she could manage as a fresh crop of tears filled her eyes and she buried her head against his chest again. The first step to making a change had gone far better than she could ever have hoped, but she knew the road ahead might still get very bumpy. Whatever happened, there was no turning back now. Her new life was about to begin and nothing would ever quite be the same again.

22

Eve and Nigel had decided to wait until Annie was further along in her recovery before Eve had the conversation with her about the need to begin moving on. It wasn't a delay tactic this time, it was just a way of protecting Annie while she was still unwell, in much the same way as they'd decided to protect Lily from the news of her mum's accident during the early weeks of her pregnancy. When Annie had insisted on going back to her favourite restaurant, Bocca Felice, for her birthday, just two weeks after the accident, Eve's heart had sunk. It was the family's 'special place' according to Annie and it had been, once upon a time. Now, going back to the place where Max had proposed, just felt like another attempt to play act that everything was fine. She knew it was because Annie loved Max, but in truth her failure to accept him as he now was, and adapt to that, was misguided at best and cruel at worst. Despite his seemingly thick skin, there was still a risk that Max would always feel less-than, and it was time to celebrate the things that made him who he was now.

They all needed to learn to laugh at the dry one-liners he could deliver like a stand-up comedian, instead of cringing and think how the old Max would never have said most of those things. Yes, his comments these days were sometimes near-the-knuckle and inappropriate, and often directed at the expense of a family member, but if they didn't laugh they'd spend the rest of their lives crying and that wasn't good for Max or for them. His idea of a good night out also looked very different now. There was an American-style diner in Port Tremellien that played loud country music and had virtual reality games, which no one could beat Max at. Eve had taken him there, three days after telling Nigel about what had happened with Felix.

'You're doing it all wrong.' Max had rolled his eyes, as she tried again to get a score on the board with the virtual reality axe throwing, but he'd been laughing as well. He wasn't frustrated or impatient, he just found her lack of skill amusing and they'd had more fun together than they'd had since before the assault.

'Can we do that again?' he asked at the end of the night and it had taken her by surprise. It had been the first time he'd made a direct request to do something with her in as long as she could remember, and for a moment panic had gripped her that finally drawing a line under what they'd been to one another might hurt him.

'Of course we can.' She'd forced a smile and then decided she couldn't just leave it there. She had to know how Max felt. 'Do you love me?'

'You're all right.' His tone had been so deadpan it had made her laugh.

'Thanks. You know I love you, don't you?'

'Yeah, but I'm great.' He'd shrugged and she'd laughed again.

'You are.' She hadn't been sure how to word her next question, or even whether she should. If it confused Max or upset him, everything could come out in a way they hadn't planned for and Annie would discover the truth before she was well enough to hear it. Eve had to get this straight in her head, though, and she had to know that Max was going to be okay with this. 'Do you remember when we got engaged?'

'Yeah.' His expression had given nothing away.

'We were going to get married. It should have happened three weeks after you got injured. That would have been almost two years ago now.' She'd bitten her lip, knowing there'd be no going back when she asked the next question. 'Do you wish we could still get married?'

'No!' He'd looked at her as if she'd suggested he might want to eat his dinner off the pavement, the lip curl giving away his feelings even if the words hadn't made them abundantly clear. 'I don't ever want to get married. I just want to be able to play my games in peace and not have to sit on the sofa and talk to someone else when I don't want to. And I want a dog. That's it.'

'Fair enough. That sounds like a good plan to me.' She'd squeezed his hand then, relief flooding through her body. It hadn't even crossed his mind to ask her what she wanted and she'd been glad about that, because she wasn't ready to admit to herself yet just how much she did want that – a married life, her own family, even the simple mundane bits that clearly sounded boring as hell to Max. She had no way of knowing if any of that would happen for her, if she'd ever find someone who didn't feel like second best after what she'd planned for with Max, but she knew now that it was at least possible. She'd thought it might be Felix, but he'd backed off completely the last two weeks, only really keeping in touch with 'How are you?' texts, the way he might do with any colleague. She might never find someone else, but knowing she had the freedom to open herself up to the possibility had been like a huge weight lifting. Now there was just one last hurdle to cross, and it came in the shape of Annie.

'Is there anything on the menu you can actually eat?' Nigel

looked on anxiously as he waited for his wife to order. Both he and Eve had tried to persuade her to celebrate her birthday some other way, but Annie had dug her heels in.

'I'm going to ask for the soup as a main course. Hot and sour chicken soup sounds delicious.'

'Better ask for a bib, you'll probably dribble most of it down your top.' Max made it sound like a statement of fact rather than a joke, but when Eve caught Nigel's eye, she couldn't suppress a smile. They'd both realised they had to lean into this, but Annie was nowhere near ready yet.

'Max! That's so rude, you know I can't eat properly yet and it's my birthday. You're supposed to be nice to me.'

'I wasn't being rude. I was giving you some useful advice, based on the way you dribbled that milkshake down your top the other day.'

'What are you going to order, Max?' Nigel cut across the conversation before Annie could respond again, but she seemed to be radiating tension and Eve just hoped they'd be able to get through the meal without Annie bursting into tears. No one should feel like they want to cry on their birthday.

'I'm getting the fillet steak and chips, but I'm going to ask for an extra portion of chips too. I'm absolutely starving,' Max announced and thankfully it proved to be the opener of a conversation about what he'd been up to that day, which provided a distraction from the tension in the air. He'd gone up another couple of levels on the PlayStation game that was his current favourite, and been out for another surfing lesson with Waves 4 Everyone, which he'd decided was the cause of his increased appetite. The tension had lifted slightly and by the time the main course arrived, Eve was almost enjoying herself. She might have been able to embrace the evening fully if she didn't feel like such a fraud for having slipped on her engagement ring two minutes before she left home. If she hadn't been wearing it, without the excuse of having come straight from work, Annie would want to know why and tonight definitely wasn't the time to have that conversation. Especially if they wanted to avoid tears on Annie's birthday.

* * *

'That was good.' Max said, pushing his plate away from him when he finished the last of his chips, before letting out a loud burp that seem to reverberate around the restaurant.

'Max, for God's sake! That's disgusting.' Annie dropped her spoon into her bowl and Eve had to admit her own half-finished plate of food suddenly felt far less appetising.

'Why? Jamie says it's a sign of respect for the chef in a lot of countries. And when we get our own place we're going to do it at the end of every meal if we want to.' Max shrugged. He'd taken a real shine to Jamie, another resident at Oakwood Park, who had been a chef in a pub before sustaining a head injury in a motor-bike accident that had left him unable to work. The current plan was for Max and Jamie to move into one of the semi-independent living bungalows together.

'Well, it's not acceptable here, or any place where I am.' Annie's voice was low but steely. 'That was not the way you were brought up and it's a repulsive thing to do while other people are still eating their food right next to you. Everyone else in this whole restaurant is looking at us.'

'Oh, chill out, you're supposed to be resting your jaw, not flapping your lips.' Max mimed the sound of a beak opening and closing with his hand. 'I never asked to come here anyway. No one cares if I burp at Oakwood Park, you need to take the pole out of your arse.'

'That's enough now,' Nigel interjected for a second time, but there was no hint of amusement on his face this time. He looked almost close to tears himself and Eve knew why. It wasn't so much Max's behaviour, even though Annie was right, he'd never have acted like that before, and if she was honest she found sitting next to someone who belched while she was still eating every bit as repulsive as his mother did. It was just another sign that trying to shoehorn Max into the outline of the person he used to be was a recipe guaranteed to make them all unhappy. If Annie wanted to have fun with Max on her birthday, she needed to focus on the things that he found fun, like the virtual reality games at the American diner where, with the overly loud music and food served 'chips in a basket style', no one would notice if Max didn't observe polite etiquette while he was eating. Annie wouldn't have to worry about people looking at them and judging them, they could just have a laugh together. It might not be Annie's idea of the perfect night out, but it was far easier for her to adapt to his behaviour than it was for Max to adapt to her expectations. He could try and learn some of those things, but it would never come easily to him and his impulse control had also been severely affected, which was one of the reasons why he'd probably never live completely independently. It turned out that was something else Annie hadn't accepted.

'I think we need to look at moving him away from Oakwood Park.' Annie's voice was shaking as she looked directly at Nigel, the rage that was thrumming just below the surface making it look as if her whole body was pulsating. 'He's not making any progress, he's going backwards if anything and at this rate he's never going to be able to leave there and get his own place again.'

'Let's not make this into a big—'

Max cut off his father's response, before he could finish. 'I don't want to leave Oakwood Park. I just want to get a place in one of the bungalows, because Bev said me and Jamie can get a dog if we live there together.'

Bev was the deputy manager who oversaw Max's care plan and she definitely wouldn't have made that kind of promise unless it was a real possibility. His eyes were shining, in much the way they had been when Eve had taken him out to the diner, but Annie was already shaking her head.

'No, no, no. You are absolutely not making that your end goal, Maximus Pascoe. You've got a fiancée here and you owe it to her to keep trying to make the progress you need to make to get back to the person you used to be.'

'No, he doesn't.' The words were out of Eve's mouth before she could stop them. It had never been the plan for all this to come out tonight and she wished it hadn't happened on Annie's birthday, because she knew it was going to hurt her, but suddenly it seemed like the perfect time to say what needed to be said. 'The only person Max owes anything to is himself, and what he owes himself is the right to be as happy as he can possibly be. I think that's what he'll find in one of the bungalows at Oakwood Park, with Jamie, and their gaming and their dog, with support on hand for the bits they need it for. Max and I had so many wonderful years together and nothing will ever change that. I'll always love him, but we can't keep pretending that it's going to go back to how it was. I just want to find a way of being in Max's life that adds to his happiness, not detracts from it because I make him feel as though he needs to be different from how he is now.'

Annie was just staring straight ahead, almost as if she hadn't heard the words and Nigel took his wife's hand.

'You know she's right, sweetheart. We all wanted Max to make a complete recovery, but we've got to acknowledge that it's never going to happen. Now, all I want is for him to be happy, and for you to be okay with whatever that happiness looks like.'

'I just don't know if I can be.' Annie turned to look at her husband and before he could even answer she burst into noisy sobs that made everyone else in the restaurant turn to look at them for a second time.

* * *

Felix was spending more of his spare time than ever volunteering at Domusamare, but that didn't stop him missing Eve. In a way it made it worse, because working for the charity had broken down barriers between them. He woke up thinking about her every morning, and she was still on his mind when he went to bed at night. He wondered how she was and he wanted to talk to her about things that had happened during his day. He'd picked up the phone more than once to call her, to talk about the fact that Sophie had finally made contact with her dad, and the tentative steps she'd been taking to get to know him and the rest of his family. It had lifted his spirits to see Sophie have new hope, and he knew the only other person at Domusamare who'd feel quite the same way about it was Eve, but he couldn't reach out to her. Every day he questioned whether he'd done the right by thing pulling away from her. But right now Annie and Nigel needed Eve. It was just that Felix wanted her, too, more than he ever would have believed.

The weird thing was that he also missed Max. Wanting to avoid the chance of bumping into Eve as much as possible, he'd asked one of his colleagues to swap with him to take over the final OT sessions that were helping to prepare Max for semi-independence. He'd also asked Nathan to take over arranging the Waves 4 Everyone sessions with Max, unsure if he could look the other man in the eye, given how he felt about the woman Max had once proposed to. He missed Max's dry sense of humour and the determination he showed when they were working on something he considered worthwhile, as well as the honesty he displayed when they were working on something he considered a waste of time. There was no hidden agenda with Max. Felix knew exactly where he stood and exactly what the other man thought of him, which was refreshing.

'Flora came back again.' Tilly who worked full time at Domusamare frowned as she imparted the information that made Felix's heart even heavier.

'She must think Duncan is still here somewhere. Did you take her back to the foster family?' Flora was a scruffy little border terrier with crooked bottom teeth and eyebrows that wouldn't have looked out of place in an *Angry Birds* cartoon. She was also gentle, incredibly affectionate and desperately sad in the wake of the death of her former owner. Duncan had been homeless and a regular client of the services Domusamare offered, often spending overnight stays in the hostel. After his death, Flora had been housed with a foster family, while a local dog rescue charity tried to find her a new forever home, but she was a bit of a Houdini and kept escaping back to Domusamare, looking for Duncan.

'Yes, Mitch from Dogs R4 Life came to pick her up, but he said they're getting increasingly worried about finding somewhere that will work for her long term, if an experienced foster family can't even keep her safe. So Flora might have to stay in the kennels at the charity for the rest of her life.' Tilly shook her head. 'It'll be like being in prison for her, she was so used to having freedom with Duncan. According to Mitch, the other problem is that they'd need to find somewhere her new owner will be home all day, and with no other dogs, because she's used to being the only one. On top of that he said the person taking her would need enough energy to take her for long walks, and that she's most likely to settle with a male owner. All of that narrows down the options even more.'

'There must be someone out there who could take on a dog like that. If I won the lottery and didn't need to work, I'd take her myself.' Felix managed a wry smile, which Tilly mirrored for a moment, but then she looked downcast again.

'Not that many lottery winners in the Three Ports area who want to take on a dog with a face only a mother could love, though, are there?'

'There must be a least one. I'll put an appeal up on all our social media pages and link it to the Dogs R4 Life website. We'll find Flora a lovely new home, I promise.' Felix was already moving towards the office, hoping that his promise to Tilly hadn't been a rash one, but he firmly believed there was someone for everyone, even when it came to matching up a dog with its new owner.

It only took him about ten minutes to write and post the appeal. He'd been just about to go and find Tilly, to tell her that the post was live, when the first comment appeared below it.

I think I might know someone who would be perfect for Tilly. What's the best way to discuss it further?

The message was from Eve meaning he finally had a reason to call her. Seeing her name was a mixture of shock and something else he couldn't have put a name to in that moment. Felix could have called her any time, but the only reason he'd have had, up until now, would have been to tell her how he felt; that the last two weeks of not seeing her had seemed like the longest of his life. Even now, all the feelings he had for Eve, which he'd been trying so hard to ignore, seemed to be flooding to the surface.

When he'd witnessed her devotion to Max's family after

Annie's accident, he'd felt certain she wasn't ready to step back enough to allow Felix to become a part of her life. It wasn't that he'd wanted her to choose between him and Max's family, he'd just needed to know there'd be room for him, and the last thing he'd wanted was to force her hand. Instead, he'd made assumptions about what her love for them meant for him and Eve. If he was honest with himself, he'd been scared of getting hurt again; his feelings for Eve already much bigger than he'd expected them to be. Stepping back had been about giving her space, but it had also been about self-preservation, or at least he'd thought so. He'd told himself it could save him from getting hurt, or his feelings for her from getting even bigger, but he'd been wrong. All he'd managed to do was to stuff those feelings down and try to convince himself that it was best for both of them. Now he had a decision to make about whether to risk getting hurt, or keep trying to convince himself that walking away was for the best. Opening his contacts, he scrolled down to her number and pressed call, still with absolutely no idea what he was going to say.

23

The day after her birthday, Annie had messaged Eve asking if they could meet up for coffee.

'I'm sorry.' It was the first thing Annie had said, before Eve could even say hello, and she'd gone on to apologise for leaning so heavily on her, and for pinning all her hopes of Max making a full recovery on his relationship with Eve. Annie had told her that she'd stayed up half the night talking to Nigel about everything and then they'd FaceTimed Lily, who'd told them about the baby.

'I know you already knew and I also know you were the one who helped Lily realise she had to get away from here.'

'I'm so sorry, I just—' It had been Eve's turn to apologise, but Annie had cut her off.

'Oh, darling girl, I'm not cross. I'm just so thankful you did it and that Lily felt she had someone to turn to, who could help her get out of a situation that was driving her to the edge. If it hadn't been for you I might have lost her too.'

'I know it feels like you've lost Max, but you haven't, not really. There's still joy in his life and if you can find ways to share in that, what happened on the night of his accident will feel a lot less like a tragedy and a lot more like a miracle that we didn't lose him completely.'

'I know.' Annie had nodded, her expression tight. 'I think it's always going to hurt that he'll never be the Max we used to have, but I'm so grateful he's still here and I've got to find ways to show him that. I also need to find something positive out of this, so that all we've been through hasn't been for nothing. Nigel spoke to me about the restorative justice thing again and I'm still not sure if I'm ready for that, but I wanted to start by putting some of my energies into fundraising for Oakwood Park, instead of spending all my spare time with Max and cramping his style. I think we'll get on much better if I learn to give him a bit of space.'

'I think you're right and it will do you the world of good, as well.'

'In that vein, I've decided when Max and Jamie move into the bungalow, that I'm going to take a little holiday. To San Francisco, to see Lily.'

'That's brilliant news!' Eve hadn't been able to stop herself from crossing the space between them and giving Annie a big hug.

'There's one more thing I wanted to talk to you about,' Annie had said, when they eventually broke apart. 'The ring that Max gave you when he proposed was my great-grandmother's and—'

It had been Eve's turn to cut her off. 'Of course, you must have it back, it needs to stay in the family.'

'It already is in the family.' Annie had put her hand over Eve's. 'You, my darling girl, are family and always will be. I knew it the moment we met you, but you've proved it over and over again these past two years. All I was going to say, was that Nigel and I would like to get the stones in the ring reset for you, so that it looks less like an engagement ring and it can be resized to wear on another finger, or on your other hand. I know it's just a silly symbol, but it would mean the world to us if you could accept it.'

'Oh, Annie.' Eve had flung her arms around the other woman again and they'd both cried for what felt like the hundredth time in the last twenty-four hours. It had been after she'd got home from coffee with Annie that Eve had seen the advert on the Domusamare Facebook page, searching for a new home for Flora, the little border terrier she'd seen come in with her owner Duncan several times. The kind of home she was searching for sounded like it might be the right fit for Max and Jamie. When her phone had started to ring within five minutes of her responding to the advert and Felix's number had flashed up, she'd realised it had been him who'd posted the appeal and she'd let the call go to voicemail.

There'd been far too much high emotion over the past couple of days and she hadn't been ready to talk to him. Instead, she'd texted back, a formal-sounding message, asking if he'd be willing to arrange for Dogs R4 Life to bring Flora to Oakwood Park, so that they could decide whether Max and Jamie might be a good fit for her. He'd replied after half an hour to say that the charity had asked him if he could act as a go-between, for an initial meet and discussion, because they were currently overstretched due to staff sickness. Now she was heading across the grounds to the bungalow that Max and Jamie were due to move into next week, so that she could be there when Felix brought the dog in. She probably couldn't have justified it if someone had asked her why she was there, but she'd told Bev she was coming in, and was committed to it now. It was too late to worry about how she was going to react to seeing Felix again, when she'd opened her heart to him and he'd turned out not to be the man she thought he was at all.

* * *

Felix hadn't expected Eve to be at the bungalow when he took Flora in to meet with Max and Jamie, and he'd found it hard to even look in her direction, as Bev, the deputy manager of Oakwood Park, did a round of introductions.

'Of course you know Max well, don't you, Felix? And I'm guessing you've met Eve a few times during your visits?' Bev's sing-song voice was like nails down a chalkboard. This didn't feel like an 'all friends together' moment. He wished he could have been cooler about it and gone back to being Eve's friend, but he liked her far too much for that and he was worried, that if he looked in her direction, he'd have no chance of maintaining the casual air he was determined to have around her.

'Yes and we both work at the hospital.' Even his words sounded stilted, but Bev didn't seem to notice.

'Of course you do, well, that's great.' Bev still didn't seem to have picked up on the tension in the room. 'And what about Jamie? Have you guys met before?'

'Yes, you joined us for one of Max's OT sessions in the kitchen, didn't you, Jamie?' Felix smiled in his direction.

'Yeah and Max nearly set the kitchen on fire when he forgot about his bacon.' Jamie had the sort of belly laugh that couldn't fail to make you smile, although on this occasion it earned him a sharp jab in the ribs from Max.

'Shut up, we're supposed to be persuading him to give us the dog.'

'You can rest assured we'll be keeping a close eye on safety and making sure Flora gets the care she needs.' Bev gave Felix an earnest look. 'We've had dogs and other pets in our semi-inde-pendent housing facilities before and we've never had any issues. Sometimes our residents have moved in with pets they owned before they sustained a head injury, but we've also done it this way around. Pets are so good for promoting the wellbeing of our residents, but we'd never do anything to compromise their safety and happiness.'

'I know you wouldn't.' Felix gave her what he hoped was a reassuring smile. His contact at Dogs R4 Life had told him about previous rehoming success stories involving Oakwood Park, and he'd been briefed just to introduce the dog to Max and Jamie and then leave them to have some time alone, which would be monitored by Bev. If everyone was happy, Flora would spend a few half days with Max and Jamie, followed by some overnight stays, before both Oakwood Park and Dogs R4 Life could formalise the adoption. 'Shall we see what Flora thinks of it here?'

Felix set the little dog down on the sofa and without Max even calling out to her she climbed onto his lap, burrowing her head into his armpit, her tail wagging from side to side like a metronome, making both him and Felix laugh. 'I think she must like your aftershave, Max.'

'I have that effect on all the women. I still can't get rid of Eve.' Max shot a look in her direction, but if his comments made her sad or embarrassed, then she was doing a very good job of hiding it.

'I haven't seen Flora looking this happy since Duncan was around.' Eve seemed to be choosing her words carefully, as if she might say something that would provoke a negative reaction from Max; like the fact that the dog's previous owner had died. He'd witnessed her walking on eggshells around Max before and Felix suddenly felt almost certain that he'd made a mistake by backing off so that Eve could continue the pretence to Max's parents that they were still a couple. That might have some benefits for Annie and Nigel, but it was costing Eve far too much. It didn't matter whether Felix was a part of her life or not; what mattered was that

Eve got to live her life to the full and make her own choices. She wouldn't turn her back on Annie and Nigel, and he found it impossible to believe they'd turn their backs on her either. The prospect of Eve moving on didn't need to stop them being part of one another's lives. More than that she deserved the right to choose where her own life went next. He needed to get out of here before he poked his nose into something that wasn't any of his concern, even if it felt like it was.

'I think I'll be okay to leave Flora with you guys for a couple of hours, Bev. What do you think?' Felix turned back towards where the deputy manager was standing, behind the sofa Max was sitting on. The little dog was now resting on her back legs, her two front paws against Max's chest as she licked the side of his face and he laughed again. It really did look as close to love at first sight as Felix had ever seen.

'That would be fabulous, would about five o'clock suit you? I can get Max and Jamie to take her out on a walk and give her an early dinner. Just so we know what kind of interventions we might have to put in place to monitor things if she comes here full time.'

'That works fine with me.' Felix nodded.

'I should probably leave you to get on with it, as well.' Eve moved towards the sofa and ran her hand down the centre of Flora's back. 'The last thing Max will want is me hanging around now that he's got Flora for company.'

'Yeah, you can definitely go now.' Max's tone was dismissive, but then he blinked slowly, almost as if he needed a moment or two to process something else that had just occurred to him. Lifting Flora gently, he placed her on Jamie's lap and stood up. He put his arms around Eve and hugged her, just briefly, before pulling away again. 'Thanks for finding Flora.'

'You know I'd do anything for you, Max.' She planted a kiss on his cheek, laughing as he wiped it away and turned back towards the dog. It had been a brief moment of connection between them, before Max had gone back to focusing on his own wants and needs, and Felix couldn't believe this could possibly be enough for her. Eve deserved someone who would put her first and would love her with the sort of passion that made everything else pale into insignificance. The trouble was, as Felix turned to follow her out of the room, he realised without any shadow of a doubt that he wanted that person to be him.

* * *

'Eve!' Felix was calling after her as she stalked across the grass, moving as quickly as possible without breaking into a run. She could have answered him, but it was far easier to pretend she couldn't hear him. She'd fought to keep a sunny disposition in the bungalow, when a huge part of her had wanted to ask him why he was acting the way he was, as if nothing had happened between them. Although maybe Felix had been pretending to be this great guy who seemed to understand her situation in a way no one else could, even if she had no idea why. Had it just been so that he could get her to let her guard down for long enough to sleep with him? She couldn't believe that was true, but perhaps that was because she didn't *want* it to be true. She'd liked Felix, really liked him, maybe even more than that. It had certainly felt like it had the scope to become love; something she hadn't even dared believe would be a possibility again. Now she just felt like an idiot and Felix was the last person she wanted to talk to.

'Eve, wait.' He put a hand on her shoulder as they reached the car park. She'd been nearly there, so close to getting back into her car that she could have slammed the door and driven away, still pretending not to see him. The peonies that took centre stage in the flowerbed outside the main house, which were swaying in the breeze, would have been the only thing waving goodbye.

'I don't want to talk to you.'

'Yeah, I got that impression.' Felix had the audacity to smile and she had to swallow the scream that was bubbling up inside her. She yanked her body away so violently that his hand fell off her shoulder.

'Okay, you've clearly got the message, Felix. So how about you just go away?'

'Because I think I might have been an idiot.' He held her gaze and she felt something inside her shift. God, those eyes of his would be so easy to fall for again, but she wasn't that stupid. What was the saying? *Fool me once, shame on you, fool me twice, shame on me.* So instead she let him have it, past caring that she was supposed to act as though the way he'd treated her hadn't bothered her, when in reality it had hurt like hell. She'd supressed her feelings so much over the last couple of years and she didn't seem able to do it any more. Maybe she'd finally found her limit and it was good that she was ready to put some boundaries in place, but after the way Felix had treated her, she was ready to erect a twelve-foot high concrete wall between the two of them. Once she'd had her say, that was.

'I just wish you'd had the balls to tell me that what happened between us wasn't what you wanted after all. I don't know if it just didn't seem like such a good idea once we were back in our real lives, or if a short-term thing was always the plan, but it would have been nice if you'd had the decency to share that with me. Whatever the reason, you could have shown me some respect by being honest, instead of stepping into the shadows, like we'd never been more than vague acquaintances.'

'Oh no, Eve, I'm so sorry if that's what it looked like, but you've got it all wrong.' He moved to touch her again and she stepped back, her eyes widening in fury.

'Don't you dare try and gaslight me into thinking I imagined all of that. You went from acting like I was the best thing to happen to you in years to almost ghosting me.'

'I know and I handled it like a complete idiot.' He held up his hands, shaking his head and she struggled to catch her breath; his straightforward admission of guilt the last thing she'd expected. 'When I went to Merri's funeral, her dad said something about their other daughter, Ashleigh, being the only thing that had got them through. I didn't think that much about it at the time, but when Annie had her accident and I saw how much she and Nigel relied on you – how you were their version of Ashleigh, especially after the rift between Lily and her mum – I felt like I'd be taking that away from them. You really are the best thing that has happened to me in… I don't know, maybe forever, but I didn't think I could do that to them. I still felt so guilty about what had happened to Merri, and so grateful that Don and Deanna still had Ashleigh. I couldn't be the cause of robbing Annie and Nigel of you, or of letting you risk losing them. I saw how much they meant to you after Annie's accident and I couldn't guarantee that what we had would be worth you putting that on the line for.'

'Don't you think that was my decision to make?' Her voice was low and she waited until he looked at her again, knowing she'd be able to see in his eyes if this was all part of some big act. It still felt like there was something else he wasn't telling her and she didn't want any more secrets.

'Of course it was your decision, but the truth is there was more to it than that. This wasn't just about protecting you or Max's family; I didn't want to risk getting hurt again either. I would never have asked you to choose between them and me, but

I knew there was a chance you might one day feel you had to.' Felix looked up to the sky for a moment and then back down at Eve. 'You saved the whole family after what happened. You've got so much capacity for doing the right thing that you even want to give the person who hurt Max the chance of forgiveness, if that makes things better in some way for Annie and Nigel. How could I ever ask you to stop being you and step back, even a little bit, a single moment before *you* decided that's what *you* wanted? I was scared if I hung around waiting there was a chance you might never be ready, and I knew how badly that would hurt me, because of how much I already felt for you. So I convinced myself it was better for both of us if I was the one to walk away.'

'And now?' She needed to hear all of it before she told him how she felt.

'I've missed you way too much to keep trying to take the moral high ground, and attempting to do the right thing, whatever that is. Whatever happens between us, you deserve to let your life begin again. So what I really wanted to tell you, more than anything else, is that you can't continue to put that on hold, not even for Max and his family. Even if you still want to tell me to get lost, I needed to say that, because I'd regret it for the rest of my life if I thought I'd contributed in any way to holding you back from living yours. You deserve to be happy, Eve, more than anyone I've ever met.'

For a moment she didn't say anything, but then she breathed out slowly and nodded. 'That's quite the speech.'

'I want to pretend it's all off the top of my head.' He managed a half smile. 'But I've been thinking about what I was going to say from the moment I called your phone, after you responded to the appeal about Flora.'

'Even with that amount of time to prepare, it was still quite impressive.' She could no longer hold back the smile that had been tugging at the corners of her mouth from about halfway through his speech. 'But tell me this, what part do you see yourself playing in this new life of mine?'

'Preferably the biggest part possible, but I'll be happy with whatever part you want me to play. I just want you to be able to be honest with Annie and Nigel, so that you have the freedom to choose.'

'They already know.' Eve laughed at the expression on his face. 'I told Nigel first and then I spoke to Max, and the rest came out on the night of Annie's birthday.'

'Oh my God.' Felix looked shell-shocked. 'How did they take it?'

'Max was pragmatic, as I knew he'd be and relieved, I think, that all expectations of what our relationship looks like now have gone.' She let go of another long breath. 'With Nigel and Annie there were a maelstrom of emotions, but they're still my family and they always will be and that was the only thing I wanted to come from this.'

'I'm so glad, Eve.' He moved towards her again and this time she let him, until they were standing just inches apart.

'The last question remains what role I want you to play...' She paused and pulled a thoughtful face. 'Hmmm, let me think about that. How about we start with trial boyfriend, for a probationary period, and see how you go with that before I make any rash decisions about this fresh start of mine?'

'That sounds pretty good to me and I think I'll be able to persuade you to keep me in the role.' He tucked a stray strand of hair behind her ear and she moved forward, pressing her lips against his, allowing her body to react to his touch and not even attempting to push down the feelings that came flooding to the surface; feelings she'd tried to pretend for so long that she didn't want or need any more. She'd never dreamt she could have it all again, to be with someone who made her feel the way that Felix did, but with Max and his family still remaining a big part of her world. Happiness washed over her and for a moment or two it was hard to think straight, but she grinned at Felix when she finally pulled away.

'I think I could get used to this new life, you know?' Catching hold of his hand, she led him in the direction of her car and the start of a journey that suddenly felt full of endless possibility.

EPILOGUE

Eve's phone pinged with another notification. It was no surprise to discover it was a message from Annie. Eve had expected her phone to be bombarded with messages from Max's mother, while she was away on the trip that she and Nigel had taken to visit Lily and Scott in San Francisco. What she hadn't expected was for the vast majority of the messages to be pictures of the 4D baby scan they'd been to, rather than to constantly check up on Max's welfare.

Stepping back hadn't been easy or instant for either Annie or Eve, but they'd both known they had to do it when Max had moved into the bungalow. Yet, somehow, despite it being what Max said he wanted, guilt had still prickled at Eve's scalp when she went three, sometimes four days without going to see him. She knew Annie still worried if he was eating the right kind of food, getting enough sleep and most of all whether he was happy. Although the latter had become more and more obvious in the months since Max had moved in with Jamie. He'd spent most of the summer either hanging out in the garden at the bungalow with Flora and Jamie, or perfecting his surfing technique under the guidance of Nathan and the rest of the team at Waves 4 Everyone.

'I can't make Dad's birthday dinner this year, because I'm going to Newquay with some of the others to watch a surfing competition.' Max had accompanied the announcement with a nonchalant shrug and when Annie had started to protest, he'd held up his hand. 'But me and Jamie are going to do a barbecue for him instead, the day afterwards. Bev said she'd give us a hand.'

Eve had been almost certain her mouth had fallen open and Annie's definitely did. She wasn't sure either of them had expected Max to deliver on his promise, but he had, and when they'd all sat out in his garden on the afternoon of the barbecue, he'd seemed to relish playing host.

'Here you go, mate.' Max had handed Felix a burger in a bun. 'Better than the baked beans on toast you were always trying to get me to make.'

'Definitely, especially when people think it's okay to microwave them.' Felix had grinned, making Max roll his eyes, but in a far more good-humoured way than he might have done a couple of months before.

'There's another burger ready, I think it's the best one yet,' Jamie had said to Max, passing it to him.

'Then it has to be for Evie.' As Max had handed her the plate, she'd once again found herself blinking back tears, at the sound of the pet name he hadn't used in two years. This time they weren't tears of sadness or guilt, just gratitude that her relationship with Max was so much better now that they'd both been freed from the constraints of other people's expectations. They'd never be Max and Eve again, in the way they'd once been, but they were still a huge part of one another's lives and there'd always be so much love between them. Moving to the bungalow had been brilliant for Max. It had been so good for all of them; the beginning of a new phase in all their lives that had been so desperately needed.

'Are you ready to go?' Felix asked now, slipping an arm around her waist.

'I am. I was just looking at the latest photos from the scan. I'm so glad the baby's okay and I think I can already see a family resemblance.'

'Yes, he's definitely got Max's chin.'

'You've already seen the photos?' Eve widened her eyes as he nodded.

'Nigel sent them to me.' The casual way Felix said it made her smile. Annie and Nigel hadn't just accepted her relationship with Felix, they'd welcomed him with open arms and he'd been every bit as delighted as she was.

'You two have got a proper bromance going.'

'I can't help it if everyone in your family falls in love with me.' Felix grinned and she turned to kiss him, pressing her lips against his just for an instant.

'They do, but it's just a cross you'll have to bear.' Slipping one hand into his, she picked up her keys from the hallway table with the other. 'We'd better hurry up or we'll be late.'

There were heading to the village hall in Port Kara, where Sophie was throwing a fifth birthday party for her son, Carter, which his grandfather had helped to organise. With her family's support, Sophie was progressing well and the plan was for Carter to eventually move back in with her, in the annex at her father's house where she was now living. She'd need to stay on track and meet all the targets she'd been set by her social worker. Even after that, she'd be monitored closely, but it was a story of hope and the power of family. It was also proof that it was never too late for a fresh start and that life could be filled with the kind of joy that was once impossible to imagine.

'There's something I need to tell you before we go.' Felix stopped, looking suddenly serious. 'I love you, Eve Bellingham.'

'That's good, because I love you too.' Kissing him again, she allowed herself to embrace the beauty of the moment, grateful for all that had gone before; knowing it meant she'd never take her wonderful new life for granted.

* * *

MORE FROM JO BARTLETT

Another book from Jo Bartlett, the latest in her uplifting, heartwarming Cornish Bay Collection, is available to order now here:

https://mybook.to/CornishBayBook2

ACKNOWLEDGEMENTS

As always, I want to start by thanking my wonderful readers. I'm so grateful to you for choosing my books and I will never take that for granted. It means so much to receive your messages of support and they really help keep me going when I'm struggling with a plot line, or another deadline is looming. Thank you all so much.

I really hope you've enjoyed the seventh instalment in *The Cornish Country Hospital* series. Returning to the setting and the characters who now feel like old friends is always a privilege. The caveat I give for each new book is that I'm not a medical professional, but I've done my best to ensure that the details are as accurate as possible. If you're one of the UK's wonderful medical professionals, I hope you'll forgive any details which draw on poetic licence to fit the plot. I've been very lucky to be able to call on the advice of a good friend, Steve Dunn, who was a paramedic for twenty-five years and to whom I can go to for advice on medical matters when I need to and, as ever, I continue to seek support and advice in relation to maternity services from my brilliant friend and midwife, Beverley Hills, whenever these arise in any of the stories.

This book features Felix, Eve and Max's story. As you will have seen at the beginning, this novel is dedicated to one of my wonderful readers, Jean, and her much loved son, Michael. I connected with Jean via my Facebook author page and when she told me that her son had sustained a serious head injury in an accident, I knew I wanted to dedicate this book to the two of them. I reached out to Jean and she shared more of Michael's story with me, which I felt honoured to hear.

If you are someone with personal experience of a head injury or love someone who has been affected by a head injury, I hope you feel that there are aspects of this story you can relate to. However, it is important to remember that head injuries affect people differently and this novel is not intended to reflect a blanket experience, as there is no such thing. For Max, the head injury significantly impacts upon his personality and his ability to live independently. This is not the outcome that will be shared by everyone and I am sure there are as many different stories of living with the after-effects of a head injury, as there are people who have sustained one. If you'd like to find out more, there are some excellent resources at www.headway.org.uk and if you haven't already watched the Louis Theroux documentary *A Different Brain*, which is referenced in this novel, I highly recommend that too.

This is the point where I begin to thank all the other people who have helped get this book to publication. At the end of all the *Cornish Country Hospital* books, I write a long list of book reviewers and social media superheroes, who have played such a big part in bringing this series to readers and spreading the word to others, including by regularly commenting on and sharing my posts. So I wanted to take this chance once again to thank as many people as possible again and, as such, my thanks goes to Rachel Gilbey, Meena Kumari, Wendy Neels, Grace Power, Avril McCauley, Kay Love, Trish Ashe, Jean Norris, Bex Hiley, Shreena Morjaria, Pamela Spearing, Lorraine Joad, Joanne Edwards, Karen Callis, Tea Books, Jo Bowman, Jane Ward, Elizabeth Marshall, Laura McKay, Michelle Marriott, Katerine Jane, Barbara Myers, Dawn Warren, Ann Vernon, Ann Stewart, Nicola

Thorp, Karen Jean Wright, Lesley Brett, Adrienne Allan, Sarah Lizziebeth, Margaret Hardman, Vikki Thompson, Mark Brock, Suzanne Cowen, Debbie Marie, Sleigh, Melissa Khajehgeer, Sarah Steel, Laura Snaith, Sally Starley, Lizzie Philpot, Kerry Coltham, May Miller, Gillian Ives, Carrie Cox, Elspeth Pyper, Tracey Joyce, Lauren Hewitt, Julie Foster, Sharon Booth, Ros Carling, Deirdre Palmer, Maureen Bell, Caroline Day, Karen Miller, Tanya Godsell, Kate O'Neill, Janet Wolstenholme, Lin West, Audrey Galloway, Helen Phifer, Johanne Thompson, Beverley Hopper, Tegan Martyn, Anne Williams, Karen from My Reading Corner, Jane Hunt, Karen Hollis, @thishannahreads, Isabella Tartaruga, @Ginger_bookgeek, Scott aka Book Convos, Pamela from @bookslifeandeverything, Mandy Eatwell, Jo from @jaffareadstoo, Elaine from Splashes into Books, Connie Hill, @karen_loves_reading, @wendyreadsbooks, @bookishlaurenh, Jenn from @thecomfychair2, @jen_loves_reading, Ian Wilfred, @Annarella, @BookishJottings, @Jo_bee, Kirsty Oughton, @kel-mason, @TheWollyGeek, Barbara Wilkie, @bookslifethings, @Tiziana_L, @mum_and_me_reads, Just Katherine, @bookworm86, Sarah Miles aka Beauty Addict, Captured on Film, Leanne Bookstagram, @subtlebookish, Laura Marie Prince, @RayoReads, @sarah.k.reads, @twoladiesandabook, Vegan Book Blogger, @readwithjackalope, @mysanctuary, @thelarlbookworm, @theloopyknot, @kirsty_reviews_books, @books,life, everything, @burrowintoabook, @thewitchystoryteller, @littlemiss-booklover87, Sapphyria's Books, @theeclecticreivew, @mrsljgibbs, @TBHonest, @annette_reads_daily, @_lozzieloves, Adventures in Reading, Running and Working from Home, Isabell from @dwoe.reviews, @maries_world_in_books, @decantingbooks and @staceywh_17. Huge apologies if I've left anyone off the list, but I'm so thankful to everyone who takes the time to review or share my books and I promise to continue adding names to the list!

My thanks as ever go to the team at Boldwood Books, especially my amazing editor, Emily Ruston, my copy editor, Camilla Lloyd, and my proofreader, Rachel Sargeant, who all helped so much in shaping this story into something I can be proud of. I also want to thank my good friend Jennie Dunn, for providing such wonderful support with final checks on the novel.

In addition I'm hugely grateful to the rest of the team at Boldwood Books, who are now too numerous to list, but special mention must go to my marketing lead, Marcela Torres, and the Directors of Sales and Marketing, Nia Beynon and Wendy Neale, as well as to the inimitable Amanda Ridout, for having the foresight to create such an amazing company to be published by.

I'm also very thankful to have such a great partnership with Emma Powell, who has expertly narrated all my novels for Boldwood Books, and who always does an amazing job.

As ever, I can't sign off without thanking my writing tribe, The Write Romantics, including my fellow Boldies Helen Rolfe, Jessica Redland, Sharon Booth and Alex Weston, and to all the other authors I am lucky enough to call friends, especially Gemma Rogers, who is another fellow Boldie.

Finally, as it forever will, my most heartfelt thank you goes to my husband, children and grandchildren. Every story I write is for you; you are my head, my heart and my everything.

ABOUT THE AUTHOR

Jo Bartlett is the bestselling author of over nineteen women's fiction titles. She fits her writing in between her two day jobs as an educational consultant and university lecturer and lives with her family and three dogs on the Kent coast.

Download your exclusive bonus content from Jo Bartlett here:

Follow Jo on social media here:

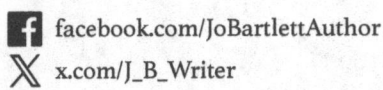
facebook.com/JoBartlettAuthor
x.com/J_B_Writer

ALSO BY JO BARTLETT

The Cornish Midwife Series

The Cornish Midwife

A Summer Wedding For The Cornish Midwife

A Winter's Wish For The Cornish Midwife

A Spring Surprise For The Cornish Midwife

A Leap of Faith For The Cornish Midwife

Mistletoe and Magic for the Cornish Midwife

A Change of Heart for the Cornish Midwife

Happy Ever After for the Cornish Midwife

Seabreeze Farm

Welcome to Seabreeze Farm

Finding Family at Seabreeze Farm

One Last Summer at Seabreeze Farm

Cornish Country Hospital Series

Welcome to the Cornish Country Hospital

Finding Friends at the Cornish Country Hospital

A Found Family at the Cornish Country Hospital

Lessons in Love at the Cornish Country Hospital

Together Again at the Cornish Country Hospital

Mending Hearts at the Cornish Country Hospital

A Fresh Start at the Cornish Country Hospital

The Cornish Bay Collection

Letting Go of Yesterday

Standalone Novels

Second Changes at Cherry Tree Cottage

A Cornish Summer's Kiss

Meet Me in Central Park

The Girl She Left Behind

A Mother's Last Wish

A Cornish Winter's Kiss

Somebody Else's Boy

Boldwood

Boldwood Books is an award-winning fiction publishing company seeking out the best stories from around the world.

Find out more at www.boldwoodbooks.com

Join our reader community for brilliant books, competitions and offers!

Follow us
@BoldwoodBooks
@TheBoldBookClub

Sign up to our weekly
deals newsletter

https://bit.ly/BoldwoodBNewsletter